Taking It Back

Book 2. White Flag of the Dead Series

Joseph Talluto

ISBN: 978-0-9871044-0-3

1

I guess I was wrong in thinking that after a winter of freezing temperatures, sub-zero wind chills, and over three and a half feet of snow would actually have an effect on the zombies. Well, it did, but not the effect I was hoping for. I was hoping the virus would have been killed off, and we would be able to just stroll back and pick up where we left off, tossing zombie corpses into the fires and becoming gentlemen farmers or some such.

No, the zombies came out of hibernation hungrier than ever, and more tenacious than ever, if that was possible. Nate had reported serious attacks on the fence down his way, and I had seen more activity in areas I thought were quiet. It was like the first wave of the virus was the opening salvo, and this increased activity was the second wave, coming forth to wipe out the vestiges of humanity that somehow made it to survive the first.

We had managed to make the move to Leport, the warming weather being a nice change from the cold we had endured. It was nice to be able to open the windows and let in fresh air. Spring was a time of renewed hope, although in our current situation, hope was a dangerous ambition.

We had decided to leave a contingent at the condo complex and I had put the question to everyone as to who wanted to leave and who wanted to stay. Charlie was coming with, Rebecca as well. Sarah and Jake were coming with me, and Jason Coleman, who was recovering nicely from his bullet wounds, along with his wife. Tommy was coming along, and John Reef with his wife, Mary as well. Mark Wells and Teri were leaving, and Stacey Wood, Tommy's new interest, was coming along too. Duncan decided to stay, likely at Pamela's urging, as well as the Kowolskis. The Stricklands were staying, as well as most of the women from Pamela's group.

I was saddened at the prospect of not seeing Duncan for a while, but I understood where he was coming from. Lately he seemed to be needing something in his life, and maybe this was it. We would only be ten miles or so down the road, but that could be a long distance sometimes.

At Tommy's recommendation, I told the group Duncan was going to be left in charge. Duncan brightened at this, and I thought I saw the smug smile on Pamela's face replaced by a serious look when she made eye contact with Sarah. I made a mental note to once again ask Sarah what she had said to Pamela that one time.

Goodbyes were difficult and bittersweet, with a lot of 'Good Luck' on both sides. I took Duncan aside and gave him his standing orders.

"Nate pushed to the river and left behind a secured area. We pushed to the river and are leaving behind a secure area as well. Nate is coming up to join us in Leport and that will be our permanent home. We will stand there or not at all. We have access to farmland, roads, water and woodlands." I walked Duncan out to the edge of the parking lot. "I need you to push north, clear the area to the canal, and then head east. Your job is to create a safe corridor for any possible survivors out there to find us. Get them to this road, McCarthy road, or the waterway. Keep the area clear. When you head east, always keep the way clear."

Duncan nodded then offered his hand. I brushed it aside and wrapped him in a big hug. "Take care of yourself, brother. You're welcome wherever I live," I told him.

Duncan smiled. "We'll see you in a while. And if there's anyone out there, we'll find them. Who knows?" he shrugged. "Besides, what could be worse than what we've been through?"

I grimaced. "Every time I hear that I feel Karma herself take a serious interest in the proceedings."

"Ride easy." Duncan said, slapping me on the shoulder.

We walked back to the vehicles and mounted up. Sarah, Jake and I took the tried and true CR-V, while Charlie and Rebecca followed in the pickup. The rest of the group was in various vehicles, but all of them capable of off-roading if needed. We had found additional vehicles to leave behind for Duncan and his crew, and we were leaving the snow plow with him as well. I had other ideas for Leport, and the snow plow wasn't needed.

We headed out and rolled down the road, moving towards what I hoped would be our permanent home. I smiled over at Sarah, and she returned the smile, giving my hand a squeeze. She and I had gotten even closer in the past couple of weeks, ever since her abduction at the hands of psychotic teens and subsequent rescue. I will admit something had been building between us for some time, but it took the possibility of losing her that caused me to finally make my feelings known. That was the plus side. On the down side, there was now another person in my life I cared a great deal for, and I had to make sure they both were safe. Up side of that, I would fight even harder to make this a safe place for them.

We moved at a decent clip, making our way once again into Leport. We had spent the last week moving our supplies and gear into the old school. It was as secure as a place as I could find, being on top of a hill and overlooking the river. It was an older building, built back when they took pride in their schools and built them to last. The doors and windows on the first floor had been secured with iron grates, and the heavy doors would be effective barriers if needed. It would only be a temporary place until homes were secured, then it would resume its duties as a school.

The areas surrounding the road seemed peaceful, the only reminder that things were out of kilter were the skeletal remains of homes we had torched. I passed by the burned-out remains of the estate home we had visited earlier, and I felt another pang of sadness as I remembered what that escapade had cost us. Jake rode alone in the back seat, sitting forward like a big boy these days, but even his little voice couldn't make me forget we were supposed to have another passenger.

Moving slowly through a wooded section of the road, I saw shades of green poking its way into view. I also saw ghostly shapes moving erratically, stumbling over vegetation and hidden pitfalls. A flash in the rear view mirror let me know that Charlie had seen them as well. I stopped the car and got out of the driver's seat, opening the back door and picking up my rifle off the floor. Jake waved his arms at me and opened his mouth to give me a squeak of greeting. God, I loved that little guy.

Sarah called out of the car. "What are you doing? Those guys aren't any danger to us."

I shrugged. "Something is bugging my spider sense. I want to check this out." I moved back to Charlie's vehicle and Sarah got out of her side and got into the driver's seat. I could hear her talking to Jake as I approached Charlie's truck. "Hi big guy!" That wasn't for me.

Charlie rolled his window down and looked at me quizzically. "Any real reason why we should care about those Z's?"

"None that I can think of, just a feeling I have." I replied, keeping an eye on our friends who had now seen our convoy and me walking, and were desperately trying to get through the brush in our direction. They weren't having much success, as their tattered clothing got caught on nearly everything and spun them every which way. Eventually they would reach us, but it would be a minute.

Charlie got out of the truck, Rebecca sliding over to the driver's seat as she had seen Sarah. He reached into the back seat for his gun and said simply "Good enough for me."

We checked our guns and clicked off the safeties, the chambers already having rounds in them. We moved towards the woods, spreading out to take one zombie each. Mine was a man about my age, completely missing his shirt and major portions of skin. His face was badly decomposed, and I realized the winter had actually preserved these things. His grey skin was pulled back from his face, giving him a skeletal look. His head flopped as he came nearer, and I couldn't figure out why. But his eyes were locked firmly on me and I believe I actually had a look into the hunger driving these creatures. It was a desperate look, a mindless look, a look that lacked intelligence but was full of purpose.

I decided not to use the rifle because for some reason I didn't want to risk a shot. I looked quickly around and found a downed tree that had several stripped branches. I kicked off a four-foot section and approached my zombie. He had never stopped coming for me, but had gotten delayed when his pants ripped on a pine tree and were now down around his ankles. He was tripping every other step and falling down, but he just kept getting up and falling. Sad, really. I waited until he fell again then quickly stepped up and smashed him on the back of the head with the branch. Splinters flew everywhere, and I managed to drive his head into the soft ground, but I hadn't finished him. His head was stuck in the mud, and his arms flailed about, searching for me even though his face was buried in the sticky forest floor. I drew my knife and punched it through his skull, quieting his thrashing forever. I noticed his neck had a huge bite out of it, exposing his backbone and that was what had caused his head to flop around.

I looked around and saw Charlie standing over his zombie, a woman in a tattered bathrobe. She actually had a few curlers in her hair, and her dead eyes stared blankly up at Charlie, who cleaned his knife off on the robe. I squished on over and used the terrycloth to clean my own blade after I had plunged it into the earth to remove most of the gunk.

"You ever see the movie Kung Fu Hustle?" Charlie asked.

I thought for a minute then laughed. "You're right, that was like that scene with the Beast. Loved that movie."

"Yeah." Charlie said wistfully. "I liked all those martial arts movies. The stuff from the seventies was the best, but they had the weirdest titles. 'Monkey' this and 'Flying' that". He sidestepped around a melting pile of snow. "Sure wouldn't mind seeing one of those again."

"Training flick?" I asked, hopping the ditch.

"You know it." Charlie said, jumping the ditch and walking to his truck. About halfway there, he stopped and cocked his head.

I looked at him. "What's up?"

Charlie seemed confused. "I heard something that doesn't belong in the woods." He started walking towards the hill, keeping his rifle ready. I waved to the vehicles and got waves back. They knew something was up and would be ready to move out at a moment's notice. I raised my rifle overhead and saw motion in every vehicle as people armed themselves and checked weapons. Probably a false alarm, but it wouldn't hurt to be prepared.

Charlie and I approached the top of the hill, while tree branches clicked gently together above us as a small breeze swept up. We moved towards the woods, making sure we were alone. The idea was to check the area while still being hidden. We stepped carefully, avoiding small branches and such that might give us away.

At the top of the hill, we crouched down and it was then I heard something. It sounded like a walkie-talkie and I was curious as to who could be out here. I couldn't make out what the person on the radio said, but I heard someone say, "Not yet. No shots yet, either." A pause, then, "We'll wait a bit longer. Maybe they had some trouble."

Charlie and I looked at each other. Someone was waiting for us. We moved silently forward until we could see the cleared area. An intersection was a little ways up and someone had moved a car to block the intersection. We could see four people standing near the car and a fifth standing a little ways off with a radio. All of them were armed with what looked like AR-15's.

Charlie looked at me and mouthed, "What the hell?"

I shook my head and motioned him to head back. We ghosted our way back down the hill towards our waiting vehicles. I thought about what we had seen and waved Tommy over. I explained what had happened and Tommy summed it up quickly.

"Looks like an ambush to me," Tommy said. "Who'd you piss off lately?"

I shrugged. "Beats me. But the best way to beat a trap is to spring it before it's supposed to."

Charlie spoke up. "How?"

"I have an idea. You and Tommy head back to the tree line and get yourselves into firing positions. Charlie, you remember the one with the radio?" Charlie nodded. "I want him alive. I have questions about this." Charlie looked grim and nodded again. I waved to John Reef and he came running from his vehicle with his gun. I sent him up with the other two, having seen him shoot and knowing he was steady.

I ran to the third car in line and had everyone get out with their stuff. It was a small car, but it would serve. The people piled their gear into other cars and watched in fascination as I went into the woods and dragged the zombie corpses out one by one. I positioned them into the car to look like living people, using sticks to prop them up. I put the car in gear and rode it to the hilltop, stopping just out of sight of the waiting men.

Charlie saw what I had done and nearly blew his cover. Tommy just shook his head and I was sure John was wondering what kind of lunatic I was. I signaled the men to get ready, then I jammed a forked stick in the steering wheel to keep it steady, put the car in gear, and hopped off. I got over to John's position quickly and watched the results of my handiwork.

As soon as the car coasted over the hill, I heard "Get ready!" The voice sounded familiar, but I pushed it back as the car picked up speed and headed towards the parked car. The ambushers must have thought they were going to lose their prey, and opened fire. The car windows shattered, and the zombie decoys jerked with the impact of high velocity rounds. The leader of the group ran out from his hiding place and waved his arms. "Stop! They're not all here! Stop! We have to wait for the Honda!"

That shook me. This was personal. I took aim with my M1A and fired at the leader. It was an easy shot, about one hundred yards. My round slammed into his shoulder, spinning him around, causing him to lose the radio. At the sound of my shot, the four ambushers spun towards the tree line, making themselves easy targets for our rifles. Tommy, Charlie, and John fired as one and three attackers went down immediately. I fired at the fourth and was rewarded with him falling to the ground, clutching his throat.

I burst from cover and ran towards the leader. I needed to get to him before he could radio whoever he was talking to. Charlie ran with me while Tommy and John ran back to the vehicles. The leader had stood up and was searching for his radio when we ran up to him.

"Don't move!" I yelled aiming at the man's back. Blood was on his shoulder and was staining his combat vest. "Get your hands up!" Shaking hands were raised and I could see sweat starting at the man's neck. Charlie checked on the rest of the crew and called out from the side. "All dead." The man's shoulders sagged at the news.

"Keep your hands up and turn around." I said. The man slowly turned and faced me, his little eyes staring hatred at me once again. I knew those eyes and I knew that hatred.

"Well, well. Dane Blake. I wondered when I would see you again." I moved in close and shoved the rifle barrel into his neck. I removed his sidearm and knife then backed up. "Put your arms down." He winced in pain as he complied. I lowered the rifle but kept him covered. "How did you know we would be coming?" I asked, keeping my voice low.

Dane looked at me sullenly, his fat face quivering with pain and rage. I repeated the question. Dane refused to answer, spitting on the ground between us. I waited a minute then punched him in the nose. Dane gasped in surprise and dropped back on his knees, clutching his bleeding face.

"How did you know?" I asked again, keeping my voice calm. Charlie was searching around and suddenly bent to the ground. He came up with the radio and brought it over. His eyes got wide at the sight of Blake, and brought up his gun.

I shook my head at Charlie and turned my attention back to Dane. I needed answers. I handed Charlie my rifle and drew my knife. The sight of the blackened tanto blade caused Blake's eyes to go huge. I walked over to the decoy car and dragged out the dead zombie. I pulled it over to Dane and threw it in front of him. I showed him the knife, then I plunged it again in the hole in its head. When I pulled it out, it was covered in zombie goo. I brought the knife closer to Blake and he recoiled as if it was a snake. It was poisoned, to be sure, with the most frightening substance on the planet.

"I'll get right to the point. You tell me who you are working with and how you knew about us, and I won't cut you with this knife. Lie to me, or try to do anything stupid, and you know what will happen to you. Understand?" A drop of muck slid off the blade and fell to the grass between us. Blake followed the drop to the ground and tried to scoot away. Charlie's rifle poked the back of Dane's neck and he stopped.

Just then, the radio squawked. "Dane? Are you there? Is it done? Report?"

Charlie and I looked at each other. We both recognized the voice. Pamela Richards.

"That bitch," was all Charlie had to say. I had other things to say but not right now. I held up the radio to Dane. "Tell her it's done."

Dane shook his head but screamed as I stabbed forward with the knife, stopping just short of his face. "*Tell her!*" I yelled in his face. Dane complied, trying to sound as normal as possible.

Pamela's voice came through again. "Did you get them all? That bitch and the kid too?" She must have meant Sarah and Jake. Rage surged through me and Dane recoiled from the look on my face.

"*Answer!*" I hissed at him, moving the knife closer. Dane spoke again. "We got them all. What do you want us to do with the bodies?"

Pamela's voice sounded scornful. "Don't bother. Let them rot. I'll call you later. Out."

I looked at Dane. "Where's your vehicle?" He motioned to the road and I could see two trucks parked out of sight in the trees.

The other cars pulled up and I could see questions in Sarah's eyes. Her eyes narrowed as she saw Dane and I went over to explain the situation to her. She gasped and looked back at Jake, her fury starting to build.

"Sarah, look at me," I said, trying to get her to refocus as Tommy and John pushed the two cars out of the way. Lisa, Jason's wife, climbed out and gathered the weapons of the attackers, passing them out equally among the cars.

Sarah's eyes calmed down enough for me to talk to her. "I will take care of this right now. Hand me the radio." Sarah took a deep breath then handed me the small two-way. I kissed her cheek and patted her arm. "It will be okay." I stepped away from the vehicles and made the call. I spoke with Duncan for a minute, then I let Charlie and Tommy talk to him as well. I could hear the pain in his voice as he took in the information, and then it turned to anger. I cautioned him not to do anything until I got there.

I went over to where Charlie and Dane were. "Get up, we're going." I said to Dane. I pushed him ahead of me and motioned Charlie over. "Head into town and get things set up. I'll meet you in a bit."

Charlie nodded. "Watch your ass."

I shook my head. "Crazy shit, hey?" I moved Dane to the vehicle and made him get in the driver's seat.

"I'm riding behind you, and my gun is in your back. Do what you're told and you might live." I was not kind as I threw him into the vehicle, a Nissan Xterra with a flatbed. Say what you want about Dane, he did pick nice vehicles. I slid behind him and showed him my SIG. "Let's go."

We passed the convoy and headed back to the complex. I could almost see Dane's brain trying to figure a way out of this. I didn't say a word, I just let the thought of my child being murdered fuel the cold fire of rage that had started when I heard the news.

I spoke when we approached the complex. "There's Pamela. Honk your horn." Dane complied and I could see Pamela's head whip around. Her eyes got huge when she saw who was driving. She couldn't see me yet, because I had crouched down. Dane pulled into the lot and parked under the building, next to the second pillar at my direction. Pamela came running over and spoke heatedly to Dane.

"What the hell are you doing?" she hissed at Dane. "You weren't supposed to come back here yet! That wasn't part of the plan!"

I popped out of the backseat and leveled my SIG at Pamela's head. "What plan?" I asked. "Was it the one where you have men kill me and my son, not to mention my friends? *That* plan?" I spat the question at her through gritted teeth.

Pamela's eyes nearly bugged out of her head when I stepped out of the car. But she recovered her composure well enough. "You can't prove anything, and even if it is true, are you an executioner? Who would follow you after that? All you have is the word of this man. Where are your witnesses that he and I had any contact?"

I kept the gun on her but lowered it slightly. "Charlie heard you talking to Dane here, same as I did. You're finished here."

Pamela laughed. "You think Duncan is going to get rid of me? You're a bigger fool than I thought. That idiot will do anything for me."

Duncan stepped out from behind the pillar that had hidden him. "Yesterday, I would have. Today? Not so much." Duncan stepped closer as he spoke. "I should have known how you felt when you kept talking about John and how he needed to be gone. This would explain those frequent trips to the adult center. You were communicating with Blake. You're right, I was an idiot, but not any longer."

Pamela laughed in his face. "What are you going to do? You haven't the guts to kill me, and I wasn't with the ones pulling the triggers on the convoy."

Duncan's eyes went cold and I knew what was going to happen. I stepped aside as he swiftly drew his Glock and shot Dane in the head, dropping him on the pavement. "The stooge is dead. Now all that remains is the mastermind." Duncan said, turning towards Pamela.

Pamela backed up, looking at Dane's body with a mixture of horror and disbelief. Her eyes drifted to Duncan who looked at her with sorrow and anger. As he raised his weapon, I spoke up.

"Wait." I said. They both looked at me, Duncan with surprise and Pamela with relief. "This shouldn't be an execution." I looked at Pamela and holstered my SIG. I waved Duncan down and stepped away from the Xterra.

I continued speaking. "You tried to have me and my son killed. Your life is forfeit around here. You have two choices. Grab your gear and get away right now, or face me one on one." I placed my hand on my SIG for her to realize what I meant.

Pamela spat at me. "Duncan will kill me if I win. No deal."

"Duncan will let you go. My orders." I said calmly.

Pamela seemed to be weighing the options. Her hand hovered near her gun, and I was waiting intently for her to make a play. Time stretched and I became aware of subtle noises around me, the slight breeze playing in the grass.

Finally Pamela's head sagged and she slumped, realizing she had lost. Duncan moved swiftly and took her weapons away from her. She actually seemed smaller, but I had no pity whatsoever. "You have five minutes to get whatever is dear to you and get away. You will have no gun, no vehicle, and you will head north. If I ever see you again I will kill you on sight. No explanation, no warning, just death."

Pamela shook as if my words were physical things hitting her and I could see anger building again in her eyes. I stepped closer and just said, "Move."

Pamela ran to the building and grabbed what she could and was out again in four minutes. Duncan searched her to make sure she hadn't stolen anything important, then pointed North. Pamela flipped us both off and ran down the street. I considered sending a shot down her way to speed her along, but figured it would be a waste of a bullet. I looked back at Duncan who was watching her run.

"She'll try to kill you again, if she gets the chance. You know that." Duncan said.

"Yeah, well, I'll just add it to the list of things I need to keep an eye out for." I went back to the vehicle and dragged Dane's body out. As I bent over a shot whipped over me, ricocheting off the car and impacting into the roof of the parking lot. I dropped to one knee and drew my SIG, pivoting towards the threat, a second bullet whipping past my ear and putting a hole in the seat. I fired three times and watched Pamela's body jerk with the impact. She screamed her rage at me and Duncan and crumpled to the ground, a dark stain spreading out over her chest. I kept my gun on her as I went closer and found she was still alive. She was drooling blood, and by the look of things, she wasn't going to make it.

"Fuck you and die, Talon," was all she said, dropping her head back and coughing blood.

I kicked her gun away, a small snub-nosed revolver. I looked her over then moved so she could see me. I bent down and quietly said, "You first." I stood up and walked away, Pamela breathing her rattling last breath.

Duncan just shook his head as I got into the car and fired it up. "She must have circled back through the pines. These kids today," was all he said.

I leaned out the window and shook his hand. "It's the new math. It just messes with their heads."

Duncan waved ruefully as I pulled away. Looking in the rearview mirror I saw Duncan dragging Pamela's body over to the burn area, and Dane's body still on the blacktop. I shook my head at the whole thing and thanked God once again for Charlie's instincts. I drove down the road towards my new home.

When I got to the school, Sarah had a question in her eyes. I summed it up simply. "Duncan shot Blake, I shot Pamela." Sarah just nodded. Gotta love a woman that understands.

2

The first week in Leport was an adjustment, as we went from comfortable condos to classrooms again, but it was necessary in order to finish the defenses for the town. Tommy and Charlie had tinkered with the backhoe and bulldozer for three days before they managed to get them running. Once they did, they dug a six foot wide, six foot deep trench around the perimeter of our town. That actually took a shorter amount of time than I expected. Tommy's arm had healed pretty well, and Jason Coleman was nearly fully healed as well. John Reef, our plumber, spent several days figuring out how to turn off the water lines to the uninhabited part of town and focus it to the habitable. He informed me that if we could get a system working where we could get water up to the tower from the river, we could have running water in the homes. I pondered that one, but after a while had to admit I was stumped. I sent the question to Nate and he had nothing for me, either. Nate informed me they would be arriving in about a week, so we had better have some accommodations ready. Nate said sixty people were coming and that was twenty more than I thought. Oh well, we had the homes.

I was keeping busy going house to house, making sure we were alone in our little slice of peace. During the thaw, the zombies that could move again were on the move and they had a weird habit of hiding out and waiting for something to happen. Sarah was helping Rebecca take care of the babies, and gave me more than a little grief for going out alone. But I reassured her I would be fine, that I needed to get this done before Nate arrived. Besides, I wasn't alone; Mark Wells was coming with me today. He was going to see about establishing a power grid isolated to our immediate area. I welcomed the company and Sarah was satisfied. She gave me a hug before I left and refused to let go until I promised her I would come back.

Mark and I were headed to the far eastern edge of our section of the town. We were going to go house to house and clear out any zombies we found. We weren't looking for any supplies, but we would mark the houses where supplies and sundries could be found for pickup later. If we found any weapons, we would bring them back immediately, but I didn't really expect to find any.

With the weather being warmer, we needed to be as careful as ever, since the ghouls were definitely up and running. We stepped down Stephen Street and worked our way to Main Street, which would then take us to our starting point. We passed several homes and businesses, and Mark began to realize just how big of a task we had ahead of us.

"We need to check all these homes?" he said, glancing around as we went downhill. We walked down the middle of the street, not because we could, but to give us the most room in case a zombie was ambling in the alleys. We hadn't encountered any Z's yet, but I knew they were around. Sounds where there shouldn't be sounds and shuffling noises coming from open windows. It felt like the town was watching us, not only the walking dead, but the souls of the people who'd died here. I didn't get the impression we were not wanted, but rather it was like the town was holding a collective breath, to see if we could actually make a stand here, and come back from possible extinction.

"Yeah, we do. I wouldn't want to give a home to some family that had zombies under the bed." I swung my carbine to cover an alleyway, but relaxed as a mouse stepped out, looked at us, then rustled into the weeds. *Good luck, little one.* I thought. I had switched back to my trusted M1 Carbine, figuring we would be in close quarters mode for a while and the M1A wasn't really suited for that, being a heavier caliber. Mark was armed with Dane Blake's Mini-14. He wasn't needing it anymore. We were also armed with our usual weapons, knives and close-in fighting tools. Over the winter I had taken a shine to Sarah's little pickaxe, but not liking the short handle, I fashioned one a little longer for extended reach. Mark had the crowbar, so he would be opening the doors.

Mark had taken to the training pretty well, and I trusted him to at least remain steady in case we got into a spot, but he had never gone one on one with a real Z yet. This little walk was as much a test of his ability, as it was of how the zombies had weathered the winter.

We came to an intersection and stopped. A small group of six zombies were slowly making their way down the street. When they saw us, it was like a switch had been turned on, and they immediately began shuffling faster, groaning and reaching. They were desperate after their winter freeze, and wanted us badly.

I wasn't in the mood to accommodate. I tossed Mark the end of a fifteen foot rope I had with me and we spread out, running at the zombies. The rope took them about waist high, and we tumbled the lot of them. As they struggled to get up, I stepped up and crushed the skull of what might have been a teenager, while Mark nailed a guy in a torn up business suit. A second zombie joined the first as I slammed the pickaxe into the skull of a zombie who was getting slowly to his feet. Mark killed another one then retreated as the remaining two came at him in a rush. He ran down the center of the street, then turned to face his attackers.

Sure enough, one was faster than the other, and they had spread out far enough for him to bury the hook end of the crowbar in the skull of the first zombie. Unfortunately, the crowbar stuck, and he couldn't pull it out in time to get to the second zombie, a kid about thirteen or so years old. Mark pulled on the crowbar, but only succeeded in burying it deeper. He walked backwards, avoiding the kid, but dragging the dead zombie with him. The zombie kid got closer and Mark swung the dead Z around, knocking the kid down, and burying him under the body.

Mark tugged and tugged, but couldn't get the crowbar out. The other zombie struggled with the weight and began to get out from under the first. I walked up to the situation, and clobbered the kid with my pickaxe to the head. His struggles ceased and Mark finally managed to get the crowbar out. We wiped off the weapons and kept moving, with only the sound of our heavy breathing permeating the air. I don't care what anyone says, fighting zombies wears you out. I was in as good a shape as I could be, but this had me breathing heavily. Maybe it was the adrenaline and the fear, mixed in with fighting for your life that took the toll. Whatever it was, I was somewhat spent.

Mark wasn't in any better shape. He had dragged that Z then swung it around, leaning back and breathing up to the sky, and coughing.

After a minute, we had recovered and were moving again at a steadier pace. We passed several houses and businesses, and made our way to a huge condo complex at the end of the street. Walker Road was the intersection, and on the other side I could see the trench surrounding our portion of the town. While it worked great on keeping any outside zombies from wandering in, it was the ones still on the inside that concerned me. There were a lot of zombies and we had a lot of work to do.

I checked the area around the complex and didn't see any activity.

"I wonder where all the zombies are?" Mark asked.

"What do you mean?" I said, looking into a garage that had been left open. There were some garden tools, but nothing of interest.

"I mean, this is a town with a population of over thirty thousand. We should have a lot of zombies here."

I thought about it for a minute as I checked the inside garage door to see if it was open. It wasn't. "Good question. I guess a lot of these people just bugged out as soon as they could, given their proximity to the interstates and the river and canal."

"Where did they go?" Mark asked as he stepped up to the door with his crowbar.

I shrugged. "My guess is they went to the state centers. Who knows? I'm sure the ones we run into around here are the ones that got left behind by friends and relatives. This was a big commuter town, with a lot of people living here who worked in Chicago, and we all know what happened there."

Mark nodded as he worked the crowbar. He and his wife had managed to get out of the city, but he would likely never forget what he had gone through to get out.

The door popped open and we both stepped back. We didn't hear anything, but that meant nothing. Stepping into the kitchen area, I looked around and motioned for Mark to move forward. He stepped in and headed for the stairs, while I checked the downstairs and the basement. The first floor was clear, and showed signs of a hurried exit. Supplies were scattered around, and some of the items were personal.

I heard Mark moving around upstairs, but he hadn't called for help, so I figured the upstairs was clear. I headed to the basement door and opened it. Immediately a decaying smell hit me, and I knew something was dead down there. Whether or not it was still moving was another matter. I grabbed a towel from the kitchen and threw it down the stairs. Nothing happened, and I didn't hear any movement. I then took a fork and threw it down, the metallic clatter ringing up as it hit the concrete floor. Nothing. I stepped down three steps and bent down to look under the wall. I shined my flashlight around and didn't see anything so I went down the stairs quickly, bringing up my carbine and scanning the area quickly. The basement was cluttered, but nothing was moving. I looked around and saw a shape in the corner. Looking closely, I saw the decomposing body of a dog. I shook my head. They probably thought he would get out on his own. Instead he died waiting for his masters to return.

I felt bad as I went up the stairs, wondering how many pets met their end that way. We had seen them in many homes, and I felt bad about all of them. They didn't understand why they were abandoned, they just waited to die.

I went back up and met with Mark, who told me the upstairs bedrooms were clear. We went outside and checked the rest of the complex, not finding anything untoward. I let Mark kill a zombie wandering the street. He moved in quickly, brushed aside the outstretched arms, and planted the crowbar in the back of its head. It went down without a sound, and he gave it another whack just to be sure. I knew we couldn't knock them unconscious, as some people claimed, but it never hurt to double check.

We decided to check out a recreation center before heading back to the school. We had secured a good piece of the area, and were going to wrap it up with the center.

I approached the glass front doors and tested one. It was open, surprisingly, and we stepped inside. Skylights lit the dim interior, and we could see the first floor clearly; the offices and back rooms looked empty. A sign read 'Courts' and pointed down a big flight of stairs. Mark and I approached and listened for activity. We heard nothing and stepped down the rubberized stairs into the darkness of the basement. The skylights' illumination could only reach so far, and it got darker the deeper we went. I flicked on my flashlight and Mark did the same. At the bottom of the stairs we went right and checked the offices and bathrooms. We could see signs of activity but nothing looked recent.

We went towards the courts and froze at the doorway. There were about a hundred cots covering the gym floor and several aid stations set up around the gym's perimeter. What spooked us was the copious amounts of blood splatter that covered the cots, the walls, and the floor. Bits of meat were scattered here and there, and under one cot I saw a severed hand. The gym had a huge canvas opaque curtain that separated it into two areas. I turned my flashlight off and Mark did the same.

We heard a shuffling sound. It sounded like it came from the other side of the curtain. I moved along the wall towards the side opening, my footsteps silenced by the rubber floor of the gym. I reached the doorway while Mark checked the aid stations for first aid supplies.

Peering around the corner, I looked into the darkness and didn't see a thing. I clicked on my flashlight and illuminated about a hundred zombies covering half the floor. The sudden illumination caused the zombies to turn around and they immediately began a chorus of moans that echoed off the walls of the gym. As one, they started for me.

I didn't hesitate, turning on my heel and running like hell for the stairs, Mark only a step behind. The zombies poured from the gym, clamoring for our blood. Mark and I bolted up the stairs and paused to throw the couches and chairs we had passed in the lounge down to the first landing to try to slow them down.

"Jesus, what the hell happened here?" Mark yelled as we levered a couch over the edge.

"I don't know, but I imagine they set up a treatment center, not knowing what the virus did, then the first infected killed the rest and the workers too." I said as I tossed my end. We threw another chair then ran into the offices to grab desks. We threw the first one down the stairs just as the first zombies were trying to climb over the furniture pile. The desk flattened one, and effectively blocked others momentarily. We grabbed two more desks and threw them down as well.

I motioned Mark to go and we ran out the front door. I looked over the parking lot and spotted the maintenance shed. Running to the shed, I pulled on the door and found it locked. Mark attacked it with the crowbar and we broke the door open. I flung the door open and looked around before grabbing two cans of gasoline stored there and ran back to the building. We checked inside and saw the zombies hadn't made it past our barrier yet. We went to the stairs and poured gasoline down on the barricade and the zombies groaned again when they saw us. Mark emptied his can and I emptied mine. I threw the can down and bounced it off the head of a female crawling over one of the desks. I dug into my backpack for my matches, and lit the whole package. I stepped back and tossed the flaming brand down the stairs.

Thankfully, Mark and I were not at the top of the stairs when the gas went up. The building shook with the whoosh of the lighting gas and the skylight above the stairs shattered from the explosion. Mark and I fell back and headed towards the entrance. One zombie managed to reach the top of the stairs, and a flaming figure limped towards us for about twenty feet before succumbing to the flames and falling to the floor, setting fire to the carpeting. Mark and I left the building, and headed back to the school. The center burning brightly, with flames shooting out of the skylight. With luck, the blaze would consume the zombies for good. If not, we were going to have to search around for a few 'extra crispy' Z's that had managed to escape.

3

When we got back to the school Sarah was waiting for me with Jake. She wrinkled her nose, and I explained to her and Jake what had happened. Sarah shook her head and handed me Jake after I had stripped my gear off.

"Got a surprise for you." She headed into the hallway.

I followed with Jake, who was pulling at my collar and cooing.

Sarah stopped at a classroom and peeked in. She stepped aside and motioned me in. I went in-puzzled, then went into defense mode as something grabbed me from behind. I held Jake out with one hand, slammed my elbow back and spun around, hoping to dislodge whatever had me.

I heard a "Whoof!" as my elbow connected and then a "Whoa!" as my spin tossed the person off of me into a cluster of desks. I put Jake down and stepped in front of him as the other person climbed painfully to his feet. Jake sat down and waved his hands, excited as he recognized the newcomer. Sarah covered her smile with her hand as Nate stood up and rubbed his ribs.

"Nice shot, John. Good to see you too."

I relaxed. "Nate!" I went over and wrapped the big man in a bear hug. Nate groaned as I squeezed his sore ribs. "Oops Sorry about that. Can't be too careful."

Nate shrugged it off. "My fault. I should know better than to mess with someone who just came in from the outside. Your nerves are still on overload."

I nodded. "No kidding. You should have seen what Mark and I found at the recreation center." I filled Nate in on the details and Sarah just shook her head and put an arm around my waist. Nate noticed her but said nothing. I finished, pointing to the burning building out the north window. "That glow? That's mine. The good news is the building is isolated so no others will go up. The bad news is the building could have been useful."

Nate shrugged. "At least you dealt with it. Some people would have stayed and fought."

I hoisted Jake and rubbed his belly with my head, getting a giggle out of him. "I didn't have enough ammo." I said. "I only brought enough for about half of them." Jake leaned towards Nate and he took him from me, giving Jake a big kiss on the cheek and smiling at him. Jake grinned and grabbed Nate's collar, burying is head in his friend's shoulder. Nate gave Jake a hug and was silent for a little while. I didn't say anything, knowing how Nate felt about Jake. A lot of people loved Jakey, and I began to realize he represented the future, something to hope for. If Jake was ever lost, that hope would be gone, and people would have nothing to live for. I know I wouldn't, Sarah not withstanding.

After a minute, Jake leaned again, this time towards Sarah. She took him and said, "Dinnertime," as she left the room. Sarah knew Nate and I needed to catch up, and to plan our next move. I winked at her as she left and she flashed me a quick grin. I looked back to see Nate looking at me.

"What?" I said, starting to feel defensive.

Nate smiled at me. "Nothing. I was just thinking it was about time you two got together."

"Why does everyone say that? Was it that obvious?"

Nate laughed. "You might not have been obvious, but she sure was. You were her pick from the first and I don't know what happened out here, but a lot of people are rooting for you two. I'm glad in this messed up world, someone has found a little happiness."

I thought about it. "Thanks, man. I kind of needed to hear that." I talked about the trip I had taken to my house and how I broke away from that old life, leaving my wedding band behind.

Nate nodded. "Good for you. At least you got the chance."

"So, getting back to the situation at hand, how are we set up?" I asked, changing the subject. I sat in a chair and pulled a table close. Nate pulled up another chair and dumped the contents of a small bag on the table, It contained some maps and lists of names, as well as a candy bar and juice box. Nate shrugged as he put the last two items back.

"We pushed hard for the river, coming up through Freeport. We managed to use all of the cargo containers from the depot." Nate said.

That raised my eyebrows. "Really? There had to be a thousand of them."

Nate laughed. "One thousand, three hundred, and forty-six. We spread out not only west but east. There was a lot of farmland to the southeast."

I nodded. It was sound move. "If ever we decide to tackle the city, there's another storage depot near Chicago."

Nate shuddered. "No thanks. I'll do that when I'm bored with life."

I smiled, wondering when that might ever happen.

"We managed to free up an additional seventy-eight people in our push west and would you believe it? Twenty of them are young guys, between nineteen and twenty-five years old who had banded together to save each other when the crap went down."

I whistled. That was a good force to send against the Z's if they were trained right. Who was I kidding? They had Nate. Of course they were trained. I motioned for him to continue.

"We have quite a few families, lots of kids, and we are in a good position for food and supplies right now. We will need to forage until the first crops come in, and we will have to start some animal raising, but I imagine we have the land for that."

I nodded. "The forest preserves we went through to get here have a lot of clearings surrounded by heavy woods. Once upon a time these were farms, so they can be farms once again. There are enough homes nearby for people to manage the herds and protect them as needed. We can trench them for defense and also to keep the animals from straying."

Nate seemed impressed. "Always looking ahead, hey?"

I shrugged. "Looking back these days puts some strain on your soul, you know what I mean?"

"Amen, brother. Amen." Nate shifted his position. "Any troubles?"

I looked at him. "Depends on your point of view." I told him about the problems I had with Pamela and Dane Blake. Nate's eyes darkened when he heard we were set up for an ambush. I told him about Sarah and Kristen's kidnapping, and Kristen's subsequent murder. Nate dropped his eyes at that. I told him about Kevin and Frank.

"Holy shit! A pit full of zombie heads! Who comes up with shit like that? Not that I'm sad to see those two gone, but that's a hell of a way to go."

I nodded. "We haven't been back since, so I'm sure there are a lot of supplies there, but I have no rush." I talked about leaving Duncan in charge and his standing orders to leave a corridor open to refugees, and also what happened to Chelsea.

Nate shook his head. "Maybe you should have stayed put."

I thought about it for a second. "No, we needed to make the push to re-establish a workable zone for survival and re-taking what was lost, and we couldn't do it from just one place. So how about you?" I asked.

Nate held up his hands. "Nothing so dramatic. We had a few bands of zombies to deal with, some survivors to train and acclimate. Most of them are anxious to meet the great John Talon."

I rolled my eyes. "The only reason I keep going out to risk my neck is because I haven't any useful skills like plumbing or electric work."

Nate laughed. "We'll get you elected yet. Anyway, in our push to the river, we happened across this home that had a ham radio set up in it."

That piqued my interest. "Really? Anyone know how to use it?" I knew ham radios were used to communicate all over the world, and if we could get one working, we might actually be able to communicate with other people and find out if there was anyone left in the world.

"As a matter of fact, Jim Bigelow knew how to work it. We didn't have a power source at the time, but we took it with us anyway."

I got the idea Nate was holding something back. "What are you not telling me?"

Nate leaned forward–and rested his elbows on the table. He looked down and it was a long time before he looked up. He sighed and said, "We're not alone."

I leaned back in my chair and stared at him. When I found my voice I asked, "How do you know?"

"We had a generator we found in the home of a carpenter, and we hooked the radio up to it. Jim worked on it for a while, then we heard the voices. We were pretty excited about that, until we started to seriously listen to the people on the radio. We got broadcasts from all over the place, all kinds of languages." Nate paused. "There's survivors all over, but not much else. Some people are screaming for anyone to help, others are just trying to find a link to keep themselves from committing suicide. Several times, we could hear the dead moaning in the background. After a while, we just turned it off."

"Must have been bad, hearing people and not being able to help or even let them know you could hear them."

Nate looked down again. "I actually felt guilty knowing what we have and hearing about people starving or about to be overrun."

I tried to be reassuring. "You can't save everyone. We're on our own as much as anyone else. We got lucky, but we fought for it too."

Nate turned cryptic. "Maybe we can save some."

"What do you mean?" I asked, looking at his maps for a clue.

"We got a broadcast we actually answered, and they know about us, and we know about them," Nate said. "Turns out they managed to escape the virus itself, and have barricaded themselves against the hordes. But they know they can't hold out forever and were wondering if we could lend a hand." Nate looked at me questioningly.

I chuckled at his look. "Phase three."

Nate's face turned quizzical. "Phase three?"

"Sure. Phase one was to survive the Upheaval. Phase two was to establish a safe zone we could live in permanently. Phase three was to go out and see who else might be out there and either bring them in or establish communication and increase the size of our community."

"Is there a phase four?" Nate asked.

"Yes."

"And?"

"You'll see."

"You haven't lost your wonderful sense of humor" Nate said.

"The secret to a spicy relationship is a little mystery. Didn't you know that?" I grinned at Nate who rolled his eyes. "Tell me about our new friends."

"Okay. Here we are." Nate opened a map of Illinois and indicated our position with a pencil. "We know that State Center Bravo is located here." He pointed to an area located about ten miles southeast of Morris in a spot that looked like it was surrounded by waterways and state parks. "The town that contacted us is located here, called Coal City."

I looked at the map. "How have they managed to survive? They're in between two interstates and a major road passes through their area. Not to mention having a state center nearby with who knows how many infected that might have headed that way, not knowing they had the virus until it was too late."

"Actually, they did it pretty much the same way we did. They are a junction of rail lines, so they used cargo containers. One of their people was a train driver and he made the run to this rail yard here," Nate indicated a spot north of the town, "and grabbed train movers and flatbeds, along with a mess of cars. They made a fence like we did."

"So what's the trouble?" I asked. "Far as I can see, they should be all right."

Nate nodded. "They were, but the situation changed and they're seeing a lot of zombie activity and they just don't have the resources to take care of it."

"And we do?" I arched an eyebrow at Nate.

"You'll think of something, I'm sure. Did I mention half the town is under the age of 10?" Nate said.

"You really fight dirty, you know that?"

"Call it revenge for my ribs, which are still sore by the way." Nate said, pulling out a pad of paper and a pen.

We planned for another two hours and then called it a night. I went to the classroom I shared with Sarah and sat down next to my son, who was just getting finished with his bath.

Sarah rubbed Jake's head dry and put him in his jammies. "How's Nate?" she asked, slipping Jake's arm through his sleeve.

"Doing his dead level best to make me age." I told her about the town and what we needed to do.

"What about Jake and me?" she asked, passing him over to me so I could help him practice his walking.

I held Jake's hands and walked backwards while Jake waddled along, babbling the entire time. We moved around the room, edging away from the desks, which Jake liked to latch on to when he wanted to cheat. "You'll be coming with. I wouldn't expect you to just stay at home with my son, fraught with worry and crying yourself to sleep each night, wondering if I will ever come home."

I had my back turned to Sarah and I tensed. Sure enough, I got punched in the back. I let Jake grab the desks and turned around, blocking the second punch Sarah aimed at me and wrapped an arm around her waist. I hoisted her up and trapped her arms with my other arm. She glared at me and tried to bite my nose.

"Easy, I was just kidding." I lightly kissed her forehead. She struggled for a second, then stopped, softening against me. I sat down with her in my lap, and she put her arms around my neck. "I need you and Jake there." I said, rubbing her back.

Sarah smiled slightly. "Really? Why?"

"If I leave you two behind," I explained, "then I might not be as careful as I normally would. If you're there, then I do everything I can to stay alive and protect the two of you. I know you can take care of yourself and there isn't anyone I would rather have watch my back."

Sarah leaned in and kissed me and I returned her kiss with the same enthusiasm. If a couple of little hands hadn't started pulling at my leg, things might have gotten interesting. I broke the kiss and Sarah and I both looked down to see Jake smiling up at us.

I sighed. "Jake, someday you need to learn timing." I lifted Sarah off and picked up my boy. "It's all in the timing, my son."

Sarah laughed and walked saucily away. Dammit.

4

The next morning I rolled out of bed and commenced my morning exercises. I included weapons exercises, and Jake watched with a bemused look on his face. Charlie showed up with Julia and the two babies played with some toys on a blanket while Charlie and I sparred. Sarah joined in and after an hour the three of us were sweating and sore from unblocked strikes and kicks. Sarah was a limber little thing and often managed a kick to the head when you weren't looking.

"Did Nate talk to you?" Charlie asked as he drank water from a bottle.

"Yeah, last night he and I went over a few things. We're going to need supplies and plan to get there."

Charlie nodded. "I saw the maps this morning and I have an idea you might like."

"Does it involve a boat?" I asked.

Charlie cocked his head and looked at me. "You're very good, you know that?"

I smiled. "I've been told, but I never believe butt kissers." I ducked as both Sarah and Charlie threw their water at me.

I stood up and thumped Charlie on the back. "Let's get moving. I want to get what we can from town today and start our supply buildup for the trip."

Charlie stood up and picked up Julia. Jakey protested until Sarah picked him up as well. They both went down to Charlie's room to drop off the kids with Rebecca, who loved watching them. They came back and we all went down to the school yard. Nate was training a man in the center of a circle of men. I was pleased to see Carl Witry again, taking up his role as trainer/zombie actor. As I watched him go through his motions, I noticed he had refined his actions and varied his approach in several ways. It wouldn't be so easy to get one past him.

Nate held up a hand as Charlie, Sarah and I approached. All heads pivoted our way as we made our way across the yard. I stopped in the ring and shook Carl's hand, happy to see him again. Carl moaned at me and I bopped him on the head with my fist.

"Nice to see you, Nate." I said, looking around. Nineteen men sat cross legged in a circle, dressed in various outfits and festooned with a variety of weapons. Not many had guns but they all seemed capable.

Nate waved the man he was training over. He was a thin young man, roughly twenty-five, with short-cropped blonde hair and light blue eyes. I was sure in the day he was pretty effective with the opposite sex. I saw him sizing me up as we came over and I smiled. Some things never change.

Nate introduced us. "John, this is Trevor Jackson. He was the leader of the group we picked up on our way here. They were holed up in an old warehouse in Molena and were running low on food when we bumped into them."

I shook Trevor's hand. He had a firm grip and looked me in the eye. Somebody had raised him right. "Nice to meet you, Trevor. Good work in keeping your men alive through the mess."

Trevor shrugged. "Just did what I thought I should do. These guys elected me leader, though I ain't sure I deserve it."

Wow. Déjà vu. "I'm sure you did."

Trevor shrugged again. "Well, they're your men now, Nate says you're the leader of this group. And since we joined up that means me too, I guess."

I chuckled. "Don't worry about it. With the group you have here I'll likely be sending you out on your own to clear homes and hunt for supplies. I can't be everywhere and groups that are used to working together are a huge asset. As a matter of fact, I have a job for you right now."

Trevor perked up and stepped closer as I pulled out a map. "We're here," I said. "The trench is here." I pointed to a line that circled the area. "I need you to take seven men and clear this area here, and send seven more to this area here." I pointed to two opposite sides of the map. "Work your way through the homes, and remove any zombies you might find. That means closets, basements - everything has to be checked."

Trevor nodded, memorizing the locations. I continued. "Meet up here, then work your way back. Don't take any unnecessary risks and don't take anything from the houses except food and weapons if you find any. The homes are going to be occupied, so no damage if you can help it."

Trevor nodded, then motioned at his group. I stopped him and said, "I need five men to come with me for a supply run. Who's steady?"

Trevor pointed to five men who stood up and came over. "This is Jim, Kyle, Carl, Steve, and Bryce," he said. Charlie, Sarah, and I shook hands with all of them.

"This is Sarah and Charlie. They've been with me since the beginning and I trust my life to them," I said. I looked at Trevor. "You still here?"

Trevor grinned and jogged over to the gate with his men. I watched them go, then addressed the five men. "I'm John Talon and I will never ask you to do anything I wouldn't do myself. I will fight with you and for you and I only ask that you try not to do anything stupid that gets you killed or more importantly, anyone else killed. Deal?"

The men agreed as one and I outlined the plan for the day. "We're taking the truck over to the strip malls on the main road past the trench. We're looking for supplies for the town as well as the trip south we're going to be taking in a few days. I figure we stand the best chance along that area. Let's go."

We went over to the side of the building where we kept the vehicles. The school had a tall chain link fence around it which served as a barrier in case of attack. A large number of zombies could tear it down, but for the occasional Z it was fine. I hopped into the Nissan Xterra with Sarah and Charlie jumped into the pickup. The men split up and we had Carl and Bryce with us, while Jim, Kyle, and Steve rode with Charlie.

We pulled out of the school and moved towards State Street, which would take us directly to where we wanted to go. We passed a number of homes and businesses and I hoped Trevor and his crew would have good luck clearing them out and we could move our people in before too long. The homes were in pretty good condition and didn't seem worse for wear for the winter. We would have to see. We also passed a lot of cars that had been moved to the sides of the roads. Tommy and Charlie had managed to do that with the bulldozer and back hoe. We could see movement in between the houses and in some of the windows, and I silently wished Trevor luck in his job.

We had just about reached the trench when three zombies stumbled out into the road ahead of us. They were about fifteen yards ahead and closing in. I stopped the vehicle and got out, pulling my crowbar out and checking my SIG. Charlie got out of the truck and joined me at the Xterra.

The zombies lurched forward and began moaning. Two of them were females and they all looked nasty. Their skin was peeling off, and white bone showed through in places. Their clothing was in tatters and decaying teeth gnashed and clacked in anticipation.

They were bunched together, which made things more difficult. I nodded to Sarah, who stepped out of the Xterra and readied the .22 I gave her before winter. She was only going to intervene if something went wrong, but I didn't see that happening. I signaled to the new guys to hold fast. "This won't take long," I said.

The zombies started to close in, and Charlie and I bolted into action, I taking the left and Charlie taking the right. We ran right at the zombies, then split at the last second, stopping directly to the left and right of the trio. Our sudden movement had confused the zombies for a split second, and that was all we needed. I slammed the crowbar into the head of the one that faced me, an average looking zombie with long, oily hair hanging in thin strips in front of her face. As she fell back I kicked the second one in the hip, sending him sprawling. Charlie buried a tomahawk in the head of the zombie on his side and swept down with his second one at the zombie on the ground. I reversed the crowbar and jammed the chisel end into my zombie's head, crushing it and ending her struggles.

Charlie was having a little trouble. He swung his second tomahawk, but the zombie moved, causing the blade to skip on the road and the only damage done was a couple of sparks. I stepped over with the crowbar and using a golf swing, smashed the zombie in the side of the head as he crawled towards me. He spun around and Charlie used the momentum to bury the second 'hawk in the zombie's head.

Charlie cleaned off his blades on the dead Z's clothing, and I looked around for more adversaries. I didn't see any in the immediate vicinity, so we mounted up and drove down the street. Leport was an old town, so the business and homes on the main streets were near to the roads. I really got a sense of closeness which made for a tense ride. Sarah picked up on it and gave my hand a reassuring squeeze. We moved towards a more open section of the town and began to see additional evidence that the virus had hit here as well. Homes with white flags on them were broken open, windows were cracked and shattered. Cars had doors open and dark stains could be seen in many places. We moved around several abandoned cars and had to move a couple out of the way. I got out and had Sarah move the Xterra up to bump the car out of the way. Carl and Bryce got out as well, and helped me move the car. As we finished, there was movement from a house. A small boy came stumbling out. His grey pallor and dead eyes marked him clearly as a zombie. He moved towards us on uncertain feet, yet clear in his purpose. His Spider-Man t-shirt was bloodstained and several wounds could be seen on his thin arms. I guessed him to be about seven years old. Carl moved towards him, but I held up a hand.

"Check the ground." I said, indicating the tall unkempt grass near the little Z.

Carl looked then whistled. "Man, I never saw that. Thanks." In the grass was a zombie who had been severely injured as a living person and was minus two legs and an arm. It was dragging itself slowly through the grass and if Carl had moved in, he would have stepped right on it. Another man once had done that and the zombie sat right up and chewed on his nuts. Didn't get through the clothing, but the man's hair changed from dark to light overnight.

The child zombie was a lot closer, so Carl moved aside and before I could stop him, fired his pistol, killing the Z instantly.

"Jesus! What the hell is the matter with you?" I hissed at Carl as the sound of the shot echoed down the street.

"What? What's the problem?" Carl asked, holstering his weapon. "Dead is dead, doesn't matter how."

I moved in close so my face was inches from his. "Dead will be us if you don't exercise some discipline. We're totally out in the open here, in case you hadn't realized. If you plan on being breakfast for some Z's, that's your business. But don't get me killed for your stupidity."

"Christ, lighten up, Trevor says..." Carl's voice drifted off as he listened. Moans and sounds of movement came from all around us, and we could see a lot of movement in between and in houses that wasn't there before. Several shapes unfolded themselves from the ground, and began that telltale lurching in our direction. If I had to guess, at least twenty zombies knew where we were and were headed our way.

I glared at Carl and shoved him towards the vehicle. He ran in, apologizing the whole way. I shook my head at Charlie's vehicle and got back into the Nissan. I threw the vehicle in gear and drove off, with the pickup close behind.

Bryce was fingering his weapon and Sarah reminded him he was in a car. "Just because your partner here is a dumb ass, doesn't mean you need to be." Bryce let go of his gun while Carl just looked down.

I said nothing as I moved quickly down the road, trying to get as much distance as I could from the sound of the shot. Zombies will triangulate on sound, God alone knows how, and will come to investigate. If we weren't there, they would lose interest and return to their wandering. If they saw us, they'd follow until the end of the earth.

We moved past more desolation and I could see many more shapes moving and heading our way. I stuck my hand out the window to signal Charlie I was going to speed up and he flashed his lights. I had an idea and with a shitload of luck we might be able to pull it off.

I moved down the street and pulled into the parking lot of a grocery store. Several cars and all of the windows of the store were smashed. I had a hunch this raid was going to be a bust, but I decided to give it a roll anyway. You never knew. Back in the old complex, I once went into a convenience store that had its windows caved in, but apart from some stuff on the floor, the place was nearly untouched.

We parked the vehicles near the front of the store, facing outwards. I did this so much out of habit that if things ever got back to normal I'd be backing into my garage for the rest of my life.

We all got out of our vehicles and Charlie and Sarah immediately swept the front of the store. Sarah nodded to me and I smiled, turning my attention to the five guys we had brought with.

"Well, gents we need to secure a perimeter before we head into this store to look for supplies. Take those cars and move them into a barricade." I indicated the abandoned cars in the lot. "Leave a space for us to get our cars out, but do it fast."

I smiled as several glares focused on Carl, but they managed to keep their complaining to themselves. I went over to the shopping carts and started moving them out to the parking lot. I had a string of about sixteen of them and I pushed them around, leaving one here and there and turning them on their sides. I went back twice and left another thirty or so around the lot, then went back to where the guys had arranged the cars. They had made a semi-circle around the front of the building, leaving a space barely wide enough for the trucks. I was actually impressed and said so.

"Thanks," said Jim. He looked at the shopping cart minefield. "What's with the carts?" he asked.

I smiled. "If we need to bug out on foot, Z's will be slowed down trying to get through that," I said. "They don't really look where they're going."

Jim smiled and said. "I'll need to remember that one."

"Let's go," I said.

The interior of the grocery store was a mess. There was stuff all over the floor and the shelves were cluttered and disheveled. But a cursory glance indicated there was enough stuff here to make the trip worthwhile. I moved towards the canned section while Charlie headed for the dry goods. Sarah moved towards the drink section and we each had a follower. Jim and Kyle went with Charlie and Sarah and Steve came with me. Carl and Bryce moved towards the gloom of the interior of the building, the morning light not casting enough brightness to see farther.

I moved quickly, gathering what I could and handing it to Steve, who took it out to the trucks. I focused on stuff we could use and stuff that had the highest potential of staying fresh. I could hear other trips being made as other supplies were scrounged and brought out to the trucks. I could hear Carl and Bryce talking as they moved along the back of the store towards the store room. I took an armful of soup cans and headed towards the front. I bumped into Charlie as he came out with an armload of baby supplies and diapers for both Jake and Julia.

"Good call," I said.

Charlie nodded, then stiffened. I followed his gaze and saw what amounted to about thirty zombies headed our way. They hadn't reached the parking lot yet, but they were coming.

I sighed. "This is not a fight I needed today." I said dropping my soup in the truck bed.

Charlie dumped his supplies. "Nobody lives forever."

I ran back to the store and bumped into Sarah and Kyle. "Zombies are outside, we need to get out very soon."

Sarah nodded and ran to the truck, Kyle right behind. They immediately turned around and ran back in. "They're at the barricade!"

I spun around. "What? How the hell did they move that fast?" I said to Charlie as we moved to look.

Charlie pointed. "Your originals are still out there. These must have come from around the building."

"Great. Let's see if there's another way out of here." I ran towards the back where Carl and Bryce were supposed to be. I stopped as Carl came out of the back storage area, his arms full of boxes. "Jackpot! We found some—"A blood-curdling, gurgling shriek came from the back room. Carl turned towards the door just as a horde of zombies poured out of the back room, overwhelming him and scattering his boxes. We didn't even have time to pull up our weapons before he was torn apart, his blood spraying out and covering the zombie that tore at his throat with its teeth. Bryce stumbled out of the back and fell down, his arm had been nearly severed, his blood pouring out. He looked up to us, his jaw torn off on one side and his bloody tongue flopped around. Two more zombies fell on him and tore at his face, ripping off chunks and stuffing them in their rotting mouths.

"Back, back!" I yelled, unslinging my carbine and firing a shot between Bryce's eyes, ending his pain. I couldn't do the same for Carl, who was buried under zombies. I could hear him scream, though, and that echoed through the building.

My shot brought heads around to our position and I looked at a dozen pairs of dead eyes as they hungrily stared at us. I moved back as the zombies regained their feet and started towards us. I could see what was left of Carl and it wasn't pretty. His face and neck had been ripped apart and an eye had been torn out. His clothes had been shredded by jagged nails and his abdomen had been ripped open, entrails spilled over the tile floor. I nearly turned away when I saw his head flop over and his one good eye looked right at me. "Sorry, Carl," I said as I fired again, sending a round through his empty eye socket and killing him permanently.

I spun around and caught up to the group at the front of the store. They were bunched in an aisle, and I wondered what the hold up was when Charlie said, "They're coming in the front too."

Shit. I looked back and the end of the aisle was filled with a pack of zombies working their way towards us. Blood dripped off their hands and mouths, and eyes gleamed in anticipation of the slaughter.

We needed breathing room. I slapped Charlie on the shoulder and said, "Up." He leaped to the shelving unit, climbing nimbly to the top, scattering rice side dishes. I climbed quickly to the top of the opposite unit then swung my crowbar down to haul up the rest. Sarah grabbed the steel and I pulled her up quickly. I waited a second for her to gain her balance, then pulled up Kyle. Jim and Steve were pulled up by Charlie just in time as decayed hands grasped and clawed at the top shelves. We moved to the middle of the units and looked down at our attackers. They filled the aisle and hungry arms reached upwards. Thank God they couldn't climb.

Charlie looked at me from across the aisle. "Hey Moses! Wanna part the Dead Sea?"

"What's the plan?" asked Steve, nervously looking down at gaping maws.

"How's the front look?" I asked, stepping back as a hand groped for my foot. Sarah was keeping her rifle trained on the horde, and thankfully, the rest of the guys were keeping their cool.

Charlie moved down the aisle, ducking under a light and sign that advertised organic foods. "Clearing. Looks like we have most of them in here with us." He had to shout to be heard over the cacophony of the dead.

"Good enough." I motioned to Steve and Jim. "We can't get out of here without a fight. Do not shoot unless Charlie tells you to." I placed a hand on Sarah's shoulder and spoke in her ear. "Go to work, babe."

Sarah opened up with her .22. The red dot sight was perfect for this close work and the GSG-5 sang with clarity. She dropped fifteen of them in about twenty seconds, a small round hole being the passage to the next life for the zombies. Others moved up as Sarah fired and we had to be careful as the second group stood on the bodies of the first and were thus closer to us. I could hear the heavier caliber guns bark as Charlie and his group opened up on his side and we cleaned out the grasping mass quickly.

We walked on the shelves until we made to the front. I jumped down and looked outside, stepping around the zombies we had killed. I didn't see any danger and motioned the rest to follow. Charlie jumped down and I helped Sarah down.

Moving outside, we spread out and scanned for trouble. A couple of stragglers were in the parking lot, but no immediate danger. We piled into the vehicles and were immediately aware of the extra space. *Can't be helped, just a freak accident,* I thought as I started the Xterra. That's why we check everything.

I pulled out of the lot and maneuvered around the carts. I stopped close to one of the zombies and let Sarah shoot it. It dropped with a grunt and I went over to the next one. She shot that one too, then sat back.

"I don't like that I'm used to it" she said, checking the gun.

I held her hand. "Me neither."

I looked in the rearview mirror and saw that Jim had tears in his eyes as he thought about his friends. *Some things you'll never get used to,* I thought as I moved towards the school.

On the plus side, we wiped out a good portion of zombies. Down side, we lost two men we could ill afford to lose. We were going to have to get back to the basics. But first, we needed to head south and see if we could help out a town that needed it. I felt something I hadn't felt for a while. Hope.

5

Despite our losses at the grocery store, we managed to press on with clearing the living area and at the end of three days people were moving into homes and condominiums. I chose a brick house overlooking the river that had a fenced, wooded yard. It was probably larger than I was going to need, but it seemed like a good place to settle into. Sarah was going to be settling in with me, so that worked out well, too.

The first thing she did when we moved our stuff in was to remove any remnants of the previous owners. That included taking down pictures and albums. I had enough ghosts on my tail, thank you very much.

I spent half a day looking for a crib for Jacob then another half day making sure the wooden shutters on the house worked. That was another reason I chose the house. It was older, but it had functioning wooden shutters which added to the defense.

I was clearing the yard when Nate rolled up in a truck. I expected him since we were going to be heading south on the river later that day to see what we could do for Coal City.

"Hey John!" Nate called.

"Hey Nate. What's the good word?" I put down the branch I was dragging and came over.

"Not much, just wanted to see what was up with the trip." Nate stepped out of the sun into the shade of a large tree that was in the front yard.

I scratched my chin. At some point I was going to have to shave again, but I was holding at once or twice a week. "We're heading out later today, using one of the boats we found up on the hill." I was referring to the subdivisions outside the trench. "We're provisioned up and ready to go. I figured we'd head out around 11:00 and see how far we drift after a couple of hours. I want to save as much fuel as I can."

Nate nodded. "Sounds right. Who's going with you?" he asked.

"Charlie and Rebecca are coming, Tommy is coming, and Sarah is coming along as well. Jason Coleman, and Martin Oso said he'd come too." I thought for a minute. "Bev Shoreman said she wants to come and Casey Steele as well."

Nate whistled. "Your boat big enough for all that?"

I nodded. "We got one of those big pontoon boats and Charlie and Tommy have been making some modifications to it, so we should be good to go."

Nate chuckled. "I can only imagine what modifications those two came up with."

I smiled. "As long as it floats I don't care."

Nate laughed. "Amen, brother. Better pack your Jesus shoes just in case."

I changed the subject. "How's things coming along here?"

Nate turned serious. "Trevor is still smarting over the two men lost at the grocery store, but he doesn't blame you. He figures they made a dumb mistake by not clearing the room first. But the incident gave his crew some fire in their bellies and they have cleared the area with a vengeance. They want to push back the trench, but Tommy wouldn't let them have the 'dozer.

"John Reef and Dean Cotton have teamed up and they have been playing with water wheels and pumps, and think they might be able to get us running water by the end of the week."

That was news I hadn't expected, but it was welcome nonetheless.

Nate continued. "Mark Wells is looking over our electrical situation, but hasn't figured out any solution yet. He's looking at water wheels too, but no luck."

I ruminated for a second. "Maybe we could do solar, or set up some windmills." I said, pointing to the highway overpass. "We could set up as many panels as we wanted up there and run the lines down to the houses."

Nate looked up. "I'll ask him about it. Good idea." He looked back at me. "Who's watching the kids? If you and Sarah are going and Charlie and Rebecca are going, who's watching Jake and Julia?"

"They're coming with" I said, anticipating Nate's reaction.

Nate responded just as I thought. "Are you nuts?" he yelled. "You're heading to a dangerous situation and you're bringing your babies?"

"What can we do?" I asked, already knowing the answer.

Nate shook his big head. "No way. Jake and Julia will stay with me and Patty."

"Patty?" I asked. "Who's that?"

Nate blushed. I never thought I would see the day. With reddened cheeks he said, "She's a survivor we found about a week after you left last winter. She's a pediatric nurse, so they'll be as well taken care of as possible."

I laughed. "I'll think about it. Now get gone so I can get ready."

Nate looked at me. "You don't have to go, you know. You can send others."

It was my turn to shake my head. "I used to be an administrator. That was what I did. After the Upheaval I became a survivor, trying to help others survive. This is what I do."

Nate nodded and got back into his truck. He headed off to the school and I went into the house to get everything ready.

Sarah was packing backpacks and making sure we had everything we needed. I figured the whole trip should take no longer than five days, but we needed to be ready for at least seven. Stuff we weren't going to carry was already on the boat and we just needed to get moving.

Jake was playing on the floor with a tool bench toy and was managing to get himself stuck every few minutes. He'd fuss and we'd free him, then he'd do it again. It was a welcome bit of normalcy. I had been getting increasingly concerned Jake was going to be adversely affected by all that has happened. But he managed to stay his happy self, and was getting bigger all the time. He was taking tentative steps more and more lately and I was sure as soon as he had his sea legs he was going to be moving all over the place.

I took out my SIG and laid it on the table. Sarah took out her Ruger and handed it over without a word. I quickly field stripped both weapons and gave them a once over with the cleaning kit. I regularly cleaned my weapons anyway, but it never hurt to run a patch through and check the actions for debris or residue. I reassembled the weapons, cursing the Ruger engineers yet again, then reloaded them and chambered a round in each before holstering my own and giving Sarah hers back. It was a testimony to the world we lived in that it never occurred to me that this was somewhat out of the norm once upon a time. I cleaned her .22 rifle and my M1A. I figured I might need the heavier firepower. I was bringing an additional AR-15 as well, which was already on the boat, so Charlie and Tommy and I could share ammo.

Sarah finished packing and handed me mine. I helped her with hers and we grabbed up Jake. Sarah looked at me. "Are we taking Jake with us?"

I thought about it and finally decided. "No. As much as I would love to bring him with to keep him close, he's safer here than anywhere. Nate will die for him if it comes to that and I can't guarantee his safety out there. We don't know what we're going to run into and I have enough to worry about with you coming along."

Sarah cocked her head at me and I continued. "I don't want to lose you, either."

Sarah's expression softened and she stood on tiptoes to give me a quick kiss. Jake leaned over for a kiss as well and Sarah laughed as Jake tried to slobber one on her cheek.

We all went out the door and walked over to Nate's house. Nate and Patty lived two homes down and Nate was waiting for us when we walked up. Jake waved his arms at Nate and received a "Hey, big guy!" in return. I put Jake down and he took three steps to Nate, who scooped him up in his big arms and held him tight.

Nate looked at me. "Good choice. Charlie just dropped off Julia, so we'll get to play family for a few days." Sarah handed over a bag of supplies for Jake, including food, diapers, clothes and toys. Nate brought Jake over to a blanket where Julia was playing. He crawled over and patted Julia on the head. Patty got up from her chair and came over to us.

"Hi, I'm Patty. Nice to meet you at last. Nate has told me a lot about you." Patty was about forty years old, with brown hair and blue eyes. She seemed nice and a good match for Nate.

"About half of its true" I said and everyone laughed. Patty just smiled. "Thanks for watching the kids." I said.

"Our pleasure" Patty replied, looking back at the babies. I got the feeling there was a sadness to her, but I wasn't going to pry. We all had stories of tragedy these days and it was a rare thing for people to survive intact.

I walked over to Jake and picked him up for a second. I looked into his eyes and he smiled at me as I silently promised to come back to him. He seemed to understand and grabbed my nose in response. I kissed him and held him, then put him down and went back to the group.

"Thanks again, Nate. I owe you." I shook his hand.

"Luck, brother. When will you be back?"

Sarah answered "We'll be back within five days, seven at the most."

I nodded. "We should have a pretty quick trip down, all things considered. Since we're not taking the highway we don't have to worry about cars and blockage and trapped Z's."

"Good luck, then." Nate shook my hand one more time, then Sarah and I walked down the road to the slip where the boat was waiting.

Charlie, Tommy, and the others were waiting at the dock. We were actually going to be following the Illinois and Michigan canal until it intersected with the Des Plaines River. I figured we could be assured of having enough water to travel by, since barges used to use the waterway. I just hoped a barge wasn't blocking the waterway.

Sarah and I boarded the boat, and I got a good look at Tommy and Charlie's handiwork. They had enclosed the aft section of the boat to provide shelter from the weather and keep our gear relatively dry. The two of them had rigged up a propane grill for cooking and cases of bottled water occupied a corner. I guessed we would sleep where we could and there seemed to be enough room all around.

I put our gear next to everyone else's and said, "Let's go."

Tommy nodded and fired up the motor. We were going to use the motor sparingly, to conserve fuel for the return trip, and would drift most of the way down. We knew where we were going, but we had to be careful getting there. Charlie, Martin, and myself all had long poles which we would use to steer around debris in the river. If we needed the motor we would fire it up, but for the most part we were returning to the days of Huck Finn.

We started downriver and moved along pretty well. The canal was slightly swollen as a result of melting snow upstream, but nothing dangerous. The good news was the extra water allowed for a swifter current, so we moved well. The trees along the waterway were tinged with green buds, which reminded us all that life goes on regardless of the circumstances. There was not enough vegetation yet to obstruct viewing the lands outside the canal and we could see wildlife scurrying about through the underbrush.

We drifted under the I-355 overpass and I couldn't help but wonder when we might be able to build such things again. Certainly not in the near future.

As we moved along, I noticed a zombie ambling along the canal bank. He hadn't noticed us yet, and was drifting back and forth. I was curious about them and water, so I whistled as we approached. The zombie's head whipped around and saw our boat. He reached out and came towards the water, stopping at the edge of the canal. His arms stayed up in a futile attempt to reach us, but he stayed put.

"Interesting," I said as I lined up the zombie in the sights of my rifle.

"What's that?" Tommy asked as he steered us closer for a better shot.

"He won't come into the water. It's like he knows it there or senses it somehow and won't go in," I said. "Wonder what it means, not that I'm ungrateful for another barrier."

Charlie chimed in from his side of the boat. "Maybe since the virus needs oxygen, the zombies are steered away from water and suffocating environments."

I fired once and the Z dropped as if someone had cut his puppet strings. I lowered my gun as the sound of the shot echoed down the canal and reverberated off the hills to the south.

Tommy chimed in. "If that's the case, then all the rivers and canals should be safe, shouldn't they?"

"Right now, I wouldn't take anything for granted until we know more, but it looks that way." I put my rifle down and picked up my pole once again to push us away from the embankment. "If so, then we can assume these things breathe in some way, although I have seen a zombie or two with their lungs ripped out." I pondered that for a minute, then realized it was way beyond me to speculate on zombie biology and turned my attention to the task at hand.

We drifted farther south and I could see another bridge in the distance. There were numerous cars on the expanse and again I wondered how they came to be there. Did they run out of gas or were they abandoned as the Z's descended upon them? We'd never know. And without the resources to get them out of the way, most roads were useless to us. Hence the river. I found it ironic that we were using the highways of the past, drifting under the highways of the present.

We moved along slowly, coming up to the town of Romeoville. Charlie suggested making a side trip to see if anything was there. I had no reason to argue so when we came to the bridge we went over to the side of the canal and Charlie and I hopped onto land. We only had to go about twenty yards before we could get onto the road and we moved quickly towards the town. We skirted around the abandoned cars and headed towards a populated area.

At least it would have been populated. A subdivision on the north side of the street had been completely devastated. Burned out homes outnumbered the remaining wrecks and they were in sorry shape as well. It was one of those cookie cutter subdivisions where the construction was cheap and the homes were not built to last twenty years. They were piled on top of one another and I am sure when the fires started, the flames just leapt from house to house. Here and there we could see fluttering white flags on the mailboxes, limp reminders of the start of the blight. We could see signs of struggles and there were numerous bodies and parts of bodies rotting in the spring sun. Fortunately, none of them were moving, so we pressed on.

At the first intersection there was a restaurant that was still standing and a gas station across the way. Beyond that were many homes and they were not in any better shape than the first. Charlie and I went to the gas station to see if there were any supplies, but the place had been cleared out. We did find a can of gas in the garage area and decided to take it along for the boat. I was curious about the rest of the town, but we had no time for a thorough investigation.

Charlie figured out a quick solution. We went over to a power line tower and with a little lifting and a lot of grunting managed to get Charlie started on his way up the tower. About halfway up he stopped and looked around, using a pair of binoculars. After about ten minutes, he headed back down.

I handed his pack back to him and said, "Well?"

Charlie took a drink. "Bad news. The whole town is gone. It's like a war zone. What wasn't burned has been turned inside out. What I thought was a burned out area turned out to be corpses covered in insects and crows. It looks like the town tried to make a stand near the high school and got overrun. There's nothing but death here. Romeoville is dead."

I shook my head. "Any good news?"

Charlie thought for a minute. "Didn't see any zombie activity, so I'm guessing they moved on. On a side note, I could see my house from up there." He flashed a stupid grin at me and for that I made him carry the gas can back to the boat.

We moved back towards the boat and when he were halfway there, realized we had company. About ten zombies had stumbled out of the burned out subdivision and were following us down the road. Charlie motioned towards the pack. "Feel like exercising today?"

I looked back and shrugged. "No need, they're not any... whoops." Three of the zombies were clearly moving faster than the others, moving at what I considered a fast walk. They would be on us if we just kept walking in a matter of minutes. "Better move to a defendable position."

Charlie looked back and saw the trio. They were moving quickly for zombies and had already outstripped their companions. Their tattered clothing hung from gaunt, burnt frames and it was hard to tell what they might have been in life. One might have been a female, but it was impossible to tell, and we sure weren't going to ask.

I started to run to gain some ground and Charlie kept up with me. We moved to the grassy area where we first got onto the road and Charlie spun around to fire at the Z's chasing us. His bullet went wide but struck one of the slower zombies. That one fell down, but immediately began getting up again. The faster zombies actually increased their speed to a trot, and started to spread out. That was new and not welcome at all. That showed some sort of modicum problem solving intelligence and if more of these things started to do that we were screwed.

Charlie and I reached the edge of the woods and managed to get about fifty yards between us and the Z's. We got behind trees and lined up our shots. I took aim at a desiccated corpse with numerous holes in his dark flesh. His fast motion made aiming difficult, but I followed his movement and fired. The bullet took him square in the face and the heavy caliber blew the back of his head completely out. He backflipped onto the ground and I swung my rifle to the next one just as Charlie fired. His bullet entered the eye of the Z on the far left, whose head flopped to the side as its body tumbled forward. I fired at the last one, but the Z tripped at the last moment, causing my bullet to go wide. Charlie took aim as the zombie started to get up again, and nailed it in the back, hammering it down to the ground. I slung my rifle over my shoulder and unsheathed my pick, moving forward to finish it off. Charlie pulled one of his tomahawks and moved forward as well.

We moved cautiously forward in the knee-high grass, keeping an eye out for the Z. Charlie may have broken its back, then again, he may not. We approached the spot where we last saw it and got a surprise. The zombie was gone. I looked at Charlie and shook my head, and we immediately scanned the area. I unholstered my SIG and Charlie did the same with his Glock. We didn't have time to hunt for the bastard, the remaining zombies were getting closer and tall grass hid them until you were on top of them, or they were on top of you.

Charlie and I stood back to back and waiting quietly, I heard movement to my right and looking down, sure enough the zombie was creeping slowly towards my leg. I bumped Charlie and he looked down and saw the Z as well. A skeletal hand reached through the grass and was just about to grab my ankle when my SIG barked and put the zombie down for good.

A groan got my attention and the rest of the zombies had reached the edge of the road and were now looking down at us. Their groans and our gunshots had attracted a lot more attention and what Charlie had said was zombie free turned out to be zombie full. I guessed we were looking at about fifty ghouls. Several of them started down the embankment, lost their footing and tumbled the rest of the way down. It was a putrid avalanche I had no intention of waiting for. I tapped Charlie on the arm and we ran back to the boat.

Tommy and Sarah and the others all had questions for us when we boarded the boat again and I gave them the long and short of it. Romeoville was dead, there was nothing to salvage that would be worth the risk of zombies. I also told them about the fast moving zombies and I saw Bev and Casey shudder as they considered the ramifications. The thought gave me the creeps as well.

6

We pushed off the canal edge and drifted away. Charlie nudged me and pointed back to where we had come and I could see several zombies, shuffling slowly along the edge of the canal, staying away from the water, but drawn to the meal that was drifting away. Charlie raised his rifle but I waved him off. They weren't any danger, so there was no point in wasting the ammo.

We drifted farther south, coming up slowly to the town of Freeport. This town was in better shape than Romeoville and had been an old river town in its day. The original I&M canal ran through this area. Nate had made his way to this town and had secured parts of it. We would eventually make our way down here and retake this town as well. We didn't need it right now, but I hoped eventually we would. There was a great stone building in Freeport that had once been a warehouse during the day of the canal, and would make a great fortification to use as a base for retaking the town.

I didn't see any zombies as we drifted past, but I was sure they were there. They would always be there until we saw each and every one dead and burned.

We moved farther south, drifting lazily on the canal as the sun climbed higher in the sky. The canal was lined with trees and we moved in relative quiet. In fact, it was kind of boring. I found my mind wandering off in ways I hadn't done for a year. It was weird how a little security made one relax.

I was in one of my mindless wanders when Sarah tapped me on the arm. We were approaching one of the locks on the canal, and there was a building that crossed three quarters of the canal. A lock system was on the left, and we would have to go through the locks to proceed further down the canal. I had considered this when we started off and we would have missed the locks had we followed the river, but we would have dealt with a lot of unseen underwater obstacles and I figured this was faster. But if the lock was closed we might be stuck.

We moved into the lock chute drifting slowly forward. We passed the lockkeeper offices and canal administrative offices of Joslin. We floated forward and luckily passed through the gigantic locks that regulated the flow of traffic on the canal. I figured the locks had been left open when everything went south, and no one had ever come back to set up the system again.

On the other side of the locks, the canal merged with the river, and the water flow was even faster. We were on the outskirts of Joslin and I was curious to see how the city had fared. We had seen bits and pieces of it when we were retrieving cargo containers last year, but we hadn't gotten as close as we were now. We began to see more buildings and homes near the river and several bridges. Coming into view as well was the appearance of several hundred zombies. In one area alone I figured there had to be three hundred zombies milling about in a perverted, slow moving dance of death. They raised their voices as we passed and several moved towards the canal, but the way was blocked and they were unable to follow us. Several fell into the canal and we all watched carefully to see what would happen, but as far as we could see the damn things couldn't swim, nor did they float.

I began to get an uneasy feeling the farther we drifted into Joslin, and the feeling was punctuated with the sounds of what was clearly gunfire. Somebody was shooting at something and by the sound of it, something was shooting back. I motioned for the women on board to go into the shelter and Charlie and I readied our weapons. We were in a bad way if someone opened up on us because we had no shelter and were pretty slow moving.

I motioned for Tommy to start the engine and get us past the town. As far as I was concerned, Joslin was a dead zone to be as avoided as much as Chicago. It sounded like there was a war going on and I personally did not want to get involved in it. Tommy fired up the engine and we moved quickly downriver, getting past four bridges and moving closer to the big interstate bridge. We saw zombies nearly everywhere and I realized this area was going to be a constant worry as long as it remained active. If someone was alive in there, they were welcome to it.

The river widened after we moved under the interstate bridge and I began to breathe easier as we were able to move farther away. I went over to the shelter and gave the all clear. Sarah glared at me as she came out.

"What now?" I asked.

"If there's trouble why would you hide the women?" she asked, poking me in the chest.

"Because you and the other women are tempting targets to men who may not have seen a woman for a while, at least not a live one," I said. "I'd rather fight just the dead right now."

"Why?"

"Because the dead don't shoot back," I concluded. I glanced over at Charlie who was getting a similar earful from Rebecca. We shared a sympathetic look and went back to our poles.

Tommy ran the engine for a half an hour and we made significant progress. I was monitoring our trip on a roadmap and judging by the bends in the river and roads we were passing, I figured we were coming close to where we were going to have to get out of the boat and walk to our destination. We passed the town of Channahon and as I looked it over I could see it had been hit hard as well. A lot of zombies from Joslin must have traveled south and descended on this area as well. Charlie looked at me and I just shook my head. We didn't have the manpower to take this on yet.

The sun was beginning to set lower in the sky and I figured we would need to camp. According to the map, we were passing the Des Plaines Conservation Area and I reasoned it would be a good place to settle for the night. I had Tommy turn down a side area on the river and we were pleasantly surprised to find a small marina nestled in the crook of the river. I could see a road that crossed the river farther up and effectively blocked any water passage in that direction.

I directed Tommy to bring us up alongside the pier and Martin and I jumped off with the mooring lines. We secured the boat and all of us got off to stretch our legs. The sun was lower in the sky and the east was darkening with purple streaks. The moon was making its appearance and I figured we had about two hours left of daylight. Tommy immediately began working on the grill to get dinner ready and the women pulled out the coolers. We were going to have hot dogs, having discovered the vacuum sealed packages lasted nearly forever. Not as long as Twinkies, but close.

Charlie and I decided to take a walk to secure the area and see if there was anything we could salvage for our trip or set aside to retrieve later. We moved down the pier and listened to the water from the river lap quietly against the supports. There were no other boats at the marina and I could only assume people used them to escape to who knew where. In the back of my mind I wished them luck.

Charlie and I approached a long building that seemed to be a maintenance shed for the marina. There were two boats in unusable condition outside the shed and scattered debris around the cleared area. We were surrounded by woods and I could see Charlie weighing in his mind what the possibilities of game animals in the area might be.

On the south side of the shed there was a pull-behind camper and a quick look revealed nothing of interest. In all likelihood this was just where it was stored until needed. Too bad the roads were pretty much unusable, this thing would have been valuable.

Charlie approached a large tank by the side of the building and tapped on it, starting high up and then moving lower. By sound, we figured there was about half of the tank left, about fifty gallons. We might need to figure a way to take that with us.

I approached the door of the shed and tried it out. It was locked. I moved over to one of the big garage doors and tried that. The door moved up about a foot and I stopped it there. I grabbed my flashlight, backed away and looked under the door. Seeing nothing, I opened the door all the way.

Inside there was a lawn mower, a small two person boat with a largish motor on it and a cluttered workbench along the far wall. I moved towards the workbench while Charlie went to the office door. A small row of lockers was next to the workbench and a cursory look into each one revealed several work shirts, a couple of towels, and decent supply of porn magazines. I smiled and turned towards the office as Charlie opened the door.

A huge zombie crashed into Charlie and bore him to the floor. The zombie had to be at least three hundred pounds and was dressed in a stained coverall with the name 'Pete' stitched on it. Charlie had his hand under the man's chin, trying to keep the snapping jaws away from him, but I could see his hand slipping. I grabbed an old, wooden handled hammer from the bench and ran over to help. Charlie managed to get the zombie off of him and the two of them were lying side by side, struggling.

I stepped up to the zombie's head and swung the hammer down, hard. The head of the hammer decided at that moment to slip off and it hurled across the garage to clang against the wall and floor. All I managed to do was bonk the zombie's head with a piece of wood.

"Play the damn drums some other time!" Charlie forced out through gritted teeth.

I reversed my grip on the handle and shoved it in the zombie's gaping mouth, barely getting my hand out of the way of the brown teeth. Charlie shoved the Z away from him and scrambled to his feet, followed by the huge zombie slowly getting up and coming at us. The handle of the hammer stuck out its mouth like the stick of a putrid candy apple.

Charlie whipped out a tomahawk and, snarling, jumped forward, burying the entire head of the 'hawk in the Z's skull. Charlie ripped out the blade as the zombie fell forward and it hit the ground with such force the hammer handle poked out the back of its head.

Charlie didn't say a word, he just went to the bench and cleaned off the blade of his weapon with a greasy rag. Coming back to the front of the garage he said, "I'd thank you, but I'm not sure what for."

I tried to look hurt. "I distracted him, didn't I?"

Charlie stepped outside and sloshed a little gas on his tomahawk then produced a lighter to set it aflame. The gas burned red off the blade, a curious side-effect of burning the virus. When the red died away, Charlie blew out the flame and resheathed the weapon.

We went back to the boat and found everyone else had started eating. Sarah handed me a hot dog and asked if we had found anything. I shook my head and said, "Just a rotting corn dog."

I ignored the piece of bun that bounced off my back.

7

I was on watch during the night when I saw the lights. We had loosened the mooring lines and allowed the boat to drift away from the dock about twenty feet. I figured that allowed us some security from any wandering zombies as well as keeping us from getting surprised by any others.

The lights were on the river and at first I wasn't sure I had seen anything, but the lights flashed on and off intermittently and after a few minutes I realized the lights were looking for something, but trying not to attract attention while they searched. That made me wonder if they were actually friendly survivors, looking for other survivors.

The river was dark as pitch, making slow slapping sounds against the pontoons. The moon offered very little light, just enough to show where the river was, but the banks were deep in shadow. If I recalled correctly, this was a Rustler's Moon. Light enough to see, but not light enough to aim a gun. I watched and saw the light again, checking the sides of the river. It was about three hundred yards upstream and moving slowly, with the river current. I couldn't hear anything other than the sounds of the river, so I had no way of knowing for sure their intent.

I stepped over to where Tommy was sleeping and tapped him on the shoulder. He awoke with a start and was reaching for a weapon when I whispered, "Shh...it's me. We've got company."

Tommy scrambled to his feet and swung up his AR. "Where, what, who... zombies," he stuttered, his head still asleep.

I grabbed his arm and shushed him, pointing upriver to where the light flashed on again. Tommy shook the sleep out and stared at the shadows, trying to see what was coming our way. I climbed on top of the shelter and lay prone, keeping my rifle trained on the dark. If they didn't notice us, my thought was to just let them drift on past and be on their merry way.

As they drifted closer, I began to hear bits of quiet conversation. It allowed me to focus more clearly on where they were. I heard Tommy shifting and knew he knew where they were as well.

"Why do we want to find them?"

"They looked dangerous."

"What choice do we have? I already explained this to you."

"The kids are tired and scared. We shouldn't have left the city."

"The gangs were going to kill us. They killed everyone else. They're worse than the zombies."

"We should have gone to the shelter."

"This is crazy."

They had drifted to within one hundred yards of our boat and I decided to force the issue, one way or another. I placed my flashlight on the roof of the shelter, away from me and turned it on. Its powerful LED beam pierced the darkness and lit up a crude flotilla. I felt like I was looking at refugee boats from Thailand. Three aluminum rowboats and two canoes had been lashed together to form a raft of a sort, and they were using the oars and paddles to move the mess downriver.

When the light hit them, several people dove for cover and I could hear the muffled cries of more than one child being desperately quieted by their mothers. I could see one man fumbling with what looked like a military-surplus style rifle. One boat was laden with garbage bags and packs, the sure sign of a hasty exit.

As the man tried to bring up the rifle, I spoke conversationally. "Don't bother." My words carried across the water, the man slowly lowered the rifle and raised his hands in surrender.

"Please don't kill us," he begged. "We're just trying to get away from the city. Please, we have children with us. Please." He looked in pretty bad shape, like he hadn't eaten in a while. Stress was in every limb as he stood there in the light.

"I'm not going to kill you," I said. I could hear stirring inside the shelter as my voice woke others up. Charlie had gotten up and was next to Tommy with his AR, trained on the refugees. "Paddle closer and we'll throw you a line. You can dock up there." I aimed the beam at the edge of the dock. "Stay there until we come for you. Get some rest. No one will bother you until morning."

The man's shoulders slumped in relief and I could hear small voices saying 'thank you' as they slowly paddled to the dock. I kept the light on them until they were secure, then sent Charlie and Tommy back to bed. I still had watch for another two hours, then it was Martin's turn. I had a few things to think about.

In the morning, after we had pulled our boat back to the dock, Charlie and I went back to the maintenance shed and hauled out the boat that was in there. There was a moment when we had to move the body out of the way, but we wrestled the boat around to the gas tank and filled the motor, hoping the gas hadn't turned to varnish over the winter.

We brought the bass boat—at least I think that's what it was— down to the water and pushed it in. I never fished, so I had no idea. Charlie reassured me it was. I pulled the boat with a line while he sat in it and steered. We brought it to where our boat was tied up and left it there. Our crew was getting up and moving about and were moving in pairs to the woods to perform morning functions. Some were looking towards our raggedy neighbors, but no one said anything. I went to the boat and put my gear on, checking my SIG and making sure my knife was in place as well as my pickaxe. My extra magazines were in place and I tucked my Walther into my leg pocket. Charlie geared up as well and with weapons in hand we went to the edge of the dock and looked over our new friends.

I motioned to Charlie. "You know, if we fall in the water, we'll sink like rocks."

Charlie looked at my gear and his own. "Don't fall in." was his sage advice.

There were twelve of them, including seven kids. There were three women and two men and the men were trying to put on a brave front while Charlie and I looked them over. I took in the poor condition of the boats, the lack of any food supplies or any supplies, for that matter. There were no other weapons evident outside of the old Mosin the leader had shown earlier.

I shook my head. Theses people were as good as dead if I let them go their way. I motioned to the leader to come up to the dock. He scrambled up and stood before me, clearly nervous and his eyes took in my weapons and gear. I didn't see any calculations going on in his head and I figured he was just a guy at the end of his rope, trying to take care of his family.

"Name's John Talon. This is Charlie James," I said.

"Bill Martinez. Thanks for letting us stay the night." Bill looked exhausted and I motioned for Sarah to come over.

"This is Sarah Greer. She's going to look after your women and kids." Sarah and Bill shook hands, then Sarah went to the boat and got the women to bring the kids onto the dock. They all ran to the woods for a bathroom break. The second man got out of the boat and walked over to us.

"I'm Jose Garza. Thanks for helping us." We shook hands and he continued. "We were in a bad way."

"I could see that," I said. "Where did you guys come from? I know you saw us and followed, but I am curious where you started."

Bill and Jose looked at each other and Bill spoke up. "We came from Joslin. I have a house near the river and we saw you drifting by. You were lucky the gangs didn't see you."

"Gangs?" I asked, having a feeling I knew the answer, but wanted to confirm it.

Bill continued. "When everything went to hell and people were trying to get out or were running from the zombies, the gangs of the city started taking over. They brutally killed any cop they could find, including their families, then declared themselves rulers of parts of the city. They demanded food and money and women and killed any who resisted. We hid from them as much as we hid from the zombies. They've set themselves up in churches and schools and the zombies can't get to them." Bill took a deep breath. "They took mothers away from their children, then fed the children to the zombies for fun. They're worse than the zombies."

Charlie and I nodded. We had seen things like this as well.

Jose continued. "I managed to save several kids who had been left alone by the gangs to die and we had just run out of food when we saw you drift by. I figured if the gangs didn't see you, maybe they wouldn't see us, either."

I looked Jose in the eye. "You saved a lot of people at great risk to yourself." I held out my hand and shook Jose and Bill's hands. "You're men I'm proud to know."

Charlie shook their hands as well. I continued, "You have no idea what's downriver, but I know what is upriver."

The rest of the group had come back and was standing on the dock with us.

"You're going back upriver and you are going to go until you reach the river town of Leport. When you get there ask for Nate, tell him I sent you. You'll get homes, food, and a chance to live again. We don't have much, but we all chip in to survive. Of course, you could go on your own, no one will force you either way. You could even stay here if you want," I said.

The group stood speechless, then a couple of the women started to cry. Jose shook my hand again and said, "Thank you."

Bill looked dubious. "How will we get upriver?" he asked.

I pointed to the boat Charlie and I had brought around. "We found this in the shed, you're welcome to it either way."

Bill finally broke down enough so I could see a tear in his eye. "Thank you," was all he said.

We helped the group load up and tied the boats in such a way as to be towed by the bass boat. It fired up when we tried it so the gas was still good. They were going to stay by the docks and wait until dusk to make the trip north. That gave them the best chance to slip by the city without being seen. We were getting ready to leave as well and I gave Bill and Jose some last minute advice.

"As much as you want to race past the city, your best bet is to go slow and make like a ripple in the water. Loud engines will attract attention. Stay to the right and when you pass the fifth large bridge, you'll be at Leport. If it's dark, stay in the boats until morning, then call out for Nate. He'll find you."

I shook hands again and two of the women gave me hugs. Sarah took it in stride, but insisted on holding my hand as we walked towards the boat. I guess she was sending a last minute message of her own.

We waved goodbye to the group as we shoved off and we kept an eye on them as we moved around a bend in the river. Would they make it? Who knew? But we did the best we could by giving them a chance. Would they get to Leport or head south? I had no answer for that one, but I hoped they made it either way.

The river forked and we took the south passage, heading towards Dresden Cooling Lake. We passed several river homes, each of them having slips for boats and I had hopes the people in the homes had made it through the mess. I didn't see any signs of life, so I wondered if they had gone to the shelter which was so close by.

I went back to Tommy and told him to just pick a house to pull up to; we were finished with our river trip. He chose a slip at the far end of the houses, hidden slightly around a bend. We pulled up and Charlie, Martin and I secured the boat. I looked around and didn't see any threats, so I gathered the group after we had off-loaded all of our supplies and gear.

"We have a little ways to go," I said, spreading the map out on a picnic table. I pointed to where we were and where we needed to go. "I figure we could find a vehicle around here somewhere, there's enough houses. I'm not looking for anything specific, just something to keep us from walking."

We split into four groups and started towards the homes, everyone getting into higher levels of defense conditions after our somewhat uneventful trip down the river. We found the houses empty, which didn't surprise me at all, and we found four cars, which did surprise me. I figured we would get lucky with one or two, but four was a bonus. Martin found some extra ammo, but since it was .32 caliber and none of us had a gun for it we left it behind. Casey found a first aid kit and Bev found a bottle of Southern Comfort. We kept both.

The cars weren't my first choice for zombie hunting vehicles, but they would have to do. All of them were sub compacts, and it was a feat of spatial engineering to get all of our gear in them. Tommy insisted on bringing the small grill and spent twenty minutes figuring out a way to pack it. The rest of us just sat in the shade and watched the sun climb higher.

Sarah and I talked about nothing and everything and it was nice to get away from the world for just a few minutes. Bev Shoreman wandered off to use a bathroom and was still gone when Tommy finished.

We split up and started to get in the cars when Charlie noticed Bev still gone. "Wonder where she is?" he asked the group.

I shrugged. "Guess she really had to go."

"For more than ten minutes?"

"You're right. We'd better go find her." I moved away from the car and went off in the direction Bev had gone. Charlie came with me and we split up, moving towards the road that made the small marina subdivision.

I circled around to the front of the homes, while Charlie went around to the back. I didn't see anything, so I started to head back when I heard a pistol shot.

I ran around to the sound of the shot and saw Charlie lining up another shot. Bev was on the ground and blood was staining the grass underneath her. It looked like she had gone to use the bushes and had been attacked. Charlie fired again and Bev's body jerked as the bullet entered her head.

I came up and looked at the zombie Charlie had shot. It was a small boy, roughly ten years old. It must have been in the bushes when Bev entered, and jumped her when she squatted down. From the wounds, it looked like her throat had been torn out, and she bled out in seconds, leaving the little monster to feed, ripping her face apart and tearing out large chunks of her throat and shoulder.

We didn't say a word as we both shook our heads and headed back to the cars. Everyone was standing by the vehicles with weapons in hand as a result of hearing the shot. When they saw just the two of us they knew what had happened and lowered their weapons. I shook my head at Sarah and she just looked down. Tommy shook his head and Martin put an arm around Casey.

I got in the car and fired it up. "Let's get the hell out of here." I could see more ghouls coming to investigate from the countryside and I didn't feel like getting stopped this far into the trip.

8

We moved out at a decent pace, drifting roughly to the south and west. We followed Dresden Road south and didn't see much in the way of devastation. We saw several farmhouses, but there didn't seem to be any signs of activity, living or otherwise. The area was actually peaceful, but that could change.

I checked the map Nate had given me and realized we were in danger of heading too far south. I didn't *need* to see State Center Bravo, but I wanted to. If it was actually still alive, I wanted to know if the people there were interested in coming back to civilization and starting over.

At Pine Bluff Road, the next intersection, I motioned for Tommy to turn right. If the center was around here, this road should take us right to it.

We drove for another half hour, then saw a hasty sign "Illinois State Center Bravo – 1 mile." I noted the abandoned shack near the road, which I assumed had been used for directing people to the center.

We crested a small hill and were able to see the center in the distance. It was located at the edge of a lake and corrugated rooftops gleamed in the morning sun. I could see it was roughly square in layout, surrounded by twin fences separated by a ten foot cleared area for patrols. Guard towers were placed every sixty to seventy feet with double towers at the corner. Large and small buildings were systematically laid out in an efficient pattern. I didn't know what the individual buildings were or what their function was, but I could guess.

Surrounding the centers were cars and lots of them. They were parked in neat rows on three sides of the center and they were parked at such angles that a person could not fit between them. I wondered about that for a second until I realized they were put that way as another line of defense, funneling potential zombies into kill zones. Of course, zombies tended to do things rather single-mindedly, so they probably tried to crawl over the cars, which would screw up their orderly disposal.

I focused on the buildings and didn't see any activity. In fact, the entire base seemed to have been abandoned. I didn't see any movement in the visible yards, but that meant nothing. I could feel the hairs sticking up on the back of my neck and it wasn't from the breeze out of the north. Something was not right with this place, but if it had the answers I was looking for, then it was worth the risk.

I put the binoculars away and turned back to the group assembled outside the cars.

"I don't see any activity, but you all know what it means to let your guard down. We're going in hot, so everybody watch your muzzles and shoot only as a last resort. We'll stop for an equipment check before the gate. Any questions?"

Tommy spoke up. "If we're expected at Coal City, why are we stopping here? Chances are anything left has been looted a long time ago."

I nodded. "You're right, I'm sure everything is gone of value. But this is the only place where we might be able to get some answers. What the hell happened to our government? What happened to our military? If these centers were to be manned by state guards, where did they go? Was there a national fall back line we missed? What about other countries? Who's left? I don't expect to find all the answers, but I hope to find out something. I'd hate to think we're killing ourselves just trying to survive when the rest of the survivors are living safe and well just a few miles away."

Tommy nodded with the rest of the group and we piled back into the cars to see what we could find out. We would likely turn up nothing, but it was worth a look.

We drove up to the front of the gate and I was surprised to see that it was wide open. I expected some sort of barricade, but there was none. The fence was ten feet high with razor wire topping the edge and there was a second fence inside the first. The area in between was covered in fine rock and I could see boot prints pressed into the gravel as soldiers went about their patrols. I could also see what looked like bare footprints and dragging marks in the gravel as well. The grass surrounding the front of the center was flattened down, as if it had been trampled by a thousand feet. A trail led away to the south, but I paid it little attention.

We turned the cars around for a quick exit if we needed it and I figured to leave the vehicles running. We weren't going to be longer than ten or twenty minutes and the sun was getting higher in the sky. I wanted to get to Coal City as soon as possible without spending the night in an unsecured area.

Once the cars were ready we checked weapons and loaded chambers. Magazines were secured and topped off if needed and clothing was checked for rips and loose material. I hunkered down into the gravel of the driveway and drew a crude map of the complex as I had seen it from the hilltop.

"Okay," I said, pointing with the stick I had used. "We're here at the front gate. Back here," I pointed to twin rows of small buildings, about twenty in total, "are what I assume was the housing for the citizens who made it here. Jason, you and Casey check these buildings, but don't dig too deeply. Sarah, you and Martin and Rebecca should check out these larger buildings here." I pointed to the huge buildings in front of the housing units. "Charlie, you check out these buildings here, I am going to assume they were barracks for the soldiers. Keep an eye out for ammo or weapons." Charlie nodded, adjusting his pack and getting an empty duffle bag from the car. "Tommy, you check these two buildings here." I pointed to another large building and two smaller ones. "But keep an eye out for any useful intelligence." I pointed to the last building. "I'm going to check out this building here, I assume it is an administration building of some sort."

I stood up and checked my watch. "We're gone in twenty minutes, whether we find anything or not." I pulled on my balaclava and adjusted my goggles. "Let's go."

We split up and headed in different directions, everyone making as little noise as possible. I didn't hear anything out of the ordinary, but while I thought that was normal, it suddenly occurred to me why my senses were tuned up. I didn't hear *anything*. No birds, no insects, *nothing*.

I stopped in front of the admin building and looked around. I could see Charlie moving towards the barracks and Tommy heading towards what looked like a garage. Neither of them seemed to think anything was out of the ordinary, but I couldn't shake the feeling that something was seriously wrong here.

I moved into the two story building and the light from the front windows was enough to illuminate the interior. The building was exactly what I thought it was, with a large central area surrounded by offices. Several hallways lead to the back of the building and I guessed that people were herded into the offices, their information taken, and then they were assigned a space in the housing buildings. It seemed very efficient, which struck me as odd for a government facility. I followed several colored lines on the floor, and most of them led to the outside, although one led to another part of the building. I followed that one to a flight of stairs and headed up. At the top of the stairs was an enclosed guard station and my sense of unease became heightened as I stepped on several spent shell casings. Someone had been shooting at something and I had a feeling I knew what they were shooting at. Bringing my rifle up to the ready, I pushed the door open and entered the hallway.

It was darker up here than downstairs, there was only a couple of skylights providing any light for the hallway. I walked slowly down the hall, passing by doors that had odd names on them, like Biolab 3, Specimen room A, Cross Contact Room. I had no desire to open any of the doors, figuring whatever might be in there was better off staying there. I was interested in the door at the end of the hall.

As I moved down the hall, my foot kicked something on the floor, causing a pinging sound to ring off the walls. I thought I heard a noise in response, but when it didn't repeat, I figured it was a mouse or something.

I reached at the door and figured this was the place for answers. The door read "State Center Bravo – Lt. Colonel Rickerson," and it seemed logical that Rickerson, whoever or wherever he was, would have some sort of information that might be useful

The door opened with a slight squeak and two desks flanked the door. This small office looked like it was for secretaries, since there was another door on the back wall. The room was sparse and utilitarian, having little more than the desks, chairs, computers, and file cabinets. I didn't bother with the file cabinets, they probably didn't have what I was looking for anyway. I did notice there were long scratch marks on the interior door's wood frame and that added another clue as to what happened here.

I tried the door, but found it locked. I took the butt of my rifle and tapped the glass, the sound seeming enormous in the quiet building. I listened carefully, but didn't hear anything else. Looking into the room through the hole I had made, I didn't see anything off kilter. I reached into the hole and pushed on the handle, opening the door.

The office was neat and tidy with a large view of the compound. The sunlight was a welcome relief to the dark of the building and I circled the desk to see if I could find anything.

Boy, did I ever. I turned the high-backed chair around and jumped back as a corpse fell towards me. It thudded to the floor and didn't move. Once my heart calmed down, I approached the body cautiously. Not seeing any movement, I put the rifle barrel into its shoulder and turned the corpse over. One look told me this one was dead for good. The man had a single bullet hole above his left ear and what was left of his brains was scattered on the far wall. I wondered if this suicide was related to the scratches on the door as I pulled the Beretta out of his hand, tucking it away for future use if needed. A quick search of the office revealed a laptop, which I took, two binders labeled "Communications", and another binder labeled "Solutions". I had no idea what might be in that one, but my curiosity was piqued. I figured if the laptop could be fired up, maybe there were files that might shed some clues on the world's situation. I found a small box of ammunition for the Beretta, so that was a plus.

I packed up the binders and ammo and tucked the Beretta into a side pocket. I heard something, but it didn't register as important. I looked out the window and I could see Tommy walking back from the building he had checked out. He was dragging something on the ground, but from that distance I couldn't tell what it was. I couldn't see anyone else, so I figured they were busy.

I left the office and headed towards the hallway. I would look through the information later. I opened the door to the hallway, then quickly closed it again. The empty hallway I had walked through earlier was now filled with ghouls. The noise I had made earlier must have stirred them. The two in front who turned to look at me when I opened the door were in sorry shape, being little more than emaciated skeletons. But their intent was clear as they stumbled towards the door with clawed hands reaching out for me. They were dressed in filthy hospital gowns, so I wondered what was going on in this building. I locked the door and backed away, bringing up my weapon as dead hands started to beat on the glass. I mentally kicked myself as I watched the glass I had broken start to develop cracks from the undead onslaught. I could see more hands start to pound the door and I knew I had little time.

I moved one of the secretary's desks in front of the door, then moved the other one on top of the first one. The desks were cheap metal government-issue garbage and not much good for anything, but I just needed a little time. The glass broke as I levered the second desk into place and I shoved the grasping hands back with it. I ran back to the inner office just as the horde of hands shoved the top desk out of the way and corpses began to squeeze through the opening, tearing their skin and clothing on shards of glass still embedded in the door.

I didn't wait for more. I closed the inner office door and slid the heavier desk in front of it. I didn't have much time and needed to get out of here fast. I figured I could make it out the window since I was only on the second floor. I grabbed the office chair and threw it at the window and watched the damn thing bounce off and clatter at my feet.

Well, try, try again as the sounds of the outer door crashing open and the desks being shoved out of the way filtered through. I grabbed the chair and threw it harder, causing only a small crack in the glass.

"Fuck this." I said as dead hands started to pound on Rickerson's office door, shaking the desk. I drew my SIG and fired two shots through the glass, the reports sounding unbelievably loud in the office and causing the Z's to groan and scrabble at the door all the harder.

I picked up the chair again and hurled it through the window, the glass finally shattering outward and cascading down like sharp rain. I looked out the window and ducked as Tommy raised his rifle at me. He didn't shoot and I poked my head up again to see him raise a tentative hand in my direction. I waved back and climbed out the window as the desk gave way and ghouls started falling through the door.

I hung down for a second, then let go, falling about ten feet and landing in a pile of leaves. I looked up to see three zombie heads staring down at me and I scrambled to my feet to get some distance in case they decided to follow me. I walked backwards towards Tommy and the two of us just watched as the office filled to capacity with dead people. They milled around the room, not really understanding where their meal went.

"Find what you're looking for?" Tommy asked, not taking his eyes off the zombies.

"Don't know yet. Got some binders that may have some answers, but there were some labs up there that might have some real interesting information" I said.

Tommy raised his eyebrows. "Labs?"

"Yeah, some strange things on the doors like Cross Contact and such," I said.

"Creepy."

"Yeah."

I checked my watch and we saw Charlie heading back our way. He was carrying a small bundle and moving quickly towards us. When he reached our position he stopped and looked back. Apparently what he saw was good news to him because he visibly relaxed.

"Well, that was close," Charlie said, putting the bundle on the ground.

"What'd you find?" Tommy asked.

"Ammo. About 600 rounds. You?"

Tommy patted his find. "Got a small output generator here. Found it in the office of the garage over there."

I nodded. That was a good find. "What do you mean 'That was close'," I asked Charlie.

I heard a crashing and looked back towards the barracks. Two soldiers, obviously dead, stumbled out of the building and lurched slowly towards us. They were dressed in full battle gear, complete with Kevlar armor and helmets.

"Oh," was all I could say.

Charlie shrugged his shoulders and I pointed to the office window, which was nearly bursting with zombies. Two of them were being squeezed out the window and grimy handprints covered the glass and wall.

Movement on our left caught our attention and we looked over to see Sarah, Martin and Rebecca heading our way and fast. On their heels were Jason and Casey and they were moving at a dead run.

A couple of seconds later a horde of zombies came pouring out from between the two main buildings, stumbling and tripping, but moving forward, nonetheless. The graying mass surged forward when they saw additional victims, and we all gaped for a second before I found my voice.

"Run! To the cars now!" I grabbed one end of the small generator and Tommy and I bolted for the cars, followed by Charlie and the rest. Sarah and Rebecca actually beat us to the cars and jumped into the driver's seats, getting the cars ready for a quick exit.

Charlie dumped his ammo into the back seat and climbed in, followed by the others. Tommy and I actually wound up bringing up the rear. As we passed the gate I shocked the heck out of Tommy by dropping the generator and running to the left, dragging the heavy gate into place. Tommy saw what I was doing and ran to the other side, swinging the right hand gate into place.

The dead were advancing steadily with a particularly gruesome individual leading the way. It was a middle-aged man who had been eviscerated, his guts hung out of his body and dragged along the ground. He jerked every time another zombie stepped on his entrails, which would then snap off, leaving bits behind. His dead eyes remained fixed on us, however, and he was going to hit us any second.

I moved the gate closed and Tommy did the same. I slid a zip tie through the bars and secured them, stepping back just as the first zombie slammed into the barrier. The gates strained the tie, but didn't break it. Tommy and I knew we needed more ties to secure the gate, but we didn't want to get caught by the grasping hands that tried to get through the gap between the gates.

Tommy came up with the answer. He waited until the push subsided, then charged the gate, keeping his hands on the reinforcing bars. The sudden push knocked down several zombies which tripped the ones coming up from behind. Using the opening, I quickly threaded three more zip ties before the hands came grasping again and I had to step back.

The zombies surged again, but the gate held. Tommy and I exchanged a look then picked up the generator and took it to the cars. We didn't have room in the back, so we used a length of cord and tied it to the roof, threading the cord through open windows. It wasn't pretty, but it worked.

Behind us, the zombies groaned and strained at their prison and I decided we needed to get out of sight before they broke free. We jumped into the cars and drove away, heading back the way we came, leaving behind yet another dead zone. Maybe we had the answers I was looking for riding with us, maybe not. I rummaged through my pack and dug out the binders and handed the one marked "Solutions" to Tommy to look through while I browsed through "Communications".

Sarah drove back the way we had come and headed south at the appropriate crossroads, leading our little convoy towards our new neighbors. I thumbed through the binder and found a few interesting pieces.

July 9 Communication from State Center Bravo: Infection spreading through housing units. Troop desertion increasing. Need reinforcements.

July 18 Communication from Governor: Contain all infected citizens.

July 29 Communication from Maryland Central: Capital has fallen, designated dead zone. Congress disbanded. President dead.

August 15 Communication from Colorado: Military in full retreat. Fall back to Cheyenne Mountain.

September 3 Communication from New York Central: UN collapsed.

October 18 Communication from California Coast: US Navy evacuate San Diego.

November 4 Communication from Houston: Dead Zone List update.

I ran down the list of Dead Zones but after four pages I gave up. I figured we were pretty much on our own and it was up to us to decide whether we lived or died. I shook my head as Sarah gave me a questioning look and turned my attention to Tommy.

"Anything good in there?" I asked, tossing the binder on the floor.

"You wouldn't believe some of the stupid things they wanted to try," Tommy said, shaking his head.

"Try me."

"Well, one of the suggestions was to douse the zombies in anti-bacterial gel, figuring it would kill them as they are walking disease factories."

I snorted. "You're kidding"

"Nope.   Here's another.   Use incendiary bombs on all population centers to burn out the infection."

I shook my head.   "Good thing we missed that one."

Tommy laughed.   "Here's my favorite.   Develop an anti-zombie spray as personal protection against the undead.   There's even a chart describing the effects of pepper spray on zombies."

"And?"

"All failed.   Test number four resulted in the researcher getting bit."

"Figures.   They'd have saved themselves a lot of trouble by just writing 'Shoot in head, then burn.'"   I turned back to the front.

"Any info in the 'Communications' binder?" Tommy asked as he put away the 'Solutions' binder.

I nodded.   "It all went to hell too fast for them to get a handle on it.   Congress and the President are dead and the list of Dead Zones is longer than Jacob's Christmas list.   The military might be somewhere in Colorado or Wyoming and there might be a bunch of people on boats in the Pacific Ocean."

Tommy and Sarah digested the news, then Sarah spoke up. "In all honesty, I'd rather be where we are than looking for help from the government."

"Amen." Tommy and I spoke together.

9

We drove for a few minutes, then Sarah slammed on the brakes, tossing the car into a shambles and nearly causing the cars behind us to pile up.

"What the hell?" Tommy yelled, pushing a pack off his head.

Sarah didn't say anything, she just pointed out the window.

A grey mist was undulating on the horizon, ebbing and flowing like a grim tide. Staring closely at it, I realized it was not a mist at all. It was a mass of zombies and they were headed in the same direction we were. I looked ahead to their destination and my heart sank. They were going to Coal City. The town was going to be hit sometime soon.

Sarah looked at me and my mind was racing. We needed to get to the town to warn them of the approaching swarm, but I didn't want to just drive ahead of the masses just to bring them to their dinner. I looked at my map and followed Dresden Road which led to Coal City. If we followed that road, we would surely be seen by the horde and they would follow us to the town. Looking at the size of that swarm, we were facing two or three thousand undead.

I stared at the map until the answer came to me. I turned to Sarah and told her to turn around and go back to the last intersection. She looked at me quizzically, but hurried to comply. When we had started east again, and were moving away from the horde, I outlined my plan.

"We're heading to the railroad. The line runs alongside the town itself and we should be able to stay out of sight of the main horde," I said, pointing to the rail lines coming up fast. "At most, we will have a few miles to go."

"Are we walking?" Tommy asked.

"Have to, unless there is a service road," I said.

As luck would have it, there wasn't any road, so when we reached the railroad, we had to ditch the cars. We packed up as much as we could, taking every weapon and round of ammo we had. We put the generator in the car and packed as much food and water as we could. Hopefully the supplies we left behind would be here when we got back, if ever.

We moved along the railroad track at a steady clip, walking briskly, but not so fast we would be exhausted if we had to run. We had about two miles to go, if I read the map correctly. Sarah walked behind me, followed by Tommy and the others. Charlie brought up the rear.

Tommy spoke up. "I really hate being exposed like this. I feel like we're going to suddenly be surrounded."

I pointed to the graying horizon. "We will be if we don't get to that town."

"What if the town is already dead?"

"We'll burn down that bridge when we come to it," I said.

"Backup plan?"

"Got one." I did, but it was iffy at best and required more than my allotted lifetime share of luck.

Tommy went silent again. We moved closer to the town, and I could see a multi-colored barrier sticking up out of the ground. It stretched for about two miles off to the west and out of sight to the south. I wondered what it was made of for a while, but when we got closer, I realized it was made of the same thing that we had made our first fence out of. Surrounding the better part of the town was a line of cargo containers. I noticed some containers standing away from the fence and wondered briefly what they were out there for, but I figured they must have been leftovers.

We moved closer to the town and I started to see people standing on the containers, watching us approach. There were three of them, all armed with what looked like to be scoped rifles. If it came to a shooting, we were going to catch the short end of it. I hoped it wouldn't but I had learned a while ago that things weren't always as they seemed.

We picked up our pace and headed towards the group. The cargo containers paralleled the tracks, so we didn't have to go far. When we were about fifty yards out one of the men raised a hand and we stopped.

"That's far enough. Who are you and what do you want?" The speaker was a graying man, about fifty years old and carrying a decent paunch. He had a badge pinned to his jacket and was keeping a hand on his sidearm.

"I'm John Talon," I called out, "and these are my friends. I believe one of you has been talking to my friend Nate Coles?"

"I'm Sheriff Tom Harlan and these two are my deputies. Come on up. We've been expecting you." The sheriff motioned to one of his deputies and the man lowered a ladder for us We quickly climbed up and introductions were made.

From our vantage point, I could see the town was well cared for and I could see several people moving around and just going about their daily lives. It was a picture of the community I was trying to build in Leport. The line of cargo cars stretched out and I could see they had encircled a water supply as well as large swaths of farmland that looked like it had been recently tilled and planted. If any town was going to succeed, it was this one. That is, if the zombies let it.

The sheriff told his deputies to see to our group and the rest of the crew headed down a ramp that went down the side of the container. I could see many of these ramps and realized they were better than ladders because there was less chance of tripping either up or down.

Sheriff Tom and I started walking along the top of the containers and I could see several spots where zombies had been killed and disposed of along the perimeter. "Looks like you managed to weather the storm better than most, Sheriff," I said.

The Sheriff grunted. "We got damn lucky. Our high school kids were the first ones to let us know something was happening and for once us adults actually listened to them. We had meetings about what to do and how to save our town. Several of our 'ol boys were survival nuts of a sort and they had some pretty good notions. We figured we needed a quick fence, something we could put up and take down if it turned out the plague was not as bad as everyone expected."

"Where'd you get all the containers?" I asked as we walked close to the reservoir.

"One of our guys is a train driver for the depot north of here and he told us about all the containers that were sitting there, doing nothing. I guess the companies that made them found it cheaper to make new ones than pay to have the old ones shipped back. Anyway, he started bringing them down and here we are."

"Are they attached?" I asked, remembering that we had a group of zombies that nearly managed to get past our fence early on until we welded them together.

"Most of them are," said the sheriff, "but I can't remember which ones aren't. We had a breach a little while back with a group of fifty zombies who pushed one out of the way and got inside." The sheriff stepped over a rise in the containers and stopped at the corner of the fence. "We lost several people before we got the better of them. That's when we got in contact with your pal, Nate. He told me if there was anyone who might be able to get us situated to where we don't have to worry about that again, it was you."

I shrugged off the compliment. "I just try to do what makes sense and try to stay alive while I do it."

"Well, I would appreciate the help," said Sheriff Tom. "Although I kinda figured you would have brought more people."

I nodded. "I wish I had too," I said, looking at the horizon.

Sheriff Harlan looked puzzled. "Why's that?"

I pointed at the advancing grey line. "Because that swarm of dead people will be here by tomorrow."

Sheriff Tom looked to where I was pointing, then said something both religious and sacrilegious at the same time. I have to admit, even for a reluctant Catholic such as myself, I was impressed.

We stepped down the first ramp we came to and hurried to the town hall. We had planning to do and lots of it. As we walked towards the center of town, Sheriff Tom grabbed his radio and called his deputies to the hall, instructing them to get the Mayor and as many of the people as they could to the hall immediately. The sun was setting, casting long shadows and as I walked through the little town, I hoped it wouldn't be the last one these people got to see.

A deputy came zooming up in a golf cart and the Sheriff motioned me to get in. We made much better time and as we drove on I could see people starting to stream out of their homes and head towards the town hall. If I had to guess, there was a lot more than one thousand people here. I figured closer to two thousand. Too many to evacuate. We had to stand and fight.

10

The Sheriff pulled up to the town hall and jumped out, surprising me with his agility. I imagined in his youth Tom Harlan was a man to step around. I walked up behind him, working my way through the people who were standing in the hallways and outside. More than one of them gave me strange looks, likely in response to my being a stranger to the town and the fact that I was armed to the hilt. Zombie Killer. That's me. Certified.

I moved into a large atrium that was doing double duty as a meeting room and the area was packed. I spotted my crew up on a landing of one of the four stairwells that led to the second floor. The mayor was talking animatedly to the Sheriff and the Sheriff was gesturing wildly. The two deputies squeezed themselves through the throng and positioned themselves on the stairs, blocking anyone from approaching the mayor.

I reached the stairs and the deputies waved me up. I moved up to where Sarah, Tommy, and Charlie were talking.

"Hey all," I said. "Everybody okay?"

Charlie spoke up. "Sure enough. They gave us food and drink and asked a ton of questions. How was your walk with the local constabulary?"

I blinked at Charlie's vocabulary, then shook it off. "Fine. He knows the horde is coming and we're going to try to do something about it."

"Do we have a plan?" Sarah asked, taking my hand.

I looked into her beautiful eyes. "Not a clue. But I'll think of something." I grinned at her and she squeezed my hand.

The noise in the room increased as the Mayor and the Sheriff tried to quiet everyone down. But everyone was shouting questions and not listening to answers. The Mayor threw up his hands and walked away from the table while Sheriff Tom continued trying to quiet the masses with no success.

I grew impatient and shrugged off the warning look I got from Sarah. I motioned for Charlie and Tommy to follow me. I released the magazine in my rifle and ejected the round in the chamber. I put it back in the magazine, then I moved to the table and tapped the Sheriff on the shoulder. His flushed face stared at me for a second, then he stepped aside. I stood on the table and held my M1A out in front of me. Behind me, Charlie and Tommy were doing the same with their AR's. I stared at the crowd, which began to quiet down at my appearance, then I deliberately charged the rifle, the bolt sounding unusually loud in the diminishing noise.

"Who wants to die right here, right now?" I boomed across the assembled town. I was greeted with shocked silence. "Who?" I yelled at them, receiving no answer. I stared for a minute. "You'd better be sure. Because if you don't start listening and don't start preparing for the shit storm coming your way right at this minute, then you will wish you had spoken up and taken a bullet when you had the chance."

I stared at the stunned audience. "My name is John Talon. I have led a group of survivors from Leport down here to lend you a hand. What I didn't know, what no one could have known, was a large horde of living dead is headed your way right now. If I had to guess, they are what is left of State Center Bravo. If I had to guess again, I would say there is about two or three thousand of them headed this way." There was a collective gasp. "You have made a good stand here and if I had to estimate your chances of survival, I'd say they were better than average. If you don't work together, your chances are none. Are you ready to listen?" A lot of heads nodded.

I jumped down from the table and rejoined my group. The Mayor looked nervous as he stepped to the table and Sheriff Tom nodded his thanks.

The Mayor spoke to the group and outlined what was expected of the townsfolk while the sheriff, his deputies, and my crew discussed plans and defenses. When the Mayor finished extolling the virtues of the town and its people and the willingness to fight for their homes and lives, he called upon the Sheriff to outline the plan.

Sheriff Tom Harlan adjusted his jacket, hitched his belt a little higher, ran a tired hand through thinning hair, then spoke to the people.

"Most of you know me as Tom since most of you grew up with me here in Coal City. I've tried to do the best I could by you and when this mess hit the world, I tried to save my town as best as I knew how." There was scattered applause. "We worked together to get the fence up and we fought together when we had that breach. We welcomed those who came to us for shelter and we never asked anything from anyone." Sheriff Tom paused to collect his thoughts. "When we had that breach, I realized we needed some help; someone who could steer us in the right direction. When I got on the ham radio I prayed I would find someone who could help save our town and ensure our survival. What I found was John Talon." Sheriff Tom motioned me over. "John has been in survival mode since the Upheaval and he has managed to save hundreds of people. I figured if anyone could do it, he could. Trouble is, I called him here just as the worst is about to hit us. I don't know if we're going to survive this, but we certainly are going to try. John here will tell you what the plan is. John?"

I didn't expect to speak, but since I was no stranger to it, I stepped up to the table. "You have a secure fence, but it has its weaknesses. Against the lone zombie or ten, it will do just fine. But against a thousand or two thousand it will eventually fail. What we need to do is engage the enemy much sooner and try to thin the ranks as much as possible. We don't have enough bullets for all of them, but we have enough to thin the herd a good deal. Me and my men will be setting up firing positions and anyone who has any long range guns and ammo will need to step up. Second, we need to make sure we have enough weapons for everyone to use in hand to hand combat. Check your homes and see what you have. Charlie here will be available to check weapons for suitable purposes. Third, we need to have fallback points in case there is a breach. All cars need to be requisitioned to form choke points and kill zones. Our final fallback position will be here, in this building. The windows are high enough off the ground that they cannot be breached and there are only two doors to block. All the people of the town not engaged in the fighting will stay here until the danger is passed." I looked around the assembled town. "I will do my best for all of you and I will fight as hard as I can for you. I expect to survive and so should you. I have a son waiting for me in Leport and I promised to come back to him. Anyone who knows me knows I never break my promises."

I stepped away from the table and Sheriff Tom stepped back up. "Get back home and get prepared. The men who live on Fourth Street, you are in charge of getting the cars to form barricades and kill zones. The men on Third Street, you get your families ready then get to the school to get the tables and such for barricades as well. Second Street, you are in charge of weapons. Everyone bring what they have and they will check them for you. First Street, you all get situated then go with Mr. Carter here. He'll get you set up along the fence. Miss Greer, Miss Steele, and Miss Maxwell will see to the children and the defenses here in the Town Hall. Let's move, people."

The hall emptied quickly and my crew members went to help where they could. I stood outside with Sheriff Tom and we watched the town spread out and get to work.

"What do you think our chances are?" he asked.

I thought about it for a minute. "Probably better than I think, but I'd say ninety percent if the fence holds."

"And if it doesn't?"

"A lot less." I was never one to sugar-coat things, especially when it came to survival.

Sheriff Harlan looked at me, then grunted. "Well, nobody lives forever."

I slapped him on the back. "No, but we're going to do our best to make sure these people live a bit longer than tomorrow."

The sheriff smiled, then moved off into the dusk, bellowing at his deputies to get moving and quit slacking. I watched him for a minute, then felt a small hand slide around my waist. I looked down and smiled at Sarah.

"Hey you," I said, putting my arm around her waist.

"Hey back," she said. "Where are you going to be? You didn't say in the speech."

"Didn't I? Hmm. That is odd," I said. "Well, don't worry. I'll have Charlie with me."

Sarah took my face with both her hands and looked me square in the eyes. "You don't have to tell me, just promise me you'll live."

I held her hands. "I promise. Now let me go. I need to get things prepared before tomorrow." I kissed her gently and she returned it with an almost desperate intensity, wrapping her arms around my neck. I held her for a minute, oblivious to the looks of the lingering townsfolk, then broke away and put her down. "I will come back. I promise."

Sarah smiled and went back into the building to get things prepared. I walked around to the side of the building and found Charlie waiting for me.

"Did you tell her?" he asked

"No. Did you tell Rebecca?" I retorted.

"Are you kidding? She'd flip," Charlie responded.

"Right. Well, we'd better get moving if we want to have even the slightest chance of living through tomorrow," I said, adjusting the rifle strap.

"We're crazy, you know that?" Charlie fell in step next to me.

"Can't be sane in this world."

"Amen."

11

I woke up smelling like laundry detergent and completely surrounded by the dead. Ordinarily, this would be cause for some concern, especially the part about the laundry detergent, but since I had planned for this to happen, I wasn't too upset about it.

Last night, Charlie and I had met with Sheriff Harlan and went over an idea I had about dealing with the dead. I figured they were going to hit the wall no matter what since the zombies could easily smell the humans inside the perimeter. But that didn't mean we had to just let them hammer away until they eventually weakened the barrier and made their way in. What I proposed was to hit them from behind and keep the horde occupied on two fronts, thinning their attack line and keeping them from seriously concentrating their efforts.

I was under no illusions. We had a thin chance at best and if we managed to get through this, I personally would be amazed.

I idly wondered what Charlie was thinking about the plan as he waited for the signal in his container. We were holed up about a quarter mile to the north of the fence and we decided to split up in case the Z's figured out that there was a snack in one of the containers. Charlie was about fifty yards to the west in a light blue container. Mine was red and we had to flip a coin to see who would be getting the blue one. I lost. We both had carried bags of laundry detergent to mask our scents as we waited for the horde to pass. I had wet down the door of the container with water from my bottle and tossed handfuls of the detergent on the door.

As far as I knew, the detergent had worked. No one had come pounding on the door in the night and I had awakened a couple of times to the sound of many shuffling feet sliding by, but as long as the door held, I was actually quite safe. Of course when I opened the door to get into my firing position I could be given a hearty good morning chomp by a lingering ghoul, but those were chances I was willing to take.

I had a lot of time to think and found my thoughts drifting to those things that I usually thought about in quiet times. I thought about Jake and idly wondered how he was doing, knowing he was safe with Nate. I worried about his future and mentally started his training and how he would deal with the world he was going to inherit. I thought about his mother and felt a pang of guilt that quickly passed. Ellie would not want me to sit around and mope no more than I would want her to if I had been the one to go. These thoughts naturally led to Sarah and the hope I would see her again. I figured she would be okay and I winced in the darkness about what she was going to do when she found out what I was up to this morning. I gave Sheriff Tom that job and I know he was not looking forward to talking to both Sarah and Rebecca.

I thought about where we were going to go to from here, what the overall plan was. In a way I felt like I needed to move quickly, that if I didn't have something set up soon everything I had worked for and people had died for would unravel. I could just hang it all up and disappear with Jake and take our chances with the dead world, but that would be selfish. Jake didn't ask to be born into this mess and it was my duty as a father to do what I could to make sure he survived. I made a mental promise to him that I was not going to roam for a long time and just spend my time making the community we lived in as good as it could be. For the moment, it was the best I could do.

The radio on my belt crackled and Charlie's voice came softly over the airwave.

"Hey, John?"

I fumbled with the radio in the dark, having a hard time getting it off my belt, and bumping my elbow on the side of the container. I cringed at the sound and hoped like hell no zombies heard it. "Hey, Charlie." I replied just as softly, my words echoing slightly in the dark container. "Good morning."

"Has the Sheriff called you yet?" Charlie seemed anxious.

"Not yet, why?"

"I think the Z's know I'm in here."

"Really? How do you know?" I thought it illogical for Charlie to be talking to me if he thought zombies were within earshot of his hidey-hole.

"Something keeps moving back and forth outside the container and I keep hearing sounds like digging." Charlie's voice seemed strained and I could only imagine what he was thinking. Being trapped inside a metal box while the dead waited for you was like already being buried. You had nowhere to go and death was outside the door. Better to put a bullet in your own head than starve to death or be eaten by zombies.

"Hang tight." I tried to sound reassuring. "I'll let you know when I get the signal to come out and start the festivities, whether or not you have anything to worry about."

"Okay. Make it soon, alright? The digging started again and it's driving me nuts."

"Done," I said, replacing the radio on my belt. If my watch was right, we should have some information soon.

Ten minutes later, the radio crackled again. "Talon?" Sheriff Harlan's voice came through. "You still there, you crazy bastard?"

I brought the radio up, more careful not to make noise this time. "Yep. Ready when you are." I adjusted my gear in the dark. "How's it look out there?"

"Well, I guess we have ourselves a regular dust up, no question about it. We got the people laying low like you said and nobody is shooting until I give the signal."

That was part of the plan. The zombies could smell the living, but if they didn't see them they would not attack in earnest. If we could keep them from massing at a single point, the fence stood a better chance of holding them off. But we needed to keep them away from the fence. Eventually they were going to try and force their way in, but not right now if I could help it.

I hit the send button. "How's the area around me?" I was ready to get out and get to work.

"Just fine, the worst has passed and they are now spreading out along the fence," the sheriff reported.

"Any activity around the blue container?" I asked. "Charlie said he was hearing digging sounds."

"Nothing on this side. His door is clear."

"Okay, thanks. I'm heading out." I wondered what Charlie had heard.

"Hey, John?" the radio started again.

"Yeah, Tom?"

"I was told to give you a message."

"Was it from a smallish, green-eyed woman with a gun?"

"Yep. Consider it *sent*. Harlan out."

I chuckled in the dark. Sarah was pissed and I really couldn't blame her. I imagine Charlie was going to get an earful as well if we lived through this.

I stepped up to the door and unlocked the chain I had wrapped around the door poles on the inside of the container. Normally these containers had all the locking mechanisms on the outside, but since I was in and wanted to keep things out, it presented a small problem. Fortunately, we were able to secure the doors and I opened one cautiously and looked out. There was no one in front of me and trusting to Harlan's assessment of the situation, I assumed there was no one where I couldn't see them.

I stepped out into the open and pulled out the small stepladder I had brought with me to the container. Charlie had one as well and I used it to quickly get up on the container. The ladder was little more than four feet tall, but it got me on top, which was where I needed to be. I hauled up a small duffle bag, which contained my ammunition, and slowly walked to the end of the container.

From my vantage point, I could see the mass of zombies milling about the fence. My original estimate had been around two thousand. Looking at the horde in front of me, I figured I was short by at least a thousand or two. I let out a long breath, then started to set up for my job.

I laid out my rifle, a scoped AR-15, and placed all the magazines I had within easy reach. Thanks to Charlie finding ammo at State Center Bravo, I had five hundred rounds with which to work. I only had six forty-round magazines, so some reloads were going to be necessary, but that didn't worry me too much.

I placed my backpack on the container, intending to use it as a rest for my sniping. The zombies were effectively three hundred yards away, and I needed every advantage I could get. I noticed movement out of the corner of my eye and looked over at Charlie's container. A small dog was sniffing around the base and scratching at whatever it was dogs scratched at when they wanted something. I laughed at the thought of big Charlie being afraid of a rat terrier.

I clicked on the radio and called Charlie into action. When he asked about the noise, I told him just to get in place and not worry about it. Within a few minutes, Charlie was on the top of his container, set up the way I was. Charlie doused the dog with water from his canteen and it ran off. In all honesty, the dog actually astonished me, since I hadn't seen one since the Upheaval. Most family pets had been devoured when the worst hit and their owners turned and the few in yards had been eaten as well. That little guy must have managed to escape and was living wild. Good luck, buddy.

Our activity had attracted the attention of a few zombies and they started to head back in our direction. They would be first.

I settled down and sighted in my first kill. It was a man in a threadbare business suit, missing one shoe and most of his face. His left eye hung out of its socket and bounced crazily as he took staggering steps across the field. I let out a breath and pulled the trigger. The rifle cracked loudly as the .223 round punched through the air and penetrated the man's grey forehead. The back of his head blew outward and he dropped backwards, his eyes finally seeing nothing. The smartass part of me wondered if his left eye was relieved from seeing nothing but feet.

The shot turned heads and the group started towards me in earnest. I shifted my aim and started to work, shooting the ones closest to me and working my way backwards. It got a little gross as the zombies got closer, not only from looking close up at dead faces and shooting them, but the ones who had fallen were pulped by hundreds of feet squishing them into the ground. Several of the ghouls were falling down, tripping over permanently dead comrades. I missed a few shots that way, aiming at a head that suddenly dropped out of sight just as I pulled the trigger.

I changed magazines when the first one went dry, adjusted the power on the scope, and went back to work, dropping the Z's as they got closer and closer. The mass of the horde started to shift my way and I was going to be facing a real dilemma soon.

When I ran out of magazines, I had left about two hundred zombies dead on the grass. They were about fifty yards from me and closing in. I worked my way back along the container, taking my supplies with, then dropped back on the ground. I tossed the materials back into the container, then scooted inside. I secured the door and waited.

Sure enough, Charlie started his killing, which was designed to draw the mass away from my container over to his. I sat on the floor reloading magazines while outside zombies died. The light from my flashlight was accented by sunlight as some of Charlie's rounds penetrated the sides of the container. That was why I was on the floor.

After about ten minutes of constant firing, the shots faded away, and I figured Charlie had beat a retreat like I had done. I waited to hear the next round of shots, and sure enough, there they were. Sheriff Harlan had gathered everyone with a scoped rifle to the wall and had stationed them at intervals. They were to pick up the firing once Charlie and I had ducked for cover. I waited until I had counted about one hundred shots, then called the Sheriff on the radio.

"Sheriff—Talon here. What's the situation?"

The radio hissed and then I heard, "Not bad. You look cleared to go."

"Thank you. See you topside."

I checked in with Charlie and he said he was reloaded and ready to go.

I shrugged into my backpack, making sure my weapons were ready and spare magazines were within easy reach. My hand tool was set and my SIG was topped of with a fifteen round magazine. I pushed open the door and walked right into the middle of five zombies. From his location on the fence, Sheriff Harlan couldn't have seen them.

Decaying hands reached for me as the sounds of hungry moans filled my ears. I had no retreat as one moved in between me and the door of the container. I ducked as grasping hands reached for my neck and I swung my rifle in a wide circle, knocking three of them off their feet. I stood up and a zombie girl grabbed the strap of my backpack and pull me close for a bite. I didn't give her the chance as I slammed my hand up under her chin, snapping her head back and causing her blackened teeth to clack loudly. I grabbed her throat with one hand while stepping back from the first three slowly getting back to their feet. I pinned her to the cargo container and dropped the rifle as the first one came close. I drew my SIG and blew a large hole in his face, dropping him in a heap. The girl I had pinned to the wall was snapping and twisting, trying to get a bite out of my wrist. I lined up the second one, a fat individual or at least he would have been if his guts hadn't been ripped out. Shreds of grey skin hung over a gaping hole in his cheek, which landed in the dirt after I shot him in the eye. I figured there was a second before the next two got to me, I spun around and shot the female in the forehead, her eyes rolling up in surprise at the new skylight in her skull.

The other two zombies were coming fast and I didn't have much time. I pivoted and shot quickly, the shot entering the first zombie's open mouth and exiting through the back of his neck severing his spine. The last Z barreled into me, knocking me back into the cargo container. I slipped on the girl I had shot and slid down just as his jaws snapped against the container. I found myself on the ground looking up at a zombie that looked down at me, his lips curling back from his mouth, revealing his broken, yellowed teeth. His head came down as my arm shot up, shoving the barrel of my SIG in his mouth. His teeth chewed the metal millimeters from my trigger finger as I fired, blowing the back of his head off and sending bits of his diseased brain into orbit.

I shoved the thin body off of me and stood up quickly, scanning the area for further threats. Not seeing any, I retrieved my rifle and hunkered down, breathing heavily and shaking my head. No matter what anyone says, no matter what all the movie hype tells you, close quarters combat takes a lot out of you.

I checked the rifle and it seemed okay, no barrel obstructions or otherwise. Sudden movement caught my eye and I stood up, watching Charlie run over from his container. Some slower moving zombies from the main horde saw the movement as well and they swung around to start their inevitable march towards their prey.

"Jesus, you okay?" Charlie asked, breathing heavily. His run had been precarious, the ground was liberally littered with newly made re-corpses.

I nodded. "All's well. Thought that last guy was going to be the end when I slipped, but thankfully he hesitated when I disappeared from view."

Charlie looked around at the bodies. "Nice work. I figured you for two or three to one, but five's impressive."

I shook my head. "Remind me never to do that again. If Sarah had been watching I'd be in serious trouble."

Charlie just smiled, then turned as low moans carried to us. Thirty or so yards away there was about twenty slow movers headed our way and we needed to get to work. "I'll take the right, you take the left," Charlie said as he lifted his rifle.

"Deal." I raised my rifle and started with a small boy on the far left. He was wearing a striped shirt and ripped up jeans. His vacant stare reminded me of students I had once upon a time when we did state testing. I dropped him with a quick shot, then moved on to the next. In short order we had killed the oncoming zombies, the last one literally dropping at our feet.

Our efforts had attracted the attention of several more ghouls and we decided we needed to get to a more defensible position. I could see more zombies coming up from the countryside, attracted to the sound of shooting, which I figured was akin to a dinner bell for roaming Z's.

"Let's get gone before we find ourselves out of ammo, trying to figure out how to spend the rest of our short lives in a cargo container." I said, moving to the east towards the railroad tracks. Charlie agreed, telling me spending the rest of his life in a cargo container with me was only attractive if I was a supermodel. I didn't bother to reply.

We ran to the tracks that paralleled the fence, since that part of the fence was not being as aggressively attacked as the north side. We ran about halfway down the length of the fence, stopping once to shoot two zombies that were coming in off the south end and getting to the ladder that had been placed there for us. I ushered Charlie up and I climbed after him, pulling the ladder up behind me. Zombies generally didn't seem to have the mental clarity to figure out what to do with a ladder and certainly lacked the dexterity to manage climbing one, but I have heard of exceptions. No point in trying to figure out if one was out there right now.

We got to the top and moved quickly towards the source of the firing as their seemed to be quite a bit and for some reason that made me nervous. As we turned the corner I could see two people firing directly down into the masses of zombies milling about. Every time they fired a body fell. All good. But the bodies were starting to pile up and they were not aware that the zombie's grasping hands were getting higher and higher.

"Step back!" I yelled. "They can reach you! Step back!" I ran faster, trying not to lose my balance on the uneven surface of the containers.

I was too late. Even as I got within twenty yards, a shooter was dragged screaming down into the teeming mass. Clawed hands ripped away chunks of flesh and chipped teeth tore at clothing and skin. It looked like someone had dropped a piece of hamburger into a pool of piranhas. Blood sprayed as arterial walls were ruptured by ghoul s' teeth. In a matter of seconds, the screaming stopped as whoever it was died. A pack of zombies stayed hunched over the body, tearing at the meat, stuffing it into their mouths. Blood smeared over hands and arms, dripping down chins and staining dirty clothing.

The other person on the container screamed, "Noooo!" and before I could get to him, he jumped off the container into the pack of hunched over zombies, shooting randomly and kicking zombies away from the body. I ducked as a bullet screamed past my ear, nearly causing me to stumble. He didn't seem to notice the zombie on his back, biting him in the neck. The man kicked away another zombie, then threw the one on his back off, knocking down a row of zombies. Other ghouls surged forward, and just before they swarmed the man, I could see the face of the shredded body on the ground.

It was Casey. What she was doing out here instead of staying at the town hall where she was supposed to be I had no idea. I turned my attention to the man fighting on the ground. He swung his rifle like a club, but he had no chance. The zombies came in from all sides and bore him to his knees. He fought up one last time and it was then I could see who it was. Martin Oso. My heart sank as his eyes locked with mine, then he disappeared beneath the wave of undead. I brought my rifle up and was not disappointed when the mass of ghouls surged upward again and I could see that Martin had regained his feet. His face was covered in bites and he was bleeding freely from numerous wounds on his arms and neck. The Z's snarled collectively then rushed him again, their hunger evident in the intensity with which they glared at him.

Martin looked at me again, then nodded as I lined up his head in my sights. A split second before the dead started tearing at him again, my rifle cracked once, the bullet putting a neat hole in Martin's head. He dropped to the ground, followed by the dead which tore at his fresh corpse. I lowered my rifle and just shook my head.

Charlie dropped his head and shook it gently, his anger at the useless-deaths evident in his slightly shaking hands.

The ghouls noticed us after they finished with the bodies of our comrades and set up another chorus of death as they moaned and surged forward. There were a lot of them in this area, but I could see pockets of more of them down the line. I took the scope off my rifle and standing back from the grasping hands that reached over the edge of the container, I proceeded to cut down the zombies that reached for me. I worked my way from the back, shooting methodically. I don't remember Charlie firing next to me, I just went on autopilot. Aim, fire, shift, aim, fire, shift, aim, fire, shift, aim fire. I started at the back of the mob and slowly worked my way forward. I saw Charlie doing the same and he was as disciplined as I was. Inside, I was furious. Martin knew better than to shoot the way he was and not only did he get himself killed, he got another team member killed as well. If he wasn't dead, I would have kicked his ass.

I emptied my magazine, replaced it with another one and then went to work again. At the end of my second clip, I had corpses laid out like a macabre carpet. On Charlie's side, the same carpet was laid off to the right. In front of us, were still the grasping hands and I put a loaded clip into the rifle, noting absently the heat coming off the barrel. I stepped carefully forward and peered over at the dead. When they saw me, they again moaned and reached for me, but I had nothing for them except release from their prison.

I fired quickly, killing six of them in short order and Charlie finished off the rest. I looked over at him and nodded, words being useless at this point. We gathered our empty magazines and began walking down the fence line, heading towards the masses of zombies in the distance. Out on the open land I could see distant shapes slowly moving towards our position, but paid them no mind. We'd kill them when they got here, no sooner.

As we reached the main point of the zombies' attack, I could see Sheriff Harlan walking up and down his line of shooters, encouraging them, and telling them to aim for the back of the horde, just like we had discussed the night before. It was hard to ignore the grasping hands that reached up, but they couldn't risk the zombies climbing up. As it was, they might have done it anyway, just from crushing each other in the press to get the succulent pink flesh just out of reach. The container we were standing on rocked gently from the onslaught, but it stayed in place, being bolted to the container next to it. On the initial tour of the defenses Harlan had said most of the containers had been secured, but not all. The ones by the lake were not, the logic being that the zombies appeared to avoid immersion in water, therefore if they made it through, they wouldn't go far.

I walked along the fence, followed by Charlie, and we saw other groups of men shooting down the ghouls and adding to the grey, lifeless mass out on the plain. A lot of ammo was wasted, but the men seemed to have enough. If we ran out, we'd have to do the job the old fashioned way, but that could be done. The focus now was to eliminate the threat of being overwhelmed.

As we turned the corner past the lake, I began to hear screams from inside the perimeter. I hadn't noticed it before, with all the firing going on, but now it seemed like there was something seriously wrong. I jogged along the cargo containers and saw what had happened. A bolt had not been tightened properly, allowing the crowd of zombies to filter in. The gap was only wide enough to allow one zombie in at a time, but it had been open long enough to allow a significant number of zombies inside the town. They had spread out as they wandered in and by the screams, had found new victims.

"Shit! They're in! Sheriff Harlan!" I yelled into the radio, attracting the attention of several ghouls on the ground.

"What you need, son?" came the laconic reply.

"There's been a breach! They're in! They're in! Fall back and get your men into the town!" I shouted as Charlie and I raced down a nearby ramp. I shot the nearest zombie and Charlie shot another one as we raced over the open ground towards Route 113. The zombies had followed the road into the town, attracted by the firing they were hearing on the north side and were headed straight for the heaviest population center. I estimated at least five hundred zombies had made it in, and the number was increasing.

12

A shrill scream sounded form a nearby house and I skidded to a halt outside the small dwelling. It was a one story house. The door hung open and another scream sounded.

"I'm in," I said and started for the door as Charlie took up a position outside the house. Five zombies were making their way across the lawn, but Charlie would deal with them.

I slung my rifle over my shoulder and drew my SIG as I approached the house. The open door allowed me to see into the small living room and I could see things were not as they were supposed to be. The coffee table was across the room and knick knacks were all over the floor. I could see into the kitchen and nothing seemed out of place in there. A scream sounded again as a shot came from outside. I could hear a moaning coming from the hallway leading to the back of the house and I circled wide, aiming down the hallway. I could see a bare foot around the corner and the missing chunk of flesh exposing the bone gave me a pretty good clue what was in front of me.

A second shot sounded outside and another scream penetrated the house. The zombie in front of me pounded on whatever was keeping it from its prey, moaning again. I couldn't risk a shot since the bullet would likely go through the zombie and the door it was in front of, so I was going to have to use my pickaxe. Trouble was, in the confines of the house, I doubted I was going to have enough room for a killing swing.

Moving to option three, I drew my knife and moved as quietly as I could. The zombie was of medium height, its clothing in rags. Hair had fallen off its decaying head in patches. I was actually glad I couldn't see its face. I stepped up and plunged my knife into the top of its head. I twisted the knife and the corpse collapsed at the foot of the door. I dragged it out of the way as more shots came from the outside.

I knocked on the door. "Anybody alive in there?"

There was a scrambling, then a young face peered out at me. "Didja kill it?" asked the boy, whose age I guessed to be around twelve.

"Deader than dirt," I said, pointing to the body.

"Cool! Thanks! I'm Cody and..." the boy's introduction was interrupted by the hand that pulled him back. His face was replaced by a woman's, his mother by the resemblance. Her relief was palpable when she saw me.

"Oh God, Mr. Talon. Thank you so much. I don't know how we would have..." she started.

"Save it for later," I interrupted, "we need to get out of here, now. There's zombies inside the fence." I ushered her and her son out of the house.

We exited just in time to see Charlie shoot another walking dead down. Cody looked around and I could see he was excited. His mother looked scared out of her wits. More zombies were heading our way and we would be overwhelmed if we didn't do something soon.

"Do you have a car?" I asked, shaking her arm.

She looked at me blankly. "I...yes...it doesn't have any gas..."

I turned to Cody. "You need to get your mother to the city hall right away. Can you do that without being seen by the zombies?"

Cody actually saluted me. "You bet! C'mon, Mom!" He took her by the hand and led her away, sneaking into the backyards of the row of houses.

As I looked around for a second, I knew we had to stop the breach. I tapped Charlie on the shoulder. "We need a vehicle that runs," I said, unslinging my rifle and shooting a stray zombie. The line of undead worked its way back to the breach and the numbers were getting heavier.

Charlie nodded. "Follow me." He ran up three houses and stopped outside a house identical to the one we had been in. Opening up the garage door, there was a dilapidated pickup truck sitting in the garage. Charlie walked over to it, hopped inside, and started it right away. I just stood there with my mouth open. Charlie backed the vehicle out and pulled up along side me.

"You coming or what?" he asked.

I was stunned. "How the hell did you know that was there and how the hell did you know it would start? Nobody's that lucky." I said as I climbed in.

Charlie grinned at me through his mask. "That's my ex brother-in-law's house. This is his truck."

I was still in shock. "Why didn't you say anything before?"

Charlie shrugged. "I never liked the asshole." He gunned the engine and sped towards the breach. "Got a plan?"

"Yeah," I said, shaking off my disbelief. "Ram this sucker into the container and close the hole."

"Works for me."

We came within sight of the opening, which trickled dead people like an hourglass from hell. They were spread out around us, but at the sight of the truck, started to converge.

"Now or never!" I said, buckling up and rolling down my window. A beer can poked me in the small of my back, but I ignored it for the time being.

Charlie gunned the engine and sped forward, knocking zombies left and right. One got caught on the hood and moaned at us until it slid off. Charlie got as much speed out of the old truck as he could, then we slammed headfirst into the container, knocking it back and sealing off the fence.

We didn't have time to admire our handiwork. We had crushed a number of zombies in the headlong rush, but there were still many out there and headed our way. I popped out of the cab and shot the nearest zombie. Another came close from the side and had to be taken down with a rifle butt to the face, followed by a boot stomp to the head. Not the neatest way to kill them, but whatever works.

I could hear gunfire to the north and I hoped like crazy the sheriff had gotten his people in place, otherwise this was going to be a long day, with house by house clearing. Fortunately, most of the townspeople were accounted for, save for the few stragglers like Cody and his mom.

Charlie slammed his door against a ghoul that had gotten too close and the door had a nasty black stain where the dead girl's goo got on it. He kicked her back when she got up, then used a tomahawk to finish her.

I jumped up into the bed of the truck, figuring to lesson the likelihood of being overrun and Charlie did the same. We pulled our rifles, checked our magazines, and started killing.

After about three minutes, my ammo ran dry. I had fifty dead people on my side and Charlie had about the same. "I'm out," I said, holding out my hand for a magazine.

Charlie slapped my hand away. "What do I look like, an ammo dump?" he asked.

"You really want to know what you look like?" I eyed a group of Z's shuffling closer. "You got ammo or not?"

Charlie fired a round, then looked at his rifle as the bolt stayed open. "That's it for me."

"Time to go," I said, slinging my rifle over my shoulder and pulling out my pickaxe. I jumped off the bed of the truck and ran towards the first zombie, Charlie right behind me. I swung my weapon hard at its head, knocking it off its feet and into the path of three of its cousins. They tumbled to the ground and we planted them for good as they tried to get up again.

Running up Route 113, I ran towards South Broadway Street, pausing once to listen to the sounds of the town. I could hear moans all around me, but there didn't seem to be any screaming. I did hear shots to the north, so I turned up Broadway and ran to the sound. In our wake, about a hundred zombies slowly worked their way up the street. Too many to handle without serious firepower. Between the two of us,

Charlie and I had about seventy-five rounds of ammo for our pistols, but since there was no immediate threat as long as we kept moving, I wanted to save the ammo for real emergencies.

We ran unopposed until we reached Third Street, then we were blocked by a small crowd of about seven walking corpses. They were headed to the sound of the shots, but when we came running up, they turned around. Various noises came out of their mouths as they saw us, and as one, started for us.

"Left." Was all I said. Charlie moved to the right without a word, his tomahawks swinging wide as he limbered up his shoulders. I moved to engage a small man, about sixty, if it was possible to judge age on a dead person who had been walking around about a year longer than he should have been. His torso was bare and a large strip of grey skin hung off of him, as if he was in the process of being skinned when he reanimated. I slammed the point of my pickaxe into his temple, dodging his long arms as they reached for my flesh. As he fell, I jerked my weapon out of his head and swinging it in a high arc, crushed the skull of a woman who wheezed at me, her throat torn out.

I stepped back, giving myself some room from the other two that had begun to crowd close. They looked like twins, roughly the same size and shape. They moved as one, which presented a problem since I could only kill one at a time.

I hit on a solution, literally. My foot bumped my first zombie and I reached down to grab him by the ankles. Swinging him around like the sack of shit that he was, I threw him at the twins. The three bodies collided and went down in a heap. I stepped up and spiked the first twin, while the second grabbed my ankle and tried to bring it in for a bite. I stepped back, dragging the Z with me, then killed it with a blow to the back of its head. It sounded like dropping a coconut off a three-story building. I was actually used to it, something a year ago I would never have thought possible.

I looked around for another enemy, but Charlie had finished off the other three. I pointed down the street and we both looked at the crowd working its way towards us. That would have not been so bad, except the crowd was dead and wanting to rip us apart and eat us. Not my party, thanks.

We jogged farther north and reached Fourth Street. I could see the town hall from where we were and things seemed to be holding. Sheriff Harlan had pulled his people off the wall and they were concentrated in a ring around the town hall. The zombies were being held back by a string of cars that had been placed in front of the building and groups of people were dealing with the ones that managed to get past the cars. I could see Tommy and Jason directing crews of people to the defense, knocking the zombies over with long poles, then rushing in to smash their heads in with hammers, sledgehammers, picks, and pipes. I wondered briefly why the firing had stopped, since I found it hard to believe that everyone had run out of ammo. Maybe they were saving it for last ditch fighting.

Charlie and I watched for a second, as I was unsure how we could help. We couldn't work our way forward without running into a mess of zombies and with the crowd behind us coming up, we were in the unenviable position of right in the damn middle. So far, we hadn't been noticed by the attacking zombies, they were focused on the meals in front of them.

Charlie bumped me and pointed to an area by the side of the building. It looked like the zombies from the side were going to get in and attack the defenders from behind. We had no choice, we had to do something or everyone was going to die.

13

I gritted my teeth and spoke to Charlie. "If you want to help them and be with Rebecca in case it all goes to shit, I wouldn't hold it against you."

Charlie shook his head. "It's a good day to die, brother."

It was my turn to shake my head. "You're a corny one, you know that?"

"Just move, I got your back." Charlie said.

I wasn't about to waste time with sentimentality. I ran to the right of the attacking zombies, my movement detected by some on the fringes and starting them towards us. I drew my SIG and shot the nearest one in the face. The sound carried over the crowd and dozens of dead faces turned my way. I shot another one, and lined up a third for another shot.

"Hey, you fuckers! You want it, come and get it!" I screamed as I fired, dropping a third one. In the abrupt silence, I shouted as loud as I could to the defenders. "You're breached on the east! Go!" I could see Tommy spin around and grab Jason and head for the side of the building.

Roughly two thirds of the attacking horde started my way, me being the easier prey and the ones coming up the street turned my way as well. All I could think of was a line from a funny zombie movie. *Oh, bullocks.*

I slowly backed away from the advancing horde, taking the time to shoot as many as I could. I could hear Charlie's sidearm barking next to me as he started dropping zombies as well. I knew we were still looking at well over three hundred zombies even after our ammo went dry, but a dead zombie was a good zombie. I wanted to draw away as many as I could, giving the defenders of the townsfolk time to deal with the internal threat and regroup. My goal was to reach the bandstand gazebo in the park. I had seen it the other night during our tour and it made the most sense as a position of defense. It was a large elevated platform, surrounded by a fence, accessible only through one stairway. If Charlie and I could make it there, we stood a good chance of being able to blunt the horde and make them attack us in fewer numbers.

I walked at a normal pace to the edge of the steps to the platform, making sure Charlie was with me and the horde had followed. Some of the back ones went after the town hall defenders again. Essentially, Charlie and I were in the fight of our lives.

I stopped about fifteen feet in front of the steps and waited. The crowd moved slowly, their shambling gait looking like a rippling body of grey water. The sun climbed higher in the sky, shortening the shadows on the lawn. None of these things was relevant, but for some reason I noticed them. A slow burning rage was building within me, causing me to grip my gun tighter and check the availability of my spare magazines. I would not go down without a fight and would take many enemies with me to pay my toll.

I looked over at Charlie, who seemed to be absorbed in the same thoughts I was, looking around, then settling into the inevitable with a cold look in his eyes and slight snarl on his lips.

"Make a barrier," I said. "Make the fuckers work for it." I was immensely glad the platform had only one set of stairs. If it had two, we'd never have a chance here.

I shot the first one to reach my killing zone and another, the sound of the shots *bawoinging* off the ceiling of the gazebo. That would have gotten old fast if it wasn't so desperate. I killed as they reached my zone, the bodies falling on top of each other and forcing the ones behind to stumble a little. It was a little uncomfortable, waiting for some to get close for a shot, but we needed to make every shot count and kill as many as we could. If we could get a barrier of bodies up, then the rest would have to work to get to us and we could have the advantage.

I shot quickly, dropping a few more as they started to get closer and attack en masse. Sometimes I got lucky and one shot would nail two of them. Not often enough, sadly. The pile of grayish bodies grew and Charlie's gun cracked as much as mine did. We piled up several bodies in succession. I didn't see them as individuals, I just saw them as targets.

I backed up a few steps as the bodies collapsed slightly towards us from the push from behind by the rest of the mob, then changed magazines again. I had one more fifteen round magazine, then I was out. I called this out to Charlie and he replied he was done in seven rounds. We backed up to the foot of the stairs and fired still, the barrels of our guns hot to the touch and smoking. The bodies were piled about five feet high, which made a decent barrier to slow down the horde. We were still in for a bitch of a fight.

My gun clicked empty and I holstered it, pulling out my pickaxe with my other hand. Charlie was ready with his twin tomahawks and we faced the oncoming, crawling horde like a couple of warriors from ancient times. If we just had a couple of half-naked buxom beauties to protect on the platform I might have actually enjoyed myself.

The horde surrounded the gazebo, cutting off any retreat we might have had and the high walls prevented them from hitting us from behind. All we needed to do was wait for them to come to us.

And come they did. The first one to cross the barrier was a small female, probably a teenager, with ripped jeans and halter top. Her mottled grey skin glinted in the sun, and her dead blue eyes stared at me with unquenchable hunger. I split her skull and, picking up the dead body, threw it on the pile, knocking back two others who were clumsily making their way across the corpses.

Figuring I was going to need another weapon, I pulled my knife, waiting for the next ghoul to come near while I watched Charlie dispatch a man who was completely naked, his pallid skin streaked with claw marks and bites. The body was kicked into the barrier as it fell, the man's big butt pointing towards us when it finished falling. I let out a grim chuckle to be joined by Charlie's soft laugh. It's not often the dead moon you, especially after you've killed them.

I kept the image of my baby boy in my mind and I fought for him. I would not allow the world to come to this, where the last few humans make a stand against the coming wave of death. My son would not inherit this world.

As I killed, once again I had to restrain myself from charging headlong into the fray and killing my enemies as they killed me. The ancient fire of battle burned in my veins and I welcomed it as I welcomed the horde with taunts and sneers. "Come on, you witless fucks. Come and die. I'll set you free." Beside me Charlie began to growl low in his chest. I recognized it as his battle cry. Let the harvest of the dead begin. "Come on!" I raged at the dead faces staring at me.

The dead began to advance and Charlie and I killed them. We killed those who came to the barrier and those who tried to climb over it. We piled the bodies up until we were crushing skulls that peered at us from behind other corpses. We fought until our arms were leaden. We fought until I broke the handle on my pickaxe and had to use a shortened grip on splintered wood. We fought until Charlie broke a tomahawk handle, leaving him to fight with a single 'hawk and his nine-inch knife. We killed the owners of the grasping, clawed hands blackened with old blood. We killed former mothers, fathers, and their children. We killed white collar workers, blue collar workers, and everyone in between. We fought until the pile of the dead fell forward from the push behind, and we retreated to the middle of the stairs, killing those zombies who crawled towards us, single-minded of purpose.

Charlie and I were covered in zombie gore up to our necks and still we fought. As I killed, a line from an ancient legend came to mind, describing a battle between a hero and a horde of advancing enemies; a hero who died so his companions could live... "He held the bridge at Gallerbru." I idly wondered if what we did here today would ever be remembered as I speared another zombie in the eye with my knife, killing him and slamming my pickaxe into the skull of another, who had grasped my shirt and was pulling me towards him for a bite.

Inevitably, we began to tire. What took only one hit before was now taking two, and the horde pressed forward, causing Charlie and I to retreat higher up the stairs. We pushed the bodies back as we killed them, trying to slow down the horde, but they pressed on. Charlie and I had to retreat to the top of the stairs and we left bodies three and four deep all the way up.

We were getting into a desperate situation. If the zombies pressed us any further, then they would be able to get around us and then it would be over. We could not retreat any farther.

We fought harder, trying to open a space where we could push back, but we had been fighting for so long that we could barely lift our arms. The only thing keeping us going was sheer willpower and the determination not to become one of the diseased husks that slobbered for our blood. I kicked at the ones coming up, tumbling them onto the zombies behind them, but they crawled back up as quickly as we kicked them away.

"We may need an exit!" Charlie yelled at me as he put down another ghoul.

"Nowhere to go!" I yelled back. "If they get farther up, they're all around us!" I jammed my knife into a small girl that tried to sneak up under my defenses. I picked up her now completely lifeless body and hurled it the horde, knocking down several of them.

"What about the roof?" Charlie asked, his hand around the throat of a snapping zombie.

"Maybe we could make it, but we would need several seconds." I said, punching a teenage zombie in the face, knocking him back slightly before I crushed his skull.

"Nothing left to lose. Get ready to push." Charlie said, picking up his dead-again adversary. I grabbed my teenager and, using them as battering rams, Charlie and I slammed them into the press, knocking down several rows of undead and tumbling several more off the sides of the stairs. I nearly slipped down after them, sliding on unidentifiable brown goo that was on the top of the stairs.

Charlie and I spun and ran for the edge of the gazebo, jumping onto the railing and climbing up onto the crossbeams that supported the roof. The timbers groaned a little as unaccustomed weight was put on them, but they held. Beneath us, the dead had surged forward and a crowd was gathering underneath us, grasping at the air and raising their dead eyes to the ceiling.

14

Charlie and I just stood there, both of us immensely grateful for the respite. My arms were nearly numb and I felt like I had been battling for hours. My clothing was soaked in sweat, and my eyes burned. I could barely see out of my goggles from all the flying zombie fluids, so in the breather we had gained for ourselves, I pulled out a small package of wipes from my pack and cleaned off my hands and my goggles. Charlie did the same, wiping off his face and hands. It was a weirdly normal moment, given the fact we were suspended ten feet over the floor of the park gazebo that at the moment was covered in living dead and very dead.

I moved across the beam and went over to the opposite side. I sat down and stretched my legs out onto the beam. I would have dangled them over the side, but there were a couple of tall zombies that might be able to grab my legs, so I left them up. Charlie followed my example and we sat across from each other, just resting for a minute.

Charlie broke the relative silence. "So what do we do now? We can't access the roof, we can't get down, and we have no ammo to kill ourselves if we have to."

I leaned my head back and closed my eyes. "Charlie, Charlie, Charlie," I said. "Have a little faith. When have I not had a plan?"

Charlie began to tick off on his fingers. "There was that house in Turley that had twelve ghouls in the basement. There was that store in Oakland that had so many ghouls in it we were on the roof for two days. There was that time in the condos that..."

I interrupted him. "You know, if you're just going to be negative..." My response was broken by a fusillade of shots coming from outside the gazebo. I plugged my ears from the echoes reverberating in the roof area, and saw Charlie do the same.

Below us, Z's dropped continuously, carpeting the platform in a pile of grayish flesh. The ones out on the lawn were cut down, and the ones on the stairs tumbled back as their brains were obliterated.

After a little while, the shots faded away. I leaned over as far as I could, but couldn't see anything due to the overhang of the roof. Shrugging my shoulders at Charlie, I swung down to the railing and looked around. Surrounding the gazebo were about twenty of the townspeople, all holding rifles. When I waved to them, they set up a resounding cheer, which was echoed over at the town hall. Tommy came forward and smiled at me and Charlie, who had swung down beside me.

"You unbelievable sons-of-bitches!" Tommy yelled above the din. I grinned in acknowledgment and thumped Charlie on the back.

"All part of the plan," I said smugly before Charlie had a chance to reply and worked my way out of the carnage. Looking back at the gazebo, I was stunned at the body count Charlie and I were able to rack up. Piles of bodies marked our retreat and dead zombies littered the once manicured lawn.

I stepped up to Tommy and nodded my thanks. "What took you so long?" I asked.

Tommy shook his head. "You two were so busy playing 'Kill the Zombie' that you wouldn't get out of the way. When you finally jumped up into the rafters we were able to open up."

"How long were we fighting?" I wondered, looking at my watch.

"About an hour and a half," said Sheriff Harlan, stepping up to us. "You all managed to draw away the worst of the horde and it took that long to clean up the ones that were left. We'd have been cashed if it weren't for you two." Harlan held out his hand. "I'm obliged to you for saving my town."

I shook his hand, then Charlie did the same. "You're very welcome Sheriff," Charlie said.

Sheriff Harlan turned around and belted out orders to the townsfolk. "We got cleanup to do! Get your shovels and your gear! We're burning tonight!" Harlan moved off to get people moving, leaving us alone.

I turned to Tommy. "What about the rest outside the fence?"

Tommy shook his head. "There's a bunch, but these folks can handle it. They got baptized by fire today and they'll be a whole lot stronger for it."

"We lose anybody?" I asked.

Tommy nodded. "There's eight that got bit, one that got overwhelmed. Overall, it could have been worse."

I agreed. "It is worse. Martin and Casey are dead. Casey got dragged off the fence and Martin went after her. I had to shoot Martin myself."

Tommy's eyes got wide, then he turned his head down. This was a cost we hadn't been expecting to bear. I told him what had happened and his response was similar to the anger Charlie and I had expressed. "What the hell was he thinking?" Tommy asked to no one in particular.

I changed the subject. "You got any pistol ammo?- I'm out and I don't like being empty."

Tommy checked his pack and handed me a handful of cartridges. I reloaded the SIG and had enough for half of a spare magazine. I would load up if we ever got back to the cars we left behind. But for now it would do.

"How come you're loading up?" Charlie asked.

"I'm going to see Sarah now. You might want to do the same."

Tommy nodded. "They both saw you draw away that horde and watched the whole fight from the upstairs windows. But they couldn't see you two climb up, so when the zombies swarmed the platform, it probably looked like you had been overwhelmed." Tommy pointed to the second story windows.

Charlie looked up for a second, then walked over to Jason to see if he had any ammo for his Glock.

15

Once we were able to defend ourselves, we walked over to the town hall, shedding zombified clothing as we went. I took off my balaclava, my gloves, and my shirt, leaving me carrying a pile of clothing and a rifle with nothing on but my pants and a t-shirt. We walked around the cars and the piles of dead bodies, the noon day sun not helping with the cleanup efforts. I stepped up to the big oak doors and stopped. I could still hear moans of the dead as they carried over the water from the fence. "I wonder if we should head over there," I mused.

Charlie laughed out loud and pushed me towards the doors. "You didn't hesitate to take on hundreds of Z's, yet you're scared of one woman?"

"If you're so brave, give me your Glock before you go see Rebecca," I retorted.

"Not a chance," Charlie said.

"That's what I thought."

We went inside as people were gathering their things and heading back to their homes. Tommy had told me Jason and a crew of men were checking the town over for strays and would personally check each house before the owners went back. Many people thanked us for what we did and I generally just smiled and said they were welcome, and that I was glad to help. Charlie took my cue and replied in the same manner, staying modest and unassuming. Several women gave us hugs and some of the older tots wanted to touch our weapons, but for the most part people were just glad it was over.

I went up the big marble staircase to the second floor, then went down the hall to the big office on the end. Charlie saw Rebecca in another office and veered off. I stepped to the door and knocked gently.

"Come in." The voice was soft and inviting and I hoped for the best. I opened the door and saw Sarah standing by the window, watching the cleanup efforts. My M1A was cradled in her arms and for a brief moment I considered drawing my SIG for comfort.

"Hey," I said.

Sarah turned around and saw me. She put down the rifle and flew into my arms. I held her tightly for several long moments, then kissed her fiercely for several more. When we finally came up for air she rested her head on my shoulder.

"When we couldn't see you or Charlie anymore, we thought the worst. Then when you came out of the gazebo, I thought my heart would explode." Sarah raised a tear-streaked face to mine. "Please don't do that again."

"Can't promise that sweetheart, you know I can't. I have to do what I need to make sure people survive."

"I know. Doesn't mean I have to like it." Sarah snuggled against my chest.

I gently disengaged myself from her. "I need to clean up. I'm covered in zombie."

Sarah smiled. "Give me your clothes. I'll make sure they get washed."

I stripped down and passed her my clothes as I changed into spare clothing from my pack. I used water from the bathroom to clean up and bumped in to Charlie on the way back to the office.

"You too?" Charlie asked.

"Yep."

I went back to the office and Sarah gathered up my stained clothing. "Get some rest. You've earned it."

I didn't think I was tired until I laid down on the couch in the office. Then exhaustion caught up with me and I fell deeply asleep.

I awoke alone to a dimming sky. I had a pain in my side where my SIG had poked me and I ached in several places, but as my dad always said, "Pain is nature's way of letting you know you ain't dead yet." Wish I had known the old man was a prophet.

I found my clothes on the desk and packed them into my bag. I didn't see my AR, so I figured Sarah had taken it. I shouldered my M1A and headed downstairs.

I was met in the lobby of the town hall by Tommy and Jason and together the three of us went out in search of the rest of our team.

We didn't have far to go. Charlie and Rebecca were out on the meeting area in front of the building, talking with Sarah.

"Hey, sleepyhead!" Sarah said when she saw me, coming over to give me a hug. "How was your nap?"

"Pretty good," I replied. "How long was I out?"

"You and Charlie slept for about four hours," Rebecca said.

"Really?" I said. "Guess I was tired."

"You ought to be," Sarah said, punching me in the ribs, "after spending a night in a cargo container, then killing zombies all morning."

I decided not to say a word at that point, figuring I would be incriminating myself even worse.

"What's the next move?" Tommy asked.

I looked around. The bodies of all the zombies had been removed, and there was a glow off to the east that I was pretty sure was a burn pile going full force. People were moving around and checking on each other and I could see some looks cast our way. We were the outsiders here, no matter what we had done for the town. They had a balance and me and mine would eventually upset that balance. We had shared a hardship and had both lost people, but we needed to be gone while the feelings were good on both sides.

"We're going to head out. I've heard from Sheriff Harlan that there may be some surviving towns farther south along the rail lines. Charlie, Tommy and I are going to take one of the Railroad trucks that Sheriff Harlan has offered and we're going to do a quick run to see if there is anyone out there. If there is and they need to settle some place, we'll direct them back here." I waited for the outburst and was surprised there was none.

"Sounds good," Sarah said.

"Sure does," Rebecca said.

Charlie and I exchanged glances. This was not what I expected. I gave Sarah a look and she squeezed my hand and laughed.

"You goof. You and Charlie just proved beyond a shadow of a doubt that you two can handle anything, including a horde of over two hundred zombies. I figured you might be doing something like this, so I sent Jason and some men to retrieve our cars and supplies." Sarah gave me another hug as I just stared at her.

Charlie shook his head and said nothing which was probably the best idea right now.

An hour later, Charlie, Tommy, and I met up with Sheriff Harlan and talked about where we were going. We had retrieved our supplies and were now fully laden with gear, including ammo for our guns. I was taking my rifle and Charlie and Tommy would be backup with theirs.

Sheriff Harlan laid out a map. "We're here. Down this rail line is Streator. We don't know if there's anyone alive in there, but considering how far they are from bigger centers, there's a good chance people are there. The rail line has about four small towns on the way to Streator. If anyone's there, they're welcome here. My brother Tim and his family live here," Harlan pointed to a small dot labeled 'Ransom'. "If he's there, I'd be obliged if you'd pass on the message that I'm alive."

I nodded, briefly wondering about my own brother, who I hadn't heard from in a year.

The sheriff continued. "We have a rail truck, so you can travel on the lines and get off on the road when you need to. We've used it to range north for supplies, but the recent uprising put a halt to that. You're welcome to it."

I could immediately see the advantages. Unless we ran into trains on the rails, we could head straight through to Streator.

"Sounds good. We'll head out in the morning."

Sheriff Harlan nodded. "Good. Your people can stay at the town hall tonight, I think there might be a small celebration tomorrow. Everyone's just too tired today."

We all laughed and after about another two hours of planning, went back to the town hall. I told Sarah about the plan and when we planned to move out. She agreed with what we were doing and then gave me some good news.

"I spoke with Nate today, Jake and Julia are doing fine," Sarah said. "Jakey misses his daddy and wants him to come home soon."

I smiled. "That's my boy." I stretched out on the carpet of the office and pulled a cushion from the couch. "I didn't think I'd be this tired after the nap I had."

"Nate also said a friend of yours showed up looking for you."

"Who?"

"You'll never believe it."

"Tell me."

"Our friend Dot."

I was amazed. "I'll be damned. I thought she was never going to leave her house."

Sarah shrugged. "Nate said she got lonely and looked for you at the condo complex, but Duncan steered her towards Leport."

I laid back. "She'll make a welcome edition to the community."

Sarah sidled down onto the floor next to me and threw a leg over my waist. "How tired are you?" she breathed into my ear.

"Remarkably well-rested, thank you for asking," I said, laughing as I wrapped her up in my arms. "What did you have in mind?"

Sarah's response wore me out much more than the zombie horde could ever have hoped to do.

16

Charlie, Tommy, and I planned on starting down the rails first thing in the morning. Sheriff Harlan had assured us that we had enough gas to get us to Streator and back, but if we wanted to take side trips, we were on our own. I did not immediately see a need to travel off the rails, but if a train was in the way and the possibility was pretty good, we were going to have to use the roads. I asked Harlan if there might be a gas can somewhere and in short order I had two three-gallon cans. Tommy and Jason managed to siphon five gallons out of one of our cars, so we were able to increase our range, if necessary. Tommy stored the gas in the back of the truck while Jason wandered off to find a piece of gum or a breath mint.

Sarah helped me pack and repack my backpack, although I did not see us being gone for more than a day, I packed enough supplies for three days. I figured we would just be scouting and seeing if there were any survivors. We stood a good chance of finding more people the farther we got from large population centers.

Sarah had a look on her face and said, "You know, it's funny."

"What is?" I asked, shouldering my pack and adjusting my holster.

"You actually sound hopeful. Before you seemed to look at what you were doing as a kind of mission, that if you didn't do it, no one else would and the world would eventually die out. Now, you're almost smiling at the prospect."

I thought about that for a minute. "Is it a bad thing? Maybe we've turned a corner on this whole dead thing."

"Actually, it is kind of nice. You used to look at situations where if it worked, great, if not, oh well. Kind of attractive, in a way."

I puffed my chest out and gave my best Burt Lancaster smile. "I won't let it go to my head. Much."

"Good," Sarah said. "You'll get yourself killed if you do and then you'll be useless to me and everyone else."

I deflated when I realized she was right. I was alive because I took nothing for granted, never hoping for too much for fear of running myself into despair when things turned south. When this all started, I had one focus; save my son. Now that I have managed to secure some relative safety for him and others, my focus shifted; finding others and making sure they survived as well. I still needed to survive for my son and when I thought about what might have happened yesterday, I just shook my head. The fight was still out there and I still had a lot of work to do.

"Thanks," I said, kissing her on top of her head.

"You're welcome," she said. "Jake needs you, the community needs you, and I need you."

"I won't do anything stupid on purpose," I promised.

"Good."

Sarah and I walked down the street towards the east end of town. The sun was just rising, the blue of the sky chasing the purple of night back to the west. The morning air was brisk, it was still spring. But it promised to be a warmer day. I could still smell a little of the decay left behind by the dead and there was a large blackened area by the gazebo where the ghouls had been burned in the piles Charlie and I had made the day before. Looking at the gazebo, I suppressed a shudder when I thought how close of a call that had been. Had Tommy and the others fallen before we could have been rescued, we likely would still be up in the rafters, slowly starving to death.

We passed through the town, raising a hand in greeting to those whose days had started as early as ours. We got many smiles and a few words of gratitude. I was grateful we were able to lend a hand here. This town deserved to live, these people were the kind that would rebuild and make things better than they were before. They had a real sense of community that would be hard to put down. And now, after they had been tested in battle, anyone trying these people would be shoved back. Hard.

We reached the fence line shortly—and climbed up the nearest ramp. On top of the fence, I saw we had climbed up too far to the north, so we wandered along the fence to the ladder that reunited us with our friends.

Charlie and Tommy were already there as well as Rebecca and Jason. Charlie was checking the mini-train wheels which kept the truck on the rails and Tommy was finishing securing the supplies on the back.

"'Bout time," Tommy said. "You wanting us to wait forever?"

I stared at Tommy. "Yes, I do," I said with a straight face. "If I let you and Charlie off by yourselves, I'd have to save your sorry asses within ten minutes."

Tommy scowled and Charlie hid his grin. It was a full minute before I cracked a smile and Tommy realized I was kidding.

"Jesus, I fell for it. Damn, it's early." Tommy tried to look busy again, poking around the bed of the truck.

I laughed and gave Sarah a kiss and saw Charlie do the same to Rebecca. Tommy jumped into the bed of the truck and Charlie moved around to the driver's seat. I waited a second, giving Sarah's hand a quick squeeze, a gentle reminder that I would be back no matter what.

"Talk to Harlan," I said to Sarah, Rebecca, and Jason. "I want you guys to work with some volunteers on Z cleanup. We got remarkably lucky yesterday." I heard an 'Amen' from Charlie. "But these people need to be trained if they hope to survive another onslaught. Make sure you include the kids. This is their world too and they should be careful, not afraid."

Sarah and Rebecca nodded and I could see Sarah already forming in her head how to get the most going at once.

"You have one day," I said. "Good luck."

Jason stepped forward. "Before you left, the Mayor wanted you to have these. One of the townspeople is a woodworker." Jason held out Charlie's tomahawk and my pickaxe. The handles had been replaced and strengthened. My pickaxe handle was wider at the head, tapering a bit towards the handle end. Charlie's tomahawk had a new, lengthened walnut handle gleaming with new varnish. Charlie's eyes grew wide as I passed it through the truck cab to him. He stepped outside and took a few practice swings, getting used to the new length and weight. I swung my pickaxe and the little weapon positively glowed with malice, wanting desperately to sink into some undead skulls. *Soon. Soon.* The additional weight would mean less fatigue in a prolonged fight.

"Tell the mayor he has my thanks." I climbed into the cab and nodded at Charlie, who started the truck and fiddled with the controls. With a final wink at Sarah, we were on our way.

According to the map, the first town we were supposed to reach was Gorman, but I couldn't find a population note on the map. Come to think of it, I wasn't even sure where Gorman was, except that the rail line went nearby. We would reach it in a few minutes, since it was only five miles away.

Charlie kept the speed to thirty miles an hour, giving us a decent chance to look around the country and see how things were. We passed a lot of farmland and there was evidence of a lot of crops that had gone to waste because there wasn't anyone to harvest them. Come to think of it, there weren't a lot of people to eat them if they had been harvested. I guess it was good to keep these places in mind in case we got big enough as a population to use all this land again.

Tommy thumped the roof of the cab and I opened the back window of the cab.

"What's up?" I inquired, not seeing anything of interest.

"Nothing. I have to take a leak," Tommy said, shifting his rifle to his back and tapping Charlie on the shoulder.

Charlie looked at me and I shrugged, figuring it wasn't a bad idea. I got out of the truck after Charlie stopped and walked down to the edge of the stones that marked the railroad. After I finished my business, I wandered back up to the truck and looked around as Tommy finished his. I could see a farmhouse in the distance, but it was too far away to see if it was occupied. It looked like a pretty decent place, neat and well-maintained, but deserted. I had a feeling we would see a lot of that on this trip. Maybe one day someone would come and make this place prosperous, but it was going to be a while.

We rolled down the rails and I told Charlie to come to a stop where a road intersected the railway. I checked my map and looked around. I asked Charlie if we had gone about five miles from Coal City and he assured me that we had. I saw a small farmhouse in the distance and another house up the way a bit. A road sign said "Gorman Road" so I referenced where we were.

"Why did we stop?" Charlie asked, looking over at the map.

"We're in Gorman," I said, looking around.

Charlie was incredulous. "Really? This place is smaller than where I grew up."

I just shrugged my shoulders and checked the map again.

"Why did we stop?" Tommy asked from the truck bed.

"We're in Gorman," Charlie said over his shoulder.

"You're kidding." Tommy stood up to look around. "I guess the town is that house over there." He pointed to a ranch house down the road.

"Guess so," I said.

"We need anything here?" Charlie asked.

"Nope. May as well move on. If we have the time, we'll check the houses on the way back," I said, scanning the map for the next town.

"Got it." Charlie thumped on the roof to get Tommy to sit down, then drove off past Gorman, the town you would literally miss if you blinked.

We passed out of the town, or what was supposed to be the town and moved down the rails. The landscape didn't change much, just expansive fields or crops and vegetation. I could see the winter-bent stalks of corn unharvested, and figured hunting Z's in that mess would be a cast-iron nightmare. Better to burn the whole field than risk an attack.

According to the map, the next town on the rail line was Mazon. This one was actually listed and was supposed to have a population of around nine hundred. Given the remoteness of the locale, I was optimistic about finding a survivor or three.

About fifteen minutes past Gorman, we began approaching Mazon. It was wide open, no sign of any defense works or provisions for dealing with the dead. I motioned for Charlie to stop on the outskirts. I had no intention of running through the town until we had an idea of what we might encounter.

I tapped on the back window to get Tommy's attention. "Scope out what you can see, I've got an uneasy feeling about this place." I did, too. Something was making the hairs on the back of my neck stand up and I had learned not to ignore the feeling.

Tommy stood up in the truck bed and used the scope on his rifle to look a little further into the town. From where I sat, I could see a number of small, ranch-style homes indicative of most of the small towns in Illinois. Here and there were older, more stately homes, and they tended to have the larger, older trees in their yards. The homes were neat and tidy, a few having some expected debris in the yards, but in general seemed to be in good shape. One house in view had several children's toys still scattered about the back yard.

Tommy tapped the roof and I stuck my head out. "What's up? See anything?"

Tommy looked down at me with a puzzled expression. "I don't see anyone, living or dead. I did see a lot of white flags on mailboxes, though."

I could feel my gut tighten instinctively at those words. The infection had made it here, then. So much for being far enough out to avoid contamination. We needed to be careful. "Keep an eye out, we're heading through," I said to both Charlie and Tommy.

"You want to head down Main Street or stick to the rails?" Charlie asked.

"Let's stick to the rails, but if we see something worth looking at, we'll take a peek."

"Will do," Charlie said as he put the truck in gear and pulled forward. Tommy stayed upright, and scanning the town, looking for any sign of life. I noticed a couple of cats running from house to house, but that was the extent of the activity. I began to get the hunch we weren't going to see anyone at all, that this whole town had up and disappeared. That hunch gave rise to the question of Where? Did the people go to the state center? Did they head to a larger town like Coal City? The empty houses and abandoned swing sets mocked us with their eerie silence.

Charlie stopped the truck on a railroad crossing near the edge of town. We could see down a main thoroughfare which I guessed was the business district. Several stores and shops were there, a couple of restaurants, a fast-food place, one gas station, and two banks. 'Earl's Rail Stop' was just across the street from us, advertising chicken dinners for under five bucks.

Everything seemed normal except there was no one around. No living, no dead, nothing. As far as I could see, the town had not been hit by looters or anyone.

"This is just weird," Tommy said from his perch, scanning the street. "I don't see anything out of place. There's not a single piece of debris, no broken glass, no sign of violence. No bodies, no blood, nothing."

"Just ghosts," Charlie said suddenly, causing me to jump.

"Don't be foolish. There nothing here for ghosts, either." I snapped, much harsher than I intended. This abandoned town was creeping me out. I looked over at Charlie. "Sorry, man. This place is just wrong."

"No prob. What's that?" Charlie pointed to an area on the outskirts of town. "That looks like smoke."

Sure enough, there was what seemed to be a cloud of smoke hovering over the far edge of Mazon. "Let's go look, maybe they're survivors who could tell us what happened here," I said, hopeful.

We stayed on the rails, the tracks taking us towards the smoke. The fire seemed to be on the other side of a small grove of trees and the vegetation was dense enough to not allow us to see through.

As we got closer, Tommy thumped on the roof. "That's not smoke," he called out. I strained to see and as we went farther, we cleared the trees and could see.

Tommy was right. It wasn't smoke. It was thousands upon thousands of flies, hovering over a massive pile of corpses. Charlie stopped the truck and I got out, covering my face with my balaclava and goggles in an attempt to keep the flies away. I crossed over the greening grass and stood at the edge of the carnage. The people had been worked over by the flies and many of the faces were gruesome to look at, especially the children. I didn't see any signs of violence or any indication of how they died. Charlie and Tommy spread out on either side, looking for clues.

The bodies were clustered in small groups and as I looked around, I began to realize that the majority of the people died as families. What in the world could possibly have happened? Were they all infected and decided to save the rest of the community by coming here to die? I didn't have any answers. One thing was curious, though. In every single group, one of the dead was clutching a small wooden cross. I started to circle the small clearing, mentally counting the number of bodies. After I reached six hundred, I gave up, figuring the entire town was here. The flies' buzzing was extremely loud, nearly masking all other sound. Maggots were everywhere, writhing underneath clothing, causing me to swing up my rifle more than once when I thought I saw movement.

I reached the other side where Charlie and Tommy were standing. "Anything?" I asked looking at another piles of bodies. This group, about thirty of them, was not as orderly as the others. In fact, they seemed to have been left where they fell.

"I think these were zombies," Charlie said, indicating with the barrel of his rifle a neat hole in the forehead of the nearest corpse. There were similar wounds in the rest of the corpses that I could see, evidence that these people were infected and put down. But if they put down the Z's, why would they leave their town and come to this area to die? It made no sense whatsoever.

I started back towards the truck, signaling the other two to follow. We wouldn't get any answers from this place and like Charlie had said, this town was full of ghosts.

Just as we passed the trees, a small figure stepped out into the open. Three rifles trained on the small man as he stood there, staring at the bodies. Flies landed on his face and clothes, but he didn't seem to notice. He was dressed in casual clothes, jeans and a flannel shirt. I noticed the bulge of a holster under his shirt and signaled to Charlie the man had a weapon. He looked to be around seventy, but was probably younger. He didn't seem to notice us, his haunted eyes were fixed on the death in front of him.

I moved closer, lowering my rifle, knowing that Charlie and Tommy had moved to the sides and still covered the old man. "Sir?" I asked, "Are you from around here? Do you know what happened here? Sir?"

"He lied to them," the old man said, his voice barely carrying over the din of the flies. "He lied to them and led them here and watched as they died for him."

Confused, I pressed for answers. "Who lied?"

The old man glanced my way, his piercingly blue eyes barely acknowledging my existence. "This town had a preacher, who told the people the dead rising was a sign of the end of the world. He told them there was no hope, that after the dead had finished, the world would be consumed by fire and cleansed by God, who was angry at the world. He lied when he said everyone was dead, that this town was the last one on Earth. He told them he had visions from God, telling him what the townspeople had to do to be saved."

I just scowled, remembering preachers and pastors from my own past who were little better than charlatans, claiming a connection to God that was more false than their claims of salvation. But I also remembered how persuasive these men were and how with just a few words they could whip a crowd up to rapturous frenzy. Opportunists, every one, and the Upheaval brought more opportunity than most dared dream.

"He had the people bring out their sick relatives, then made them watch as they turned into those nightmares. He said it was God's curse on the land and the only way to heaven was on his path.

"I didn't think they would believe it, but they had no way of knowing they weren't alone. Out here they were cut off and the preacher wouldn't let them leave. He then told them that the day to get to heaven was here and he would help them along."

The old man brushed an errant tear that had strayed down his cheek. "He led them here and gave them pills and prayed over them as they died as families. This town died from lack of hope. They had no hope." The man's reedy voice faded off.

I found it ironic that had the town just waited, we would have proven this preacher wrong on all counts.

"What happened to the preacher?" I was curious to see if the man had moved on or followed his own teachings.

The old man's voice hardened. "I found him going through people's homes, taking what he thought would be valuable. I gave him his reward."

I didn't ask what that was, already guessing the answer. I backed away from the old man and signaled Tommy and Charlie to head back to the truck. We trotted back to the vehicle and spun around as we heard a shot behind us. The old man's body lay crumpled in the grass, his blood showing bright red on the brown landscape.

As I got into the vehicle, Charlie spoke up. "You knew he was going to shoot himself, didn't you?"

I nodded. "He had nothing left to live for. Not even revenge."

"Is what happened to this town why you keep going, why you keep trying to find people?" Charlie pressed, asking a more personal question than he had ever asked before.

I nodded again. "Think about it. If you figured there was nothing left to live for and the rest of your life was going to be a struggle just to survive, wouldn't you trade that for a promise of salvation? If this life was over anyway, what would be the point? We'll never have the lives we once had, but we can at least live. That's our revenge against the dead. That's how we drive back the nightmare. We make what we have left worth fighting for."

Tommy spoke through the back window. "We gonna go back and see if there is anything worth bringing back to the community?"

I shook my head. "That place is dead. Worse than if it had been overrun by zombies. The soul of that town is dead. I don't want anything from it."

Charlie nodded and hit the gas, sending us on our way to Verona, the next town on the map. As I looked in the rear view mirror, I could have sworn for an instant I saw hundreds of people in the tracks behind us, watching us leave. When I blinked, they were gone. Ghosts, indeed.

17

We traveled down the rails, keeping an eye out for anything unusual, although finding something more unusual than the last town we visited would be a stretch. We plowed ahead and in short order came to the outskirts of Verona. It was easy to see the differences. Verona, while a small town, was ringed by a six-foot tall earthen hill, the dirt and clay being used from the ditch that was directly in front of the hill, making it a twelve-foot obstacle to any roaming dead. The hill had an opening for the railway, and I assumed others would be found where roads entered the town. Across the opening was a wooden door made from four by fours, hung on a frame that was set into the hill. I could see the door swung outward, so it would be doubly hard to break it down. The rail bed fell away into the ditch, so any attacking horde would only be able to hit the door one, maybe two at a time.

"Stop here," I said to Charlie as we pulled closer. Put your rifle down and sit in the back of the bed," I called over my shoulder to Tommy.

"What's going on?" Tommy asked.

"Protocol." "We have to wait for them to notice us and decide if they want to talk to us. If we stand around holding weapons, they might decide to shoot first. I'm not willing to get into a firefight without better cover than the windshield of this truck."

Tommy grunted, but put his gun down and sat back where he could be seen. Charlie and I waited in the cab and after about ten minutes, two men with rifles crested the hill and waved us towards the gate. We pulled forward slowly and the gate opened as we passed through. On the other side, another man with a shotgun signaled us to stop. I could feel Charlie tensing beside me and I shook my hand at him, trying to calm him down. The gate closed behind us and I hoped everything was going to go well.

We were surrounded by at least ten men, all armed in some fashion. I tried to remain pokerfaced, but after a minute of silence, I was starting to inch my own hand towards my SIG, with my other hand getting ready to open the door. Beyond the armed men, I began to see a growing crowd of onlookers, curious as to who the newcomers were. No one was smiling and I was getting curious as to what the deal was.

A heavyset man in a brown jacket made his way through the crowd and stood in front of the truck. He stared at Charlie and me for a second then gestured for me to step outside.

I got out of the truck and stood a couple of feet from it. I was already calculating who I was going to shoot first if things went south and it was going to be the sorry looking bastard to my right who was standing too close pointing a rifle at my head. I glanced up at Tommy who gave me a slight nod. His rifle was likely near his hands and would be in action at the first sign of trouble.

The man in the brown jacket spoke. "Howdy. I'm Bob Larkin. Who might you fellas be?"

"I'm John Talon and these are my companions Charlie James and Tommy Carter. We've come from Coal City to see if any towns on this line were still alive. Obviously, you are," I said, looking pointedly at the man holding his gun on me.

Bob nodded. "How's Coal City doing? I haven't heard from the sheriff in a while?"

"It lives, and Tom Harlan is fine." I still didn't take my eyes off the man next to me.

"Good enough. Put your gun up, Ed, these men are fine. Sheriff Harlan and I spoke over the radio this morning and he said to expect you three. He told me you three were bonified deader killers and we should be glad to know you. Just by appearances, I figured he ain't too far off the mark." Tensions suddenly erased and trigger fingers eased up.

I had to smile. 'Deader' was a new one to me, but it fit. Didn't really matter what we called them, they were the enemy and that was it.

Bob Larkin and I spoke while the rest of the town was dismissed. The town basically had barricaded themselves when the first wave of 'deaders' came over the horizon and started attacking people. Bob, who was the head of the town council as well as being an insurance salesman, decided the best thing to do was to build a wall around the town, using what they had in abundance, which was dirt. The wall and ditch were very effective and I had to agree, since we were using the same approach in Leport.

Bob told me that essentially people here had gotten on with their lives. They were used to the fact that electricity might not be coming back for a while and if they wanted to make a life they are pretty much going to have to work together. Bob was happy to hear about Coal City making it through the invasion and after about an hour, I was ready to get moving.

I climbed aboard the truck and Charlie, Tommy and myself were rolling through Verona. We waved to the people we saw and they smiled and waved back, the news about us having traveled through the small town faster than modern communication could ever have hoped to achieve. Bob and I set up a communication network, using the rail line as the means of transporting news and items of trade. Bob said one of his friends was putting the finishing touches on a pedal-powered rail car, which would be used for the trade effort. I had some serious doubts about that, but kept them to myself.

For my part, I warned Bob about Mazon, and he shook his head at the waste. He was going to have to let the town know, since several people had relatives there and would want to bury them. My suggestion was to burn the whole lot, but Bob just shrugged.

We passed through the town and out the other doors. It wasn't until we were about a mile away that Tommy poked his head through the back window.

"I have a question," Tommy said. "If they knew we were coming, why the chilly reception? I thought you were going to kill that guy holding the rifle on you."

Charlie nodded. "Seems a little out of place, given their defenses."

"I asked Bob about that and he said it was because they've been having trouble lately," I said.

"What kind of trouble?" asked Charlie

"Apparently there's some sort of rogue group terrorizing Kinsman, Ransom, and Kernan. They're demanding 'protection goods' and such. They originally came in showing themselves as capable of handling the zombie problem, but they disarmed the populace and now are essentially running things. They tried to run a fast one on Verona, but got knocked back. The people of Verona are wary of strangers, which is why we got that reception. If we hadn't known Harlan or been from Coal City it might have gone down differently."

"So what you're saying is we're heading to a fight we may not want, against a group we have no knowledge of, supported by a bunch of weaklings too afraid to fight for themselves?" Tommy asked.

"Possibly."

"I'll be in the bed, cleaning my guns, if anyone needs me." Tommy said, withdrawing to the back of the truck and pulling out his cleaning kit.

I chuckled and looked over at Charlie. "We could pull out, head back to Coal City on the roads."

Charlie just looked at me.

"You're right," I sighed. "This is what we do."

"At least it's not boring."

"True."

We moved down the rails as the sun was getting to its highest point. The landscape sloped gently in various places and I could see homes here and there in the distance. We were coming up to a farm that had the house relatively close, so I told Charlie to pull up so we could take a look.

We stepped out of the vehicle and crossed the field to the growing grass of the farmhouse lawn. The house was typical of the area, two stories, whitewashed, with a few outbuildings. There was a barn, a garage, some sort of long building I couldn't identify, and something that appeared to be a chicken coop. They were all in need of repair, but that was something I suspected was necessary before the world died.

Tommy wandered over to the barn while Charlie and I checked the house and other buildings. Charlie moved around to the windows and looked in while I stepped up onto the expansive front porch. I guessed the farm had to be somewhere between fifty and one hundred years old. I looked in the front window and saw a family room with several pieces of furniture and old antiques. All that wasn't as interesting as the legs I saw sticking out from behind the lounge chair.

Great, I thought, *here we go again*. I pulled my pickaxe and held it ready as Charlie stepped onto the porch. He saw me arm myself and pulled one of his tomahawks as well. I tried the door and found it open, so I pushed it slowly in, stepping back to allow anything in there an opportunity to come out and play.

Nothing happened, so Charlie and I stepped into the room. I went over to the legs and saw they belonged to what I assumed was the owner of the farm. He was a fairly big man, dressed simply and would be mistaken for sleeping except for the large, gaping wound in his chest. I figured he had been shot close range with a shotgun and judging by the looks of him, this had happened a while ago. The blood around him on the floor had turned black, as well as the mess on the wall behind him.

I turned to Charlie. "Murdered. I'd bet if anyone else was home they're dead too."

Charlie pointed to the family photo on the mantle. "It's a family of six," he said.

"Shit, not again." I remembered the last time we came across something like this. A rogue group had killed a family and very nearly killed us, but we burned their world down around their ears.

Charlie and I split up, Charlie taking the upstairs and I took the downstairs and cellar. I opened the door to the cellar while Charlie headed to the stairs at the back of the kitchen. The kitchen had been completely ransacked and I did not expect to find anything useful in the basement, but the opportunity was there.

Down in the basement, I looked over several workbenches and found a few road flares, which I added to my pack. Tools and such were of no use right now, but I did find a small refrigerator. Looking inside I found four beer cans. I placed them on the stairs to take later.

It'd been a long time since I had a beer, and I thought I'd earned one. Normally I didn't drink, but I had a feeling I was going to need it.

As I turned to head back up the stairs, I noticed something odd. The back wall wasn't made of flagstone like the rest of the walls. It was made of cinderblocks, painted the same color as the stones. Looking closely, the wall seemed a lot closer than the wall upstairs in the kitchen. Walking over to the bench that lined the wall, I looked over a bookshelf that seemed oddly out of place. I looked at the floor and could see scuff marks where the bookshelf had been moved.

Intrigued, I wrestled the bookshelf away from the wall and flashed my light in the revealed opening.

I was pleasantly surprised. The area behind the wall was a secret storage place, with canned goods piled high. I found stacks of batteries, emergency radios with a crank handle, and several boxes of MREs. There were backpacks hung on pegs by the opening and several stacks of bottled water. In addition, there was a shotgun, a .22 rifle, and boxes of ammo for all, including ammo for a .38, which I didn't see and for a .45, which I didn't see, either.

I grabbed a duffle bag from the corner and filled it with canned goods and water. I took one of the backpacks and emptied it, filling it with MREs. I emptied another backpack and filled it with ammo for the shotgun, the .38, and the .45.

I hauled all the bounty back upstairs and met Charlie in the kitchen. His eyes widened at the haul, but then turned cold.

"What's up?" I asked.

"Come upstairs and see."

Puzzled, I followed him back upstairs. At the back of the hall was the master bedroom and inside was a nightmare. A body was on the floor, a single gunshot wound to the chest indicating how he died. He was dressed in jeans and a leather coat and appeared to be young, maybe twenty years old. That wasn't the nightmare. The woman on the bed was the nightmare. She had been stripped and presumably raped, then methodically mutilated until she bled to death from hundreds of cuts and stab wounds. Whoever killed her, wanted her to suffer. If I had to guess, the body on the floor was some sort of relation to whoever had savaged the woman. This was a revenge killing if I had ever seen one.

Charlie reached into his pack and retrieved a Smith & Wesson Model 66 and a Springfield Armory Mil-Spec 1911. Both were stainless steel and in good shape. "Found the revolver on the bedside table, probably left there to taunt the woman as she suffered. The .45 was in the dresser."

I didn't say a word. I was too angry at a world that allowed this to happen. I pulled my knife and cut the woman loose, wrapping her up in the bed sheets and carrying her downstairs. I barely noticed her weight as I walked outside, Charlie stopping to pick up the bags I brought up from the basement.

Outside, Tommy was working at the ground, digging a shallow trench. I walked over to where he was and placed the woman on the ground. I looked over to the side and dropped my head.

"Oh no."

Tommy stopped what he was doing and looked off into the distance. He didn't look at the two small bodies lying side by side in the sun. "They hung them." Tommy's voice was barely above a whisper. "Two little boys who probably never hurt a thing in their lives. They hung them like they were useless pieces of meat. I mean, what kind of animal..." Tommy's voice cracked and he looked down, resuming his digging.

I had nothing to say. I had seen a lot of things since the world went upside down and I had thought I had seen the depths of depravity humans were capable of. But every time I thought I had seen the bottom, another layer got exposed. Was the line of lawlessness that close? Was the beast of man that close to the surface, waiting to be loosed? I didn't know. But the cold fire had started burning and I did know one thing and I said it aloud, more to myself than anyone else, although perhaps it was to the dead family.

"Men will die for this. I promise."

Charlie nodded, then went to the garage for more shovels. I headed back to the house to bring the father out to be buried with his family.

It took an hour, but we buried the family together, hoping that wherever they were, they would appreciate the effort. I found a couple of boards and fashioned a crude cross to place at the head of the grave. We stood silently for a moment, each of us reaching out to the deceased family with our prayers.

We gathered our supplies and as we were putting them in the truck, Tommy said, "Hold up." He walked off into the field on the other side of the tracks and looking around, I saw what had attracted his attention. A lone zombie was wandering through the field at a snail's pace, tripping over vegetation and the uneven ground. Tommy walked straight to the zombie, which raised a groan at his approach and lifted its hands to the oncoming meal.

Tommy never slowed his advance, never took his eyes off his target. He unslung his melee weapon, a length of gas pipe that had a t-junction on the end, hammered into killing points. Just as the grasping hands nearly had him, Tommy hit the zombie in the head with the makeshift mace. The power of the swing smashed the zombie's head off the body. Charlie and I watched as Tommy followed the head into the brush and repeatedly smashed it.

I understood how he felt. I wanted to crush something, make it suffer for what had happened here, and the frustration of not being able to strike out made it worse. There would be a reckoning.

Tommy walked back, dragging his weapon through the grass to get the worst of the ghoul gore off it. He wiped the rest off with a bit of cloth taken from the dead body, then climbed back into the truck.

None of us said a word. We had things to do. The sun was high and we had to hit three more towns before the end of the day.

We drove on, sighting Kinsman relatively shortly. I didn't see the landscape pass by, didn't pay attention to anything, really. My mind was wrapped around the family that had been brutally murdered. What kind of monster could hang little children? What monster lurked out there that had just waited for the veneer of civilization to erode away? I had killed and based on the way I was feeling, I was going to kill again if I had the chance to even the score. Was I any better? I liked to think so, but some might argue not. I never killed anyone who did not wish to harm me and I liked to think I was protecting a larger ideal. Just because the trappings of civilization had fallen away did not mean we had become uncivilized.

We pulled into Kinsman and immediately I could see something wasn't right. There were people about, but they didn't look at us, or if they did, they tried not to notice us. That was weird. I could see several people out working in a field, most of them older men, women, and children. This wasn't adding up at all.

Charlie and I got out of the truck and walked over to what looked like an old fashioned feed store. There were three men standing outside the store and they looked down as we approached.

"Excuse me. Is this Kinsman?" I asked, knowing full well it was, but I had to start the conversation somewhere.

The man in the middle looked up at me. He was about fifty or sixty years old, wearing a faded flannel shirt and stained work coat. His tired blue eyes looked into mine.

"Yes, sir, it is. Can I help you in some way?" His voice was full of fear and I couldn't figure out why.

"Just glad to see I'm headed in the right direction. My name is John and this is Charlie. We've come from Coal City to let anyone still alive know they're welcome to come live there if they want to. But you all seem to have a decent town here, people working to grow food and such. We'll let you get back to what you're doing." I turned to walk away when the man grabbed my arm.

"You ain't with them, then?" His voice was a hushed whisper and the other men with him quickly looked around.

"With who? You saw me and my friend come down the rails. Who do you think we are?" I was more than curious as I disengaged my arm.

The men looked around again. "A group of about twenty came in at the end of the winter, looking for supplies and a place to rest. We obliged, them being the first people we'd seen for a while. Well, they had another notion, and we were overwhelmed in short order. They took our food, took our young women, shot a few who resisted, and made the rest of us work to keep them in food and supplies. They threaten to kill the kids unless we help them." The man's voice shook with anger as the other men nodded their agreement.

The man continued. "They say they have a horde of zombies at their place that they'll let loose on the kids if we don't do things their way and then tie up the parents for the kids to eat." The man hung his head. "We don't have any weapons and we can't leave. We're trapped."

I thought about this for a second. Rock and a hard place, for these people. I made a decision. "Where is their base?"

The man on the left, a shorter, heavyset man of around sixty said, "We don't know for sure. They tend to head back in a northerly direction, so we figure they're up that way, but the last guys to go looking came back as zombies."

"What protection do you have from the occasional zombie or three.?" Charlie asked.

"We use garden tools, even though the group said they would protect us. The attacks have been less, lately, but there's still one every other day or so."

My response was interrupted by the sound of a vehicle coming down the road at a high rate of speed. Charlie and I sidled into the store so as not to be seen. I could see Tommy slide out of the truck bed and work his way into the ditch by the tracks so he could see under the truck. Charlie opened a window up on the store and knelt down, aiming his rifle in the direction of the noise. I waited by the door to see what was going to happen.

I didn't have long to wait. A black truck barreled around the corner, screeching to a halt in front of the general store. The three men out front looked very scared and tried to keep their eyes down.

The truck belched out four men, all in various clothing, most of it black. Two of the men wore t-shirts that had large skulls on them and the other two, teenagers, wore typical youth dress. All of them sported earrings and necklaces and all of them were wearing black leather jackets. I was reminded of the dead man we found at the farmhouse and the cold fire began to burn again. All of the men were armed with a pistol in their belts, ala Pancho Villa style, with two of the men carrying AK-47 variants. I was a little disappointed, since we wouldn't be able to use the guns once we dealt with this.

The leader of the group immediately started screaming at the men at the store. "What the fuck is going on? Whose truck is that? You know the goddamn rules, no fucking strangers! Do I need to make an example out of you, you old fuck?" The screamer was a man about twenty-five years old, with dirty blond hair and what I called 'trouble eyes'. His tirade caused the men to flinch, but he didn't notice the fist the oldest man clenched at being addressed by this punk.

"No, sir." came the reply.

"I better not, you useless piece of shit. Boxer!" the leader called.

A small specimen by the truck spoke up. "Yeah!"

"Check out that truck. Tell me what you find."

"You got it, Van." The little guy ran over to the truck, opened the door and brought up his rifle dramatically to cover the interior. I nearly laughed. I could see Charlie just shake his head in my peripheral vision.

Van, the leader, shoved his nasty face into the oldest man's face. "Where are the people who drove that truck?" No answer. Van's face got red and he pulled out his pistol and aimed into the face of the man next to him. "I don't like to repeat myself, fucker. I'm counting to three, then I'm killing your friend and feeding him to the zombies. Got it? One..."

I stepped out of the store and pointed my rifle barrel at Van's forehead. "Two," was all I had to say. Behind Van, the other two men were caught off guard and fumbled for their weapons. I could see Tommy coming around the black truck, his gun up and ready. Behind him I could see the inert form of Boxer on the tracks.

To his credit, Van didn't flinch. "I'll still kill this fucker, unless you drop your gun, hero." Van sneered at me.

I pressed the barrel of the rifle into Van's head. "What makes you think I'll let you live one second after that gun goes off? Kill him, he's nothing to me." That earned me a panicked look from the man under Van's gun.

Van worked that one around in his head and I could tell he wasn't good at math. "Boys! Shoot this asshole!" Van yelled to his men.

Nothing happened. Van was becoming confused. Something was wrong, but he didn't dare take his eyes off me. Behind him, Tommy had effectively disarmed his cohorts and they were kneeling on the ground, hands on their heads, mumbling threats I couldn't hear.

"Question for you, Van," I said.

"Fuck you."

"What comes after two?"

Van's eyes got wide and it finally dawned on him that he was going to actually die if he kept this up. He reluctantly lowered his gun and I used my left hand to take it from him. It was an engraved, ivory stocked Springfield .45. Very nice. I wondered who he stole it from. I passed it over to Charlie who came out of the store aiming his gun at Van as well. I figured Van's eyes were going to pop out of his head if we offered up any more surprises. Resistance was the last thing he expected. Instead of tired, scared old men, he was suddenly facing battle-hardened veterans of the Upheaval. I'm sure had he suspected we were there, we would have had a more serious disagreement.

I shoved Van out into the street where he landed unceremoniously in front of his men. He jumped up immediately, but I was ready and slammed a fist into his head, knocking him back face first against the truck door, denting the panel. Van slid down, holding his nose, which seeped blood through his fingers.

I hunkered down in front of the two men and they stared hatred at me. "Howdy," I said. "I need to know where your base is and if you tell me, I'll let you go warn them. If you don't, I imagine things will go badly for you."

"Fuck you," the older of the two said. "We'll kill your punk ass. Who the fuck do you think you are? We own this area which includes you."

I was unfazed. "Okay. The hard way it is." I stood up and Charlie and I gathered up the weapons. I walked back to the men at the general store, and handed them the guns.

"These are yours. Do what you want, but I would suggest you get everyone out of here. Head down the tracks and get to Verona. They'll take you in." Several people had wandered over from the fields and were standing in the distance.

I addressed the people. "My name is John Talon. You people need to decide how you want to live. If you stay here, you'll likely be killed by the group that has been terrorizing you or fall prey to the next gang that comes along. Verona is alive and so is Coal City. Take the tracks and move quickly."

I started to walk back to the truck, Charlie following with Tommy bringing up the rear. The old man called out, "What do we do with these guys?"

I turned back and smiled at him. "They're all yours." I watched the people of the town surge forward and as I climbed into the cab of the truck, I could hear a high pitched scream as the people took their revenge against their oppressors.

"Three," I said to no one in particular. Charlie chuckled and Tommy looked at me like I was nuts.

18

We found more of the same in Ransom with the populace being cowed by the group of renegades. Ransom had actually put up a fight against the group and had several people hanging outside town as an example to the rest. Another score to settle.

Ransom had about three hundred or so people living in it and they were all looking for a way out. I pointed them in the direction of the tracks and when we pulled out, a long line of people and belongings was headed northeast. None of the gang showed up, so I imagine they were in for a surprise when they came back to a ghost town.

Kernan was similar to Ransom with the exception that we managed to get into a little firefight with the representatives of the renegades. Charlie took a graze to his upper arm and I got nicked in the leg because I wasn't bright enough to get myself fully under cover, but neither was serious. We killed four of the group with the remaining two beating a hasty retreat to the north. I came to the conclusion that we were not going to finish this unless we went after the rest of the gang, so after a brief powwow, it was decided that Charlie was going to take the survivors of Kernan over to Streator, if anything was left of it, and establish connections there. We did manage to find Tim Harlan, who was overjoyed to hear his brother was still alive.

For Tommy and myself, it was time to go hunting. We had a pretty good idea where our quarry was, but it was still going to take some doing to find them and deal them a blow they would not forget. As Machiavelli once said, "If you must do injury to a man, it should be so severe that his vengeance need not be feared." So it would be.

I pulled out the map that had brought us this far and I outlined what we knew so far. "The farmhouse was about here," I said, placing a small pebble on the map. "The group had extended its activity over these towns here." I placed additional pebbles on Kernan, Ransom, and Kinsman. "Everyone says that the scumbags always went north in some fashion. Since most scumbags rarely show any incentive beyond really lazy, I'm going to hazard a guess that our little friends are probably here." I pointed to a spot labeled LaSalle Lake Fish & Wildlife Area.

"What's there?" asked Tommy.

"As far as I can tell, water. But without any serious intelligence or someone telling us where to go, we have to start somewhere." I wasn't sure, but I did have a gut feeling about the place.

"Are we leaving in the morning?" Tommy wanted to know.

I hesitated. "We may have to do this one at night."

Tommy stared at me. "Are you nuts? We never go out at night. The Z's are always more active at night. It would be suicide!"

I shrugged. "What choice do we have? We go in the morning, they'll see us miles before we will see them. We at least know that they won't be out at night, for the same reason we shouldn't be, so we can move around without alerting anyone."

"Fine." Tommy said grudgingly. "But I get the shotgun."

"Deal. But get some rest. We move out in 3 hours."

"Oh, like I'm gonna sleep *now*."

We moved out just as the sun was setting. It was the best time to be moving since it was hard for zombies' vision to adjust between the light of the sky and the dark of the ground. With any luck, we would be past any problems before they could figure out where we were. We couldn't find a vehicle to take us where we wanted to go, but we did manage to scrounge up a couple of usable bicycles. In all honesty, if I had to travel at night, I would rather have the bike. It was quiet, it was quick, and could go overland much easier than a car could. Besides, with the way my luck was running, we probably wouldn't have been able to find anything better than a beat up Cutlass with a bad muffler and out of time cylinder.

Tommy and I pedaled north and based on the map we had roughly ten miles to go, five miles north and five miles east. We were going to stick to the roads since we were not sure of the overland route and we really didn't want to have to sidestep any natural barriers.

I didn't relate this to Tommy, but I had a dark suspicion that wherever we wound up, the local ghouls might be out in force because these yahoos had been tearing up the countryside for a while with their travels back and forth. Too much activity tends to cause zombie investigation, and if they had been taking shots at the Z's they'd come from even farther away.

We pedaled quickly on the road, passing by untended fields and empty farmhouses. I didn't feel the remotest desire to check out any of the farms, the memory of the last one we checked out too fresh. The evening air was cooler and the moon hadn't risen yet. The land was darkening with the sky following suit. I was hoping for a clear night sky to give us some light to work with, but that was really out of my hands.

We passed the first crossroads without incident and moved along the road towards the next. The nice thing about country roads in Illinois is they are laid out in one mile square increments. At each mile was a crossroad. If you didn't know where you were going, you could still do a decent job just following the pattern of the roads. I told this to Tommy who seemed dubious.

"How do you know this stuff?" He whispered as we worked our way past another farm.

"My wife's family is from downstate. They own a farm and she told me. Never thought it would be useful." I swerved around a large pothole.

"Never thought the world would end, but here we are."

"Yep."

Our conversation seemed normal, but underneath we were both wired as tight as snare drums. I knew we were being heard by Z's in the area, and in all likelihood many zombies were rousing themselves out of their holes and on the prowl for prey.

We traveled down the road, glancing briefly at the dark homes that rose up out of the darkness like gravestones. Not a light was seen, not a sound was heard. I felt like a trespasser, like we were intruding on a world no longer ours. Stay in the light children, for the dark hides monsters.

Tommy raised a hand as we approached the second mile road crossing. The stop signs looked lonely and out of place, and the street lamp that once lit this little intersection stood silent and dark, watching sentry over its little corner of the world. We slowed to a stop in the middle of the intersection. I looked over at Tommy, and his eyes were locked on the road ahead.

"See something?" I asked

"Hang on." He looked off to the left a little bit.

"Yeah, there it is. It's in the ditch on the left side, about fifty yards up," he said, pulling out his blunt weapon.

I squinted into the darkness. "What's that weird glow?"

"I don't know. Never saw that before."

I shrugged and pulled out my own weapon, the handle-modified pickaxe. "I guess we should go see."

I pedaled a bit forward, then parked the bike. I was not about to engage a Z while still straddling a bicycle. I got off and stood in the center of the road, figuring it gave me the best purchase for fighting. I listened as the zombie made its way along the ditch, aware of me now, and zeroing in for the kill. As it approached, I could see more details in the waning light. Its clothes were in tatters, hanging off more than hanging on, its dead skin stretched over its dead features. Its nose had been torn off, giving its face a more ghastly, skeletal appearance. Wispy hairs stuck out from its head, and its glowing eyes focused on me as its mouth opened to reveal jagged teeth.

I did a double take. Glowing eyes? When the hell did that start happening? I didn't think it was possible to make a creepy dead thing creepier, but here it was. The eyes of the zombie actually glowed with a mild luminescence, like a glow in the dark toy that was starting to fade.

As twitchy as glowing zombie eyes made me, I was actually curious how it happened. Was this a side effect? Had it always happened and we just never noticed because we didn't go out at night? On the plus side, it sure made it easier to spot them at night. On the minus side, it gave me the willies.

The Z scrambled up the ditch and crawled out onto the road. Before it had the chance to get up, I ran up to it and hit it on the head with my pickaxe. The new handle worked well. I didn't take as large a swing as I normally did, but the additional weight carried well and the pointed end crushed the ghoul's head easily. I pulled out the pick and noticed that the zombie's brains were glowing as well. Stranger still. I wiped off the pickaxe and climbed back about the bike. Tommy stepped down to inspect the corpse.

That's just wrong," he said, getting back on his bike.

"Makes them easier to spot at night, now, I guess," I said, putting my weapon back into its place.

"Some consolation," Tommy said. "Can you imagine hiding in a dark room only to see glowing pairs of eyes coming at you from the blackness?" He shuddered for effect.

"You mean like that?" I pointed to a very dark spot in a small grove of trees. Sure enough, three pairs of glowing eyes could be seen, weaving back and forth, unblinking, unwavering. They had seen us and were now coming for us.

"I will never look at fireflies the same way again," Tommy said as he started his bike. I pedaled after him. We could have stayed and killed the converging dead, but we had places to go and we only fought when we really had to. I had run into lunatics who felt it was their mission to eradicate the undead threat and wound up taking chances that got themselves killed.

We moved steadily north without further incident, although Tommy and I saw several more zombies in the countryside as the sky grew darker and darker. No doubt, there were a lot more we couldn't see, since the glowing eyes weren't like flashlights, more like a slow dull glow. If they had hair falling in front of their faces we could not see their eyes.

Still, it was creepy as all hell to be riding through the dark country and seeing spots of lights dancing in my peripheral vision and I knew they weren't little harmless insects.

We reached the five mile crossroads and finally turned our bikes east. The sky was even darker and the stars were coming out in force. Without the glow of civilization muting the light of the stars, the night sky was amazing. We could see thousands of stars and a couple of planets low in the sky. The arm of the galaxy could be seen, something I had only seen once a long time ago when Ellie and I visited the southwest deserts.

We pedaled steadily for another twenty minutes and with the night breeze coming out of the east, I could smell water on the wind, enough that I knew we had to be coming near a significant body of water. Remembering the map, I reasoned the LaSalle Fish & Wildlife area was getting close.

I let Tommy know we were getting close and he just nodded in the dark, his eyes straining and his hands gripping the handlebars tightly. I didn't blame him. Up ahead was a pack of zombies, around ten of them, walking along the road, and headed towards us. Their glowing eyes marked each one and I had to decide what to do. We were near enough to where I thought the renegades were that I didn't think we could risk a shot and there were too many of them to take out in hand to hand combat. There was no cover and the Z's would simply overwhelm us.

"I'm going to head right at them to bunch them up, then I'm going to swerve to the edge of the road and go around them," I said to Tommy as I pedaled faster. I could hear the groans of the dead as they saw us coming, carried on a wind that brought also the scent of decay and death.

"Gotcha." Tommy braked a little to get behind me and then pedaled to catch up so he was only a foot or so behind me. He had the more dangerous position, since the zombies would be reacting to me, but Tommy would be closer to their reaching hands. I pedaled quickly, staying close to the right side of the road, as I approached, I could see several of the zombies moving to the right, trying to cut me off. A couple moved too far, falling into the ditch on the side of the road. I sped towards the groaning mass, then just before I would have plowed into them, I swerved sharply to the left, veering away to the other side of the road. Tommy followed closely behind and we pedaled furiously away from our now confused pursuers. I chanced a glance back and saw they had turned around and were now chasing us, although they were fading quickly into the darkness.

I breathed a sigh of relief. "That went well," I said, as Tommy resumed his place next to me.

"If we never do that again it will be too soon. I swear that last guy nearly caught my shirt. I felt a tug as I went past."

"Any encounter you walk away from uninfected..." I said.

"Yeah, I know."

"Did you notice the eyes?" I queried.

"What about them? Were they different colored this time?"

"Only four of them were glowing."

"Perfect," Tommy said, bouncing over a bad repair to the road.

I smiled as we went farther east, passing the fourth mile crossroads. I began to wonder if I had guessed wrong and we were risking our sorry necks for a wild goose chase. If that was the case, we were going to have to find a place to spend the night and in the middle of nowhere that would present a few problems.

19

We came across the power plant unexpectedly, with the dark building looming large in the night. I could make out the outline of several utility towers stretching away from the plant and the complex was ringed with a tall, barbed-wire tipped chain link fence. Off to the east, I could see stars reflected in what appeared to be a significant body of water and I could see several buildings in the outlying areas. We moved closer for a better look and I could see three buildings which looked like maintenance sheds off to the west. We crossed a parking lot and moved into the shadows by a maintenance office building. There was a large guard house at the entrance to the plant with a gate that slid out of the way. The fence was impressive, two parallel lines with a walkway in between large enough for a vehicle to travel. There was an administrative building about seventy-five yards back from the gate and I could see several large trucks parked in front of it.

Tommy touched my sleeve and pointed to the second story of the admin building. There were small flashes of light and I realized the windows had been covered or painted and we were seeing light through the cracks. Pretty smart. Whoever was running this show was smart enough to realize a light would attract every Z for miles.

As it was, we could see several pairs of glowing eyes in the darkness, headed our way, attracted by our scent and sound. We had very limited time before we would be in a serious fight.

I motioned for Tommy to follow me and I sprinted for the gate. It was the only part of the fence that didn't have barbed wire on the top. I jumped for the fence and climbed over the top, dropping down and looking around. The parking lot had several zombies shuffling across and I could see more on the road and fields outside the area. There was no guard posted outside and I could see why. The fence was more than sturdy enough to withstand an assault and with two lines running completely around the complex, this place was as secure as any. Had I lived in this area, I would have chosen this place as a good spot to make a stand.

"What's the plan?" Tommy asked as he dropped down beside me.

"I want to make sure this is the place we have been looking for. I wouldn't want to wipe out a group of people who were just trying to survive. So let's scout a bit and see what's here," I said, unslinging my rifle from across my back. Tommy did the same with his AR, checking the magazine and making sure our ride hadn't moved around his spare magazines too much.

We moved towards the office building and when we were about twenty yards away, we could hear faint sounds of activity from within. There seemed to be muted cheers and yells and what sounded like a bottle breaking. We may have found the right place after all.

I moved around to the corner of the building and stopped. I caught the scent of something odd in the wind and when I smelled it again I recognized it. Blood. Something had lost a lot of blood recently and it was on the wind. I signaled Tommy to circle wide and together we rounded the corner, guns at the ready.

Sprawled out on the grass was a man or what was left of him. He had been completely wiped out, not enough of him left to reanimate. Some of the bones had even been cracked open to get at the marrow inside. His head had been smashed open and his brains were completely missing. Blood was all around, leaving a large dark stain on the greening grass. Bloody footprints lead away into the dark, dark blotches on the sidewalk.

I looked at Tommy and we both realized the same thing at the same time. There were dead things out here. We didn't want to alert anyone to our presence, so we reslung our rifles and pulled out our blunt weapons, trusting in our side arms for firepower as needed. We stepped farther around and I could see the power relays in the distance, dwarfed by the tall towers as they reached for the dark of the sky. I could see several shadowy shapes moving among the towers and I knew them for what they were.

I pointed them out to Tommy and we moved quickly, spreading out and trying to take out as many as we could before they could swarm. The grass gave way to sand, which muffled our approach. The wind was still coming out of the east, which allowed us to attack from downwind. The gross side was we could smell the bastards and I have yet to meet a walking corpse that didn't smell like someone had microwaved a bag of garbage. The sad part was I was used to it. I came to one zombie who was just standing still, swaying slightly as it smelled the wind. I swung the pickaxe and sent the Z back to oblivion.

The sound of my pick cracking the Z's head open carried like a shot and three more turned in my direction. Tommy put his down and was approaching a third when I sprang towards the ghouls.

The first one rushed at me with slavering teeth only to be driven back by a spike to the head. The next one, a slight female with half her hair torn off, came slowly forward, her right foot turned around backwards. I hooked her foot and sent her tumbling, finishing her off with a spade to the head. The third one caught me by surprise, moving a lot faster than I had expected. He plowed into me, knocking me down and clawing at my back. I shoved back as hard as I could, but he was on too tightly. I couldn't do much except watch as he brought his teeth down onto my shoulder. I felt his teeth bite something and then he brought his head back. I felt a tug at my back and realized he had bitten my backpack shoulder strap and had it in his teeth. I drew my knife as he chewed the strap and when he realized he hadn't bit me, he leaned back for another lunge. I took that opportunity to shove my knife up under his chin and into his brain, ending his career as a deader. His glowing eyes looked into mine as he died and if I hadn't known better, I would have sworn there was a spark of recognition.

I threw him off of me and climbed slowly to my feet. Tommy was finishing off his second with a golf swing to the Z's head. He walked over to me as I was inspecting the damage.

"Holy shit. He got that close, did he?" Tommy said, peering at the teeth marks.

"Yeah." I said shakily. "One inch left or right and Sarah would be raising Jakey alone."

Tommy had nothing to say. I needed to get through this one on my own. I had just nearly bought the farm and brushing that close to death had a tendency to refocus your priorities.

I shook myself and looked around. There weren't any more immediate threats but that didn't mean they weren't out there.

Tommy was inspecting one of the corpses, then he walked over to another, and another. "That's weird," he said, half to himself.

"What is?" I asked, cleaning off my weapons.

"All these Z's have a stab wound in their throats."

"Really?"

"Yeah, and it looks like it was done after they had turned."

That was odd. "Any theory as to why?" I asked.

Tommy pondered for a second. "Its almost like they wanted to make sure they couldn't moan, like when people used to do that surgery on dogs to keep them from barking."

That made no sense. Why would someone go to the trouble of silencing Z's and not finish them off altogether? Oh well. We had other things to do. I motioned for Tommy to follow me and we went over to a small building next to the main administrative building. I saw a lot of footprints in the sand going to the building and was curious.

I tried the door with Tommy standing guard and I was surprised the door opened. I let the door swing outward and was rewarded with the foul odor of sweat, urine, feces, and something else I couldn't identify. I didn't smell the dead, so that was a good sign. I couldn't see in the darkness very well, so I unholstered my SIG and pulled out my flashlight. I scanned the building and saw it was a warehouse of sorts. A skylight allowed natural light to illuminate the interior, although that didn't help at night. There were boxes of supplies and alcohol, stacks of dried goods, and piles of clothing and shoes. Walking into the stores, I was surprised at how much there was. This group had done well, considering where they were.

As I walked slowly down the center aisle, I became aware of a sound. It wasn't loud, but it was there. It sounded like crying, but it was muffled, like someone was trying to keep themselves from sobbing out loud. I still hadn't found anything that created the smell and it was getting stronger as I moved farther back.

Towards the back of the building it looked like where they had stored the leftover material for the fence that went around the complex. I flashed my light over this material and froze as I shone the light on a living face.

I stopped suddenly. It was a woman, but it was difficult to tell her age. She was thin and filthy and her clothing barely covered her. Her hair hung in dank strips over her face and outside the circumstances, she might have been pretty. She was in a cage fashioned out of the fencing material and as I played my flashlight over the area, I could see several more cages similarly occupied. I could hear shifting as more women moved to see what had disturbed their sleep. In all, I counted sixteen cages, all of them occupied. They were roughly eight feet long and eight feet wide, six feet in height. Each contained a bucket, a cot, and a threadbare blanket. The blankets were whatever was grabbed in a hurry and some of them looked like children's blankets.

"Tommy." I spoke softly, but the woman I was looking at flinched as if I had struck her. She looked like she had been used badly and had resigned herself to the fact she was going to be used badly again. I could see the remnants of a bruise on her cheek and could see more on her arms and legs.

Tommy trotted over and turned on his flashlight, the beam playing over the cages and captives. "What the hell?" he said softly, as more women woke up and looked out at us.

"What's going on here?" I asked the nearest prisoner.

"We're the slaves," came a voice from the center of the cages. "That's what they call us. Didn't they tell you that?"

20

I walked down to the center and looked at the woman who had spoken. She was a thin blonde with a decent figure, dressed in a threadbare sundress that barely covered her. She looked at me with large brown eyes that had seen a lot of nasty things in recent times.

"I'm not with them," I said, noting the stir that caused. Several women stood up and came to the doors of their cages, holding the chain links and looking at Tommy and me with new eyes. I imagine we looked different than what they were used to. I was dressed for combat in my jacket, cargo pants, and vest, festooned with weapons. Tommy was similarly dressed.

"Who are you?" The woman's voice lost its disinterested drawl and became much more alert, more hopeful.

I thought for a second. "I'm John Talon. This is Tommy Carter. I'm here to kill the sons of bitches that slaughtered a family and terrorized the towns around here. I didn't expect to find anyone here worth saving, but I guess I was wrong. If you want to leave, you're coming with us right now."

The women rushed the doors of their cages and in short order we had freed them from their prisons. After being hugged and kissed several times, I told them to get to the stores and help themselves to whatever they wanted. Several grabbed bottles of water and headed off to the corner to wash up, while others picked through the clothing for more appropriate attire. While we were waiting for the women to get their fill of food and water, as well as being washed and dressed, Maggie, the woman who first spoke to me, filled me in on what had happened and what was going on around here.

The men had descended on the towns like thunder, sweeping through and taking whatever they wanted, including women. When they met resistance, they killed the dissenters and cowed the rest. They took the women back to this complex and kept them in these cages to be used however the men felt fit. No women were allowed in the "command center" as the men called it. The leader, a man called Art, was as ruthless as they came, killing with impunity any who crossed him. His favorite method of dealing with dissent was to release someone out into the yards where a few zombies were allowed to roam freely. The hapless victim would run themselves ragged until eventually being torn apart by the zombies while Art and his cronies watched from the rooftop. The zombies had their throats cut, so they couldn't moan and warn their victims. The women couldn't go anywhere if they got out of their cages, since the zombies would get them, too.

"Sounds like this Art guy is a real sweetie," I said to Maggie.

"He's a bastard," Maggie said around a mouthful of dried apricots. "And he's gotten meaner since his brother was killed on a raid."

Well, well. Now I knew I had the right place. I waved Tommy over from his discussions with two other women and filled him in on what I had been told.

Tommy nodded. "Sounds like what I had been hearing as well. What do you want to do about it? We can't find bikes for all these women and some of them are in bad shape, needing medical attention. We can't fight 'cause some of them will get killed for sure. I don't want to run, but I don't know what we're going to do."

Tommy had good points. As much as it galled me not to be able to put a bullet in Art's face, I had another job to do. I walked outside for a second and looked over the area. From where I was standing, I could see a fairly large crowd of zombies wandering around the outside fence. That wasn't too much of a concern, since zombies were usually easily distracted. But transportation was my big problem. I looked over to the trucks parked in front of the main building and realized suddenly that I could do both.

I went back into the building and outlined my plan to Tommy. He looked at me like I was nuts, but as the plan unfolded, he got a grin on his face that got wider as I explained further.

We waited for the lights in the building to die down, Maggie explaining that the men talked about plans and such before going to bed. They were not allowed to visit the women every night, since Art believed that the men had to "Earn their Turn" as he called it. The more loot a man produced, the more action he could get.

When the last light was out, Tommy and I ran around the front of the building and inspected the trucks. The only one that had the keys in it was the smallest one, a Chevy S-10. Cursing my luck again, we pushed the truck over the grass and near the building. I was dubious about all of the women being able to fit in the truck, but Maggie assured me that they would find a way, even if they had to lay on top of each other. I could understand their desire to get away. I was disappointed that we couldn't take any of the stores, but if things went well we could always come back and get them. I was interested in seeing if this power station could be restarted, but that would have to wait.

Tommy and I trotted towards the fence for the second part of my plan. We split up as we passed another building, with me ducking behind it and moving towards the far edge. I looked out as Tommy approached the fence, exciting the glowing-eyed ghouls on the other side. He moved slowly down the fence, drawing the crowd away, taunting and waving at them. When he had led his undead groupies away, I ran to the fence and opened the railway gates, an opening that allowed a small train to pull into the yard. I secured the gates open and ran back to the harem building.

"Okay ladies, let's get going," I said as I reached into my pack and pulled out a couple of flares. Maggie looked at me quizzically, but didn't say anything. I went over to the main admin building and opened a side door. I sparked the flare and stuck it in the sand next to the door. I ran back to the truck and climbed in. The truck bed was dangerously low, but we had to risk it. I started the engine and pulled away from the building, wincing as I hit unseen bumps and dips. I heard squeaks and gasps as knees and elbows bumped the truck bed walls. When I reached the train opening, I parked the truck and waited. About a minute later, Tommy came running in out of the darkness.

"They're coming! They're about to round the bend!" he panted as he jumped into the cab.

I stepped out and lit the second flare, planting it in the ground in the middle of the opening. The zombies would flock to the light and find their way in to the compound. The second flare would draw them to the open door to the gang and to dinner. With the men sleeping, they would likely wake up as zombies in the morning.

Not a perfect plan and there was a possibility that Art and his men would be able to regain control, but they would be severely weakened. I personally hoped Art got his nuts chewed off while another lovely nibbled his face away.

We pulled away from the compound, following a maintenance road that paralleled the railroad. I didn't want to go too quickly, since I couldn't afford a blowout. We reached the main road that went in front of the power plant and turned left, heading back to Coal City. I figured our little foray was finished. Charlie was probably sleeping in a nice bed, after a good meal. Oh well. Glancing in the rearview mirror, Maggie caught my eye and smiled.

Okay, I thought, *it was worth it.*

We drove quietly through the night, passing the occasional zombie or two, but nothing that was really a threat. Tommy was looking over the map, and glanced at the speedometer.

"I figure we have about twenty miles to go to get us to Coal City," Tommy said. "If we stay at this speed, we should be there in about an hour."

I looked at the dashboard. "No we won't."

"What? Why?" Tommy looked over and saw what I had seen. "You gotta be kidding me."

"Nope. We're almost out of gas." I shook my head as the empty light came on, indicating I had a gallon of gas left in the tank.

Fifteen miles later, the S-10 gave a lurch. I knew what that meant and increased the speed of the truck, figuring to coast as long as I could. With a final surge, the truck shut down, coasting to a stop. We had turned north at Mazon, skirting the death field, and were sitting on Route 47, according to the map. We had roughly six miles to go. If it was just Tommy and me, it would have been feasible, but trying to herd sixteen unarmed, untrained women through the dark made it mission unbelievable.

But we didn't have any choice. We couldn't stay where we were, since the ghouls would be able to find us and there was not a farmhouse in sight. We had to go, and go now, since I was sure we had attracted the attention of a lot of the local dead with our truck driving. Even though I had run with the lights off, the noise was such that it carried a good distance out here.

We got the women off the truck and I was grateful to see that all of them had managed to get some sort of footwear. I had no illusions about being able to carry someone for six miles. The wind was dying down and the moon was finally cresting high in the sky, casting a pale light over the landscape. Cornstalks rustled in the wind, causing Tommy and I to finger our weapons and glance around. We needed to move.

I took point, walking in front of the women, while Tommy brought up the rear. We had the women walk in a single file line down the middle of the road, the reason being if something came out of the fields in the center of the line, there would be a few seconds to react and deal with it.

We walked for about an hour, passing by two farm houses. I didn't bother to stop and look around or even consider them as a stopping point for the night. White flags fluttered in the night breeze from the lonely mailboxes by the side of the road, indicating these homes' surrender to the disease.

It wasn't until the fifth mile that we saw our first zombie. He was moving down the center of the road, ambling along as if he owned it. He was pretty tall for a zombie, roughly six foot three, with broad shoulders and long arms. At the sight of him, several of the women gasped, but to their credit, they didn't scream. I limbered up my pickaxe and advanced on the ghoul who hissed as he saw me and moved quickly forward.

Damn. A fast one. His success as a zombie was evident by the copious amount of dried blood about his face and hands. His shirt was filthy with blood. As he reached out I ducked aside and swung my pickaxe as hard as I could. The chisel end connected solidly with the

Z's knee, cracking it and tumbling the large zombie to the ground. It tried to stand up, but its leg buckled and wouldn't support it. A large hand reached out to grasp me as I got closer and I used a baseball swing to crush the skull of the ghoul at the temple. He went down with all the grace of a falling tree and I hooked his belt with the pickaxe. It was a trial trying to get this thing into the ditch, since he weighed over two fifty if he weighed an ounce.

The women cautiously moved forward. Maggie approached me as I wiped off my weapon.

"You've done that before, I guess?" she asked, looking down at the body.

"Yes." I was getting tired and was not in the mood for conversation. Any further explanation would have been pointless and likely last until morning. We needed to move.

I figured we had two miles to go and the horizon was starting to look a little lighter. I started walking again and Maggie fell back in line, understanding the need to continue.

We walked for another half hour, passing field after field. It wasn't until I began to see homes closer together that I realized we were nearing Coal City. Staying on the road, we passed the high school, and I could swear I saw a zombie wandering around the running track.

We stopped at a restaurant that had a beer garden and made our way inside. The garden had several tables and a wrought iron fence that enclosed it. Tommy did a quick check of the premises and declared it clear. Exhausted women collapsed on the tables and chairs, several of them lying out on the floor. I stretched out on a table and Tommy sat next to me.

"We going in?" Tommy wanted to know.

I closed my eyes. "Not 'til morning. We don't need to wake anybody just yet."

Tommy just nodded, then nodded off. I spent a moment with a lighter, burning the virus out of the strap on my backpack.

I was nearly asleep when a felt a touch at my shoulder. My eyes popped open and I looked into the startled face of Maggie, who was looking down the barrel of my SIG.

"Sorry about that," I said, putting the weapon back in its holster.

"I just wanted to say thank you," Maggie said. "We figured our lives were over until you and Tommy came."

"You're welcome," I said, closing my eyes.

In the morning, Tommy and I went over to the wall and shouted until someone noticed us. I climbed the ladder and spoke with one of Harlan's deputies, conveying our needs and leaving him to alert the rest of the town. In short order, Tommy was leading the women to the main gate, with a lot of people gawking at what we had accomplished. Sarah gave me a fierce hug and when she saw the chewed-on strap of my backpack, she looked into my eyes and started to cry. I didn't have anything to say, I just held her close.

After the women had been taken in, thanks to the arrangements made by Sarah and the women of Coal City, I gathered our band together. Charlie had arrived early in the morning, riding nice and easy in a comfortable truck on the railroad tracks. After hearing what Tommy and I had gone through, he muttered something about the luck of fools again and thumped me for nearly getting killed.

We were heading out today, going back to Leport. We had a long way to go and with the stars in proper alignment, we'd make it without incident. I told Sheriff Harlan about our plans and he wished us luck, thanking us for all we had done. He promised to stay in touch and we would be setting up some sort of regular communications soon. As it was, several towns were now in contact thanks to our work on the rails and with good fortune, we'd be able to get more going.

As we gathered our things for the trip north, I reflected on what this trip had cost us. We lost three people, but we gained several towns. I'd take that any day.

We drove out of Coal City to the waves and gratitude of the town. I felt good about what we had managed to do, but I knew we had other things to take care of first. One thing had been nagging me for a while, ever since Tom Harlan had mentioned his brother.

Where was my brother? The question would not leave me alone, and when we got back to Leport, I intended to do something about it.

After I spent a lot of time with Jake and Sarah.

21

We made it back to the boat and returned to Leport later in the day. Nate came down to the dock to greet us, bringing Jakey and Julia along as well as a large number of other people. There were a lot of questions, not the least of which was why we were three people short. After hugging Jake for a while, I explained to the people what had happened, what we had accomplished, and what had happened to our lost companions. There were head shakes all around, but no looks of blame. I downplayed what Charlie and I had done at Coal City and only briefly mentioned what Tommy and I had done. Everyone was excited about the prospect of new people and possibly being able to communicate and trade. We had realized on the trip up that the tracks that ran through Leport ran all the way down to Streator. We could set up a line of communication or we could get a train or something running.

While we were away, Duncan had been sending people back at a steady pace, with the list of incoming survivors reaching over two hundred. Tommy realized he was going to have to dig another trench, this one farther out as people moved into homes outside the safe zone. Everyone had to be quarantined for a bit to make sure no one was bringing the infection into the area, but no one complained.

One real piece of good news was the town had running water. Our plumbers and engineers had rigged up a pump system using a big water wheel and a whole lot of garden hose, not to mention the judicious use of gravity, and there it was. Not a ton of pressure, but it beat walking to the river with a bucket every day.

I spent the next few weeks just taking things easy, dealing with minor problems as they came up in the community, talking to newcomers, working out on the farms. I spent three interesting days with Nate as we scouted the local area, trying to find a suitable place for livestock. Eventually, we settled on a spot north of the farms. It had decent water, plenty of grazing and was surrounded on three sides by water. The only way any zombies would get at the livestock would be to come through a narrow gap and we had posted men to keep an eye on it. Charlie took off into the country side and came back later with a few cows, a horse, and several goats. It was a start and the animals actually seemed to be glad to have human company again.

Charlie and I spent a little time with our doctor because she wanted to run some tests on us. We shrugged and gave a vial of blood each, not thinking about it, or questioning her motives. I figured she'd tell us in time.

Summer was getting closer and more and more I was finding myself looking up the river, wondering about things that had no answer. On one such occasion, I was holding Jake, rocking him gently in the evening breeze. His little head rested on my shoulder, while his feet occasionally kicked at the SIG on my hip. I kept my eyes on the north and began to formulate an idea which refused to let go. It was one of those things that stayed with me. No matter what I was doing, during any down time my mind went back to it.

I whispered to Jake and he smiled sleepily, his little hand hooking into the collar of my shirt. I felt a ghost of a touch on my shoulder, and turned to see Sarah at my side. Jake saw her and reached out with a hand, wanting to go over to her.

"Hey, big boy," Sarah said quietly, rocking Jake and putting his head on her shoulder. In her arms, Jake looked twice as big, even though he was still tiny. He was roughly fifteen months old, give or take, and was walking around and getting himself into all kinds of trouble. I didn't mind any of it, I was just glad to have him with me.

"How's the school coming along?" I asked, curious as to its progress. Sarah and three other women were getting the school in shape for classes. We had several teachers and they were willing to pick up where they had left off after the Upheaval. We had enough children to actually have a couple of classes, although the children's ages varied widely, it wouldn't be anything different from turn of the century schools. Being a former administrator, I had been asked to head the school, but I declined. That was something I did before, not something I did now. Besides, it was my opinion that the best teachers did their best work when they were allowed to be creative and have few administrative restrictions.

"It's fine," Sarah said, settling Jake on her hip. He played with her hair, which looked lighter in the waning sun, then leaned his head into her neck and shoulder. "We've finished the classrooms and the teachers have the textbooks, getting themselves familiar with the lessons and what they want to teach. Nate says he wants to run P.E."

I thought about that for a second and let out a short laugh. "Sweet Jesus, those kids will learn a new language as well as physical education."

Sarah smiled. "Nate thinks it would be good for the kids to be trained to defend themselves, like we train everyone else."

I thought about it for a second, then nodded. "In ancient times, the Spartans did not bother with any walls or fortifications, relying instead on the strength of their people to be the wall. I can see his point. Let's do it."

Sarah looked at me funny. "I used to teach world history before I became an administrator," I said to her.

"Can I ask a question?" Sarah said after a while. Jake was falling asleep, his little hands curling his hair and his eyelids were struggling to remain open.

"Sure. Anything."

"When are you leaving?"

I smiled. "Is it that obvious?"

Sarah didn't return the smile. "I've known you for a while and when you get that faraway look in your eyes, you're thinking about heading out to some other place, looking for God knows what."

I couldn't deny it, I was thinking about another trip, and this time I was heading into the mouth of the monster. I decided to be candid. "I need to know what happened to my brother. The last time I spoke with him it was a year ago. I would like to try to find out what happened, if anything."

Sarah contemplated in silence, then her eyes got wide and she shook her head. "No!" she whispered, since Jake was asleep. "You can't go there! You know it's suicide!" A tear began to form in her eye. "You can't, please don't."

I took Jake from her and put him to bed, covering him with his blanket, watching him for a moment. I went back outside where Sarah was sitting on the porch, watching the river as tears fell down her face. I pulled her to her feet and held her close. She held me tight, burying her face in my chest.

"Please tell me you're not going." She said.

"I have to. For a few reasons, not the least of which is my brother. I need to see what's left and I need to see if there are any survivors. Duncan cleared the road on this side of the river and the only thing we have on the other side is our farms. We don't know anything else. Lastly, I will not send anyone else on this mission. I can't and you know it." I kissed her on the top of her head and she raised her face to mine. "You couldn't be with a man like that, could you?"

Sarah stood on her tiptoes and kissed me. "If you were anyone else, I probably would have killed you by now."

I smiled. "That's my girl."

In the morning, I called a meeting with the council, a group of people elected by the populace to voice their concerns and to keep people informed as to the goings on. I tried to have a meeting once every two weeks, but sometimes things needed to be discussed earlier.

Nate was there, as was Charlie and Tommy, and various others representing parts of the community. Trevor was there and so were Rebecca, Dot, and Sarah. I headed the council and gave the general direction of the agenda, but I had passed over my full leadership role for a more democratic one. Except in times of emergency, then I was the sole authority. That was something Nate put in there, since he realized that a council cold not effectively make timely decisions when needed. Besides, Nate told me, nobody else was stupid enough to take the job.

We met in the town's old community center, the newer one having been burnt down by yours truly. It was a nice old brick building that once had been a high school. We gathered in the conference room and I got things under way.

"I know we weren't supposed to meet for a couple of days, but I am going to be heading out and I wanted to make sure everyone knew the where's and why's."

Charlie looked at me with a knowing eye and Tommy just rolled his. Nate shifted his chair and I was sure he was curious.

"Things have been going pretty well here. We've established communication and trade with the towns on the rail line, except for Joslin, and we have taken a number of steps to ensure our long-term survival. What I am going to do is both for the community and for myself." I paused, keeping the attention of everyone in the room.

I took a deep breath and let loose the bomb. "I'm going to the city."

Everyone tried to speak at once and I managed to hear tidbits here and there. Words like 'suicide' and 'dumbass' assailed my ears, as well as 'crazy' and 'stupid'. I had thought this out and didn't really believe it was going to be too bad. Of course, that's what I thought about Coal City and nearly got chewed in that one.

When the commotion died down, I raised my hand for silence. Nate was glaring at me and Charlie was sitting with his arms crossed. Tommy was shaking his head and Trevor was eyeing me funny.

"Look, I know it sounds crazy, considering there are likely millions of zombies in the city. But I'm not asking anyone else to go, not asking anyone to risk themselves in what may be a wild goose chase. But lately I have been getting the feeling my brother is still alive and I need to try to do something about that. I am not abandoning the community, nor am I asking anyone to understand why I need to do this. But I need to be able to look myself in the eye and believe I tried my best to see what happened to him and his family." There were understanding nods. "Besides, it's been over a year since the Upheaval and things may not be as bad as we believe regarding the city. We just don't know."

Things calmed down a bit after that and we hammered out the details. Sarah insisted and got a concession regarding timelines. I was to be gone three days, no longer, regardless of what I found or didn't find. I was not going alone, as Charlie and Tommy were coming with me.

I wanted things done as well. I assigned Trevor and five of his crew to go out to State Center Alpha and see if there was anything left. They were to seek out and report, find out if there was anyone else out there, maybe find some more answers about the state of the country, if possible. They were going to be going cross country, but since it was in the middle of farm country, they should actually have little problems. Trevor had come a long way and his men worked as well together as Charlie, Tommy and I did. I could have sent more of them, but in all honesty, if the expedition went south, I wanted to minimize the losses.

Charlie, Tommy and I would head out first thing in the morning, and we would take the pontoon boat. I had looked over the map and saw that the canal was the way to go. We would head north until the canal forked, then we would head north farther until we could see what we could see. The eastern portion of the canal made more of a direct route to the lake, which might have been useful later, but not now. The northern route actually led near where my brother used to live in the city, so if he made it out, he made it one of two ways: he took the canal or he took the railway. I wasn't sure about the railway, since it went underground and in a zombie infested city, the last place I would go is underground. My brother and I tended to think alike in a lot of things, so I was hopeful he made the right choice. I was going to find out.

I spent the rest of the day getting ready, making sure I had enough ammo and supplies. I spent a brief time with Trevor, talking to him about what I found at State Center Bravo. Trevor was all ears, taking in each detail and committing it to memory. I drew him a route that should take him to the center without too much interference. I warned him about what we had found on one of the farms and what we had done to the renegade group. Trevor's eyes had widened, it was something that Tommy and I hadn't talked about. I also warned him about the glowing eyes of the zombies and he was sufficiently seasoned enough to appreciate what kind of effect that could have on his men.

When I had finished, Trevor and I shook hands and he gave me what amounted to high praise. "You sure are one high-octane son-of-a-bitch."

I waved off the comment. "I just do what needs to be done, nothing more. You'd have done the same."

"Not sure about that, boss. Walking at night with sixteen women through dark country—whew! No thanks."

"Get moving," I said with a smile.

While I was getting things together, Sarah, Jake, and I had a visitor. Dot came by to talk. We caught up for a while, then Sarah went off to feed Jake his lunch, leaving Dot and I on the porch.

"Been busy, hey?" Dot asked.

"Yeah, it's been a trip. Several, as a matter of fact," I said, shaking my head at the rush of memories.

"You're doing fine," Dot said. "As a matter of fact, I'd say you're doing ten times better than anyone could have hoped for."

"Thanks."

"Tell me one thing, though, John."

"Sure, anything."

"Why haven't you told Sarah the other reason why you are taking this trip?" Dot asked, seeing through me better than anyone had ever done before. It was downright creepy.

"It wouldn't be fair to her and might cause feelings to get hurt. Besides, I need this closure. I thought I had it at my house, but over the last few months, it's been like a cobweb in my head, tickling me from time to time, never letting me forget it's there." I looked down. "I hope you won't tell Sarah," I said.

Dot smiled at me. "I won't on one condition."

"What's that?" I asked, giving her the same look I give a zombie right before I plant a chunk of metal in its frontal lobe.

"That you marry that girl before you get much older," Dot said, standing up and patting me on the arm. "No telling how much time you have, especially these days."

My mind was paralyzed for a moment, then I managed to speak. "Deal," I said, before I fully understood what I was saying.

"Good. Tell Sarah I'll be by to help her with Jake while you're gone." Dot walked off, whistling an old Irish tune, her rifle slung over her shoulder like she was heading off to war.

I had the feeling I had just been bamboozled, but in all honesty, couldn't find a downside. I finished packing up and joined Sarah and Jake, trying to squeeze in as much quality time as possible before I headed out. I was sure Charlie and Tommy were doing the same.

22

In the morning, we packed up the pontoon boat and shoved off. The enclosed space had been taken off and the deck was surrounded by a small wall of wood secured to the railing. The wood only went waist high, but it was sufficient cover if we needed it. It wouldn't stop bullets, but it would allow you a small measure of security in case things got ugly. We each had our packs, rations, and weapons. I was back to the M1A and Charlie and Tommy were carrying their AR's. Charlie had done some modification to his AR, swapping out the carbine upper for one with a flat top and lengthened bull barrel. He topped it with an ACOG site he had recovered from State Center Bravo, so he was clearly ready. I preferred iron sites myself. Tommy did as well. We had enough ammo for defensive killing and escape, not eradication. I carried a lighter and small squeeze bottle of kerosene for that.

We drifted north, the purr of the motor moving us at a decent clip. It hadn't rained in about ten days, so the canal wasn't moving as fast as it could have. We were all quiet, each of us tucked away in his own thoughts, wondering what this trip might bring, wondering if we had sufficiently said our goodbyes in case this trip was our last. I had left before Jake had awakened for the day and as usual, I had made my promise to return to him. Despite all the progress we had made, he was still my whole world. Sarah had gotten up with me to send me on my way–and the way she was smiling made me wonder if she and Dot hadn't cooked up something between them.

At first we didn't pass anything of interest and for the most part, couldn't see that much beyond the foliage on the banks of the canal. After about a half hour, we reached the split in the canal that would take us east and to the lake. There was a refinery on our right, the silent storage bins seeming to watch us pass on the canal. I didn't see any activity on the ground, but that wasn't much of a surprise. Big refineries and places like this weren't attractive to zombies as a source of food. There just weren't enough people outside of a skeleton crew to watch the gauges and make sure everything was running smoothly. Besides, when everything went south, anyone who worked here would have tried to go to their families.

The sun climbed higher, throwing a wave of brilliance that promised to be a beautiful day. Because of the depth of the canal, we were still in shadows, which helped us move relatively unseen. We couldn't do anything about the noise of the motor, but a pontoon boat was meant for quiet cruising anyway, so the motor wasn't that bad.

We moved on and in a little ways we found another industrial area. This one looked like a power transfer area, but I couldn't be sure. There were actually zombies here, and they shambled over in our direction, but we were going to be past them long before they reached the canal banks.

The only real indication of zombie activity was the roads that crossed the canal and through our binoculars and rifle scopes we could see several of the cars that were occupied by the undead and several other zombies wandering among the vehicle debris. They raised a forlorn moan at our passing and one actually fell into the canal and disappeared beneath the dark waters. We kept a close eye on that situation, since we were pretty certain the zombies stayed away from water for a reason, although we weren't entirely certain it killed them. If it did, it probably took a long time, so caution was necessary.

We went past a huge complex big enough to be seen from where we were and it took me a minute before I realized what it was. It was a distribution center for a parcel carrier, one of the largest in the area. I thought about all the undelivered items stored there and made a mental note to check it out in the future. I had no idea the canal went right past it.

"Big place," Tommy said from his perch at the steering wheel of the boat.

"It's huge and full of goodies," I said, shifting my pack.

"Really? How do you know?"

"It's the distribution center for United Shipping."

Tommy looked around. "So that's where we are. I thought this area looked familiar, but I've only seen it from the expressways. Weird how things change when you're moving slow and from a new direction."

Wasn't that the truth. Charlie nodded in agreement and returned to watching the canal. He was making sure the way was clear of obstacles, like branches and other debris. We hadn't seen much so far, but in the catches along the canal banks we could see things like suitcases and other floating castaways, reminders of people who chose the canal as their escape route. I idly wondered how many people drowned just trying to get away any way they could.

"Contact," Charlie said from the front and I shifted my weapon to the ready. Tommy steered the boat towards the middle of the canal and I could see what Charlie was talking about. On the right side of the canal was a subdivision and from what we could see this one had been hit hard. Burnt out homes and smashed windows, doors torn off their hinges, black marks everywhere. We could see rotting corpses down every street and it took little imagination to figure there were more in the homes. Several cars had smashed into homes and blood splatter was all over the interiors. The streets had dozens of zombies lurching around and for the most part, they were ignorant of our passing.

I looked at Tommy and shook my head. There was nothing here. It wouldn't even be worth it to try and scavenge something from the homes. Until the zombies eventually rotted away on their own, they were the lords of this area.

Some of the zombies turned our way on account of the noise of our motor, but they didn't do much, just shuffled in our direction. By the time they reached the road that ran along the canal, we were past them. There was also a fence that ran along the road, so we were in no danger. As I looked back at the subdivision, I saw the telltale white flags adorning nearly every mailbox.

We passed a rail yard and a little farther up there was what looked like a truck shipping yard. Trailers were arranged neatly along the canal and there was a small pavilion for the workers near the water. Overhead was the expressway and even from our vantage point, we could see it choked with cars. I couldn't see the status of the vehicles, but I assumed there was the usual carnage and abandoned vehicles. I gave it little thought. The road wasn't going anywhere I wanted to be and since the canal was just as useful and relatively safe from attack, why bother?

We moved on and came to the beginning of the true Chicago suburbs. There were smallish homes everywhere and from what I could see, they were all destroyed. They were the little bungalow style homes with detached garages. Flags flew on the mailboxes, grim reminders of the hope that people once had for help during the Upheaval. As we moved past, Charlie and I could hear the echo of thousands of undead moans, as the ghouls wandered in search of prey. Whatever might have survived this long wasn't going to survive much longer.

Suddenly, we heard something out of the ordinary. The moans of the dead seemed to grow louder and the ones we could see were clearly agitated by something. I couldn't see anything and Charlie shook his head that he couldn't see anything, either. Judging by the sounds the dead were making, something was in there they wanted and wanted badly. Anything the dead wanted was usually alive.

I signaled Tommy to steer over to the bank under the overpass. Charlie looked at me and I shook my head.

"Don't worry, we're not going in there. I'm climbing the bank of the overpass to see what's going on." I jumped off the boat and onto the bank of the canal.

"Good. I'd hate to risk my ass for something like a cat or a dog," Charlie said as he joined me.

"Who are you kidding?" I asked as I headed up the steep bank of the overpass. "You chased a cat three miles just because Rebecca thought it would be nice to have a kitty for Julia."

"Yeah, but that was in the country, not in the middle of an infested suburb," Charlie retorted.

"If I recall correctly, it was in the middle of downtown Freeport, through an area that hadn't been secured yet and six zombies were chasing you as you chased the cat."

"Still doesn't change how I feel about this little hike," Charlie said as he slipped on a bit of wet grass.

"No one asked you to come along," I said, stopping near the top and checking for roaming Z's.

"After all we've been through, you knew I'd be along, just like you'd come with me if I was going somewhere, no matter how stupid," Charlie replied as he joined me near the top, his rifle balanced in one hand as he kept himself from falling with the other.

"True." I didn't see any immediate danger, so I hoisted myself up and over the guardrail. There were several cars on the bridge, but none occupied. By the looks of things, it seemed like someone had arranged the cars as a sort of defensive barricade. Nothing that would stop a determined zombie, but it would slow them down. The position of the cars made me wonder what was on the other side and if there were survivors somewhere.

Charlie tapped my shoulder and brought my attention back to the situation at hand. I looked out over the vast subdivision with its rows upon rows of houses, stacked neatly up against each other. If I had to guess, I would have said there were thousands of them, making the approximate number of zombies in the tens of thousands. But what really held my attention was the lone figure running down the street, pursued by roughly five hundred walking dead, with that number growing by the minute. Their groans were awful to hear, a wail of anguish and never-ending hunger.

Charlie sighted in the figure with his scope. "Woman. Early twenties. Looks like she's been surviving for a while. Got a pack, gun, knife, and what looks like a pipe."

"Any cuts or blood on her?" I asked, bringing my rifle up and attaching my scope. I didn't use it often, but it did have its purposes, since I never got around to carrying a pair of binoculars.

"Not yet, but if she keeps on going the way she is, she's going to be bloody," Charlie said.

When I looked through my scope, I could see why. She was running towards us, but a group of zombies was coming at a cross road and would make the intersection before she would. On top of that, there were other zombies coming out of homes and holes, attracted to the noise of their brethren. In short order she was going to find herself surrounded and eaten. It wasn't going to be pretty. The down side was we really couldn't help her. Sure we could shoot down a bunch, but that would actually just waste ammo and only prolong the inevitable.

Charlie looked at me as if to ask the question we were both not wanting to answer. I shrugged and couldn't see a solution. There was no way she was going to get out of this one unless she learned to fly in a hurry.

Suddenly, it hit me. Fly! Of course! "Cover me!" I yelled as I sprinted down the road. I needed to get to where I could be seen and heard by the besieged woman. Charlie moved over to the side of the road where he could brace his rifle to shoot more accurately. I ran down the road, making sure there weren't any lurkers to make my life miserable and stopped within what I hoped was earshot of the running woman. The zombies who were going to cut her off had just emerged from the side street and I could see the woman pause. She drew her sidearm, looked at it, and then holstered it. I figured she was dangerously low on ammo and was contemplating finishing herself off as a last resort.

I jumped up onto a car so I could be seen. "Hey! Hey!" I yelled, waving my arms. The woman looked at me with a stunned expression, like the last thing she expected to see was a lunatic jumping on a car in the middle of zombie infested territory. Can't say I blamed her. "Get up on the roofs and head this way! We have a boat!"

Hope surged in the woman's young face as she sprinted for the nearest house and clambered up the iron railing on the side of the porch. There was a desperate moment when it looked like the gutter wasn't going to hold her weight, but she swung her legs up just as the first zombies reached up to try to drag her down. She rolled up onto the roof and scrambled to the peak.

Sitting down and taking a breath, she looked over at me and yelled "Watch your back!"

I spun around on my car roof and fired a rifle round through the head of a small zombie that had managed to sneak around behind me. The heavy bullet blew his head apart like a ripe melon and he dropped into a pile of decaying flop. The shot galvanized the zombies on the ground who saw their original prey climb out of reach. The horde that was chasing the woman turned their attention to me and started to head my way.

"Cross the houses on the roofs, head for the canal. We'll wait for you there!" I yelled as I dropped off the car and sprinted back the way I came. I had no intention of sticking around any longer. I gave the woman a chance and if she chose to take it, great. If not, I tried.

Stealing a look back I saw the woman running down the shingles and leaping across the small space between the homes. It was only a six foot jump, but if she slipped she was dead. Talk about your hurdles of death.

I quickly outstripped the horde and headed back towards Charlie. He waved me past him and I took a breather as we watched the progress of the woman. The line of houses she was on took her on a curving path towards the canal and if she could get ahead of the horde, she stood a good chance of living. I glanced over the bridge and waved to Tommy, who brought the boat around.

"We have a survivor and she should be showing up downriver about two hundred yards. I'll be down in a sec and we can go get her."

"What about Charlie?" Tommy hollered about the growing din of the undead.

Charlie poked his head over the side. "Right here, dickhead. Go get the girl with John and swing back towards the other side of the bridge, I'll see you there."

Tommy waved. "Go swim, loser," he joked. I just shook rolled my eyes at the two of them, as I climbed over the guardrail and slid down to the banks of the canal. The zombie horde that had chased me was advancing on the road, and Charlie was going to keep them distracted while we picked up the woman. As I jumped aboard the boat, I heard Charlie's rifle crack as he sent a hot .223 round into the head of a nearby Z.

Tommy moved the boat farther ahead, then cut the power down to keep us relatively motionless in the water as the current gently tried to push us back. I could see the woman still on the roofs, jumping from one to the other and gaining ground on her pursuers. She had about four homes to go before she would have to abandon the houses and make a sprint for the canal. I heard Charlie's rifle crack again and I saw several ghouls break off their pursuit to head in his direction. Push came to shove, Charlie could jump off the bridge. It was only about a thirty foot drop into twenty-foot deep water, so he would be okay if we could keep him from sinking with all his gear.

Tommy watched the woman closely, trying to time his approach to the bank as she got closer. When she reached the last house, she slipped down to the gutter and hung for a second. Dropping to the ground, she raced past a tangle of children's toys and jumped the fence that circled the yard. Zombies came pouring through the houses in their attempt to get to her and I took the liberty of shooting two of them that were faster than the others. The woman scrambled to the edge of the canal and leaped on board the boat as soon as it was in range. I directed her to a chair in the front while Tommy spun the wheel and headed to the bridge to pick up Charlie who was standing on the far bank of the canal, his rifle trained on the bridge.

When Charlie was safely aboard, Tommy swung the boat back north and moved away from the hordes of zombies that stared at us helplessly from the shores and bridge. I moved up to where the woman was seated and handed her a bottle of water.

"Welcome aboard. My name is John Talon and these are my friends, Charlie James and Tommy Carter. Who might you be?"

The woman took a long drink of water and then eyed me warily. "I'm Angela Brooks. Thanks for your help. I figured I was done for sure that time." Angela had dark hair, bright blue eyes, and a homespun face that was handsome rather than pretty. She had smudges of dirt on her face and looked like she hadn't seen a good meal in days, but she seemed healthy enough. She was wearing a dark blue hoodie and faded jeans. Her backpack looked like it was from a junior high. Her weapon was a Glock 9mm, the handle protruding from a holster on her belt.

I nodded. "Glad to help. God knows there's few enough of us left these days. Before we get to know each other better, I need you to hand over your weapon." I held out my left hand, keeping my right hand near my SIG. Charlie shifted his grip on his rifle so it was across his lap, but the muzzle was pointed in Angela's direction

"Why do you want my gun?" Angela said, her eyes narrowing.

"Honestly? I don't know you and until I do, I'm not having you armed on this boat. I've gone through too much to have everything I've fought for lost because I turned my back on someone with a personal agenda. I've been shot at by females before and I would rather not repeat the performance. Now please hand over your weapon."

"And if I refuse?" Angela said, shifting in her chair.

Charlie stood up and held his rifle casually, the muzzle now directly pointed at the woman. The look on his face clearly said he would kill without hesitation if the wrong move was made.

"We put you on the bank of the canal immediately and say our goodbyes and good lucks. If you take a shot at us, we'll kill you. We'd rather not." My smile didn't reach my eyes. I had no patience for this sort of thing.

Angela considered the proposition and with a resigned sigh handed over the weapon. I looked at it, ejected the magazine and shook my head at the two rounds left. I asked if Angela had any more magazines or bullets and she shook her head. I passed the gun to Charlie, who field stripped it at the little table on the boat and started cleaning it.

I sat down across from Angela. "Now, what brings you to that little piece of hell?"

Angela seemed to deflate and leaning back in her chair, told me how she was working downtown as a nutritionist for a health club when the world ended. She and a friend named Dana had managed to escape the city when the Upheaval had started and had stayed in the woods that were across the canal for the last three months. Before that, they had been on the run, hiding where they could, looting what they could find for food and supplies during the winter. She and her friend had hooked up with some other survivors, but their shelter had been overrun, and she and Dana barely escaped with their lives. The rest of the group had been torn apart. I nodded. It was not an unfamiliar scenario.

Angela and her friend had headed south and taken shelter in the woods. The zombies didn't seem to want to cross the river or the canal, so it seemed like they would have been safe for a while. Then during the winter, her friend got sick and died from pneumonia. Angela buried her friend and resolved to go on when the weather was good enough for travel. She was doing a supply run in the subdivision when the zombies woke up and came after her. That's when we showed up.

When she finished, I started explaining who we were and where we came from. I told her about Leport and the community we had built there. Her eyes widened when she found out we had nearly four hundred people living there. I told her about the other communities we had contact with and how we were managing to take back what we had lost. Her eyes drifted for a minute and I knew she was reliving some memory from her past. We all did that from time to time.

When I finished, I had a question for her. "If you're interested, you're welcome to join the community. We can give you a place to stay, friends to make, and a chance at life. We could use a nutritionist to help with the kids and our limited food supply. Interested?"

Angela's eyes misted, then she buried her head in her hands and sobbed. I got up and left her to sort things out for herself. I had seen this before from survivors who suddenly found themselves safe, able to relax and not worry that the bump in the night was going to try and eat them.

I sat down by Charlie as he finished putting the Glock back together. "Will she join us?" he asked, casting a glance her way.

"Probably," I said. "She's seen a lot and we've only scratched the surface of her story, but it will take a while to come out. I'm just stunned anyone is alive out here."

Charlie nodded and handed the Glock back to me as well as a fully loaded magazine. I took both and headed back to the front. Angela seemed to have composed herself and looked up at me with red eyes.

"Sorry," she said. "I haven't been that emotional for a while. I guess the shock of suddenly being offered a chance to live after nearly dying for so long catches up to you."

I waved it off. "Happened to a lot more people than you think." I handed her weapon back and the full magazine. "Charlie cleaned it and loaded the magazine for you. You're good to go."

"You're trusting me with my gun? What if I shoot you and try to take this boat?" Angela asked, inserting the magazine and chambering a round before returning it to its holster.

"It's been tried before. I take a lot of killing and you'd be dead before you got the gun out of the holster."

"You're pretty sure of yourself."

I shrugged. "Goes with the territory. My girlfriend thinks it makes me cute."

Angela rolled her eyes and turned towards the canal. We were making good time and passed quite a few communities and industrial parks. We saw zombies nearly everywhere and in each community I saw the telltale white flags fluttering uselessly in the morning breeze. When we passed the train depot, with it's thousands of train cars, I started to pay close attention. My side trip was getting close and I wanted to make sure I didn't miss it. I hadn't told Tommy and Charlie about it yet and was likely going to get some fierce opposition, but I didn't care. I needed to do this.

23

Around a small bend in the canal, I saw what I was looking for. It was a ten story, modern-looking building with a curved design that arched towards the canal. Two round lower buildings connected to it. The whole thing was white facing with black steel and deep blue tinted windows. It was a striking building completed within the last ten years.

Fitzgerald Hospital had been a world leader in cardio care and doctors from all over the world came to hone their skills and learn the latest techniques for treating heart disease. Now it was a haven for the dead, one of the centers of the Upheaval. It was where I needed to go.

I told Tommy to pull over to the building. He headed that way and asked me why.

"I'm taking a side trip." I said.

"What is this place?" he persisted.

"A hospital."

Tommy was speechless for a moment, then he recovered his voice. "Are you fucking insane? Hospitals are loaded with the dead! That's where a lot of the shit started and spread. You want to go to one?" He was incredulous, which put him on par with Angela and Charlie, neither of whom could speak.

"I know it doesn't make sense, but lately I have been feeling that unless I find out exactly what happened to Ellie, I can never go forward with Sarah. It will be a wedge of guilt that won't ever go away," I said.

Tommy shook his head. "You're not thinking this one through, hoss. You go in there, you will probably not come out, and if you do find Ellie, she may be a zombie. You gonna be able to pull the trigger on her? I've seen too many people hesitate when a loved one comes close and they end up dead because of it."

"I can't ask you to understand, Tommy. I don't understand it myself. It's like something is pulling me here, wanting me here. I can't call this one off. If you don't want to head over, fine. I'll swim if I have to, but I'm going."

Tommy looked at me for a long moment, then shook his head. "If we hadn't just pulled off a night raid and gotten out with our skins intact, I'd say swim for it. But you know I won't just leave you, brother. So I'm in. Here we go." Charlie shook his head at me, then topped off his rifle magazine. Angela just looked at me like I was growing a second set of ears.

We pulled up to the hospital landing. Few people actually knew it was there. The canal had been accessed during the construction of the new wing as an experimental route to the facility's sister hospital, which specialized in children's care and cancer treatment. Ellie told me that a boat from Fitzgerald Hospital could reach Mercy General a full thirty minutes ahead of an ambulance leaving at the same time. Ellie had estimated they had saved probably about 200 lives a year using the hospital ferry.

Tommy cut the motor and we drifted to the little dock. I jumped off and secured the boat, scanning the area as I did so. The ferry boat was long gone, likely taken by someone fleeing the hospital. Bits of debris littered the dock and long black smears painted a grim mural on the ramp leading to the hospital doors, gaping open like a forbidden portal.

I stepped back aboard the boat and traded rifles with Tommy. I didn't need a heavy battle rifle for indoor fighting and his AR carbine would work well. In addition, Charlie and I could share ammo as needed.

"You sure you want me to stay with the boat?" Tommy asked, looking tentatively at the dark opening. "More firepower might be a good idea."

"Yes, I need you to stay with the boat," I said. "We may need to move fast out of here and having the boat already running would be seconds we don't have to spare.

"Besides, someone needs to bring the news to Sarah and Rebecca if Charlie and I get killed," I said casually, adjusting the spare magazines on my vest.

I stepped off the boat with Charlie beside me. I glanced back to see Angela sitting there with her mouth open.

"Three hours, no more. If we don't find anything, we'll be out sooner. Any more and something found us." I moved up the ramp, Charlie behind me. I smiled when I heard Angela say, "Is he always like that?" to which I heard Tommy say, "Let me tell you about those two..."

The rest was lost as I moved to the doorway. I could see an overturned gurney just inside the door with a disemboweled corpse still attached to it. It used to be an old woman, but her skull had been cracked open and large chunk of missing brain explaining why she hadn't returned. Sunlight filtered through the windows at the end of the hallway, but it was still very dark in places. The small reception desk by the entrance was abandoned, the computer overturned and the chair knocked sideways, as if whoever had worked there had been dragged over the counter. Dark streaks on the surface indicated this was likely the case. The hallway was a mess with bodies lying about, body parts strewn in corners and brownish streaks and handprints all over the walls. The ceiling even had sprays of dark on them, clear evidence of arteries being ripped open to bloody the area.

I pulled a marble from my pocket after checking with Charlie to make sure he was ready. We were in a good position. No hallways led to either left or right and no doors were any closer than twenty feet. Our backs were to the bright opening of the canal, so we had a decent amount of light to see. I threw the marble down the hall, listening to it bounce loudly on the tile floor, clacking along the hallway before smacking loudly against the window on the far end. I waited for a full twenty seconds, then watched as several dark shapes slid from doorways and hallways in response to the noise. A low, hungry moan began from the nearest one, echoed in chorus by the crowd behind. I could see movement near the floor as additional Z's dragged themselves forward.

"Mine," Charlie said, moving his rifle around to his back and pulling out his tomahawk. I hung back, but kept my carbine trained on the advancing ghouls.

Charlie stepped around a stain on the floor and advanced on the zombie. It was wearing hospital scrubs and raised a rotting arm towards Charlie. Its face was skeletal with large holes showing dark bone underneath. Black stains streaked its clothing and its left arm dangled uselessly. A large chunk was bitten out of its neck, I imagined this might be one of the first zombies in this area.

With a meaty smack, Charlie crushed the zombie's skull. His tomahawk easily broke through the head and exited out the other side. Charlie nearly over swung and had to check himself as the corpse fell to the side.

"Damn," he said, looking down at the body. "These older ones are barely holding themselves together."

"Good," I said, pulling out my pickaxe and adjusting my rifle so it hung down my back. "This should be better than I had hoped. If they're that delicate, then we can save some ammo." I moved ahead of Charlie and popped a crawler in the noggin, stepping around its grabbing, skeletal hands. I was amazed at how easy it was to penetrate the skull. It seemed the oldest zombies were decaying to the point where they were increasingly fragile. Anywhere they hit their head could literally kill them. For some reason, this seemed to make them a little less scary.

My reflections were interrupted by the advance of the rest of the zombies. Charlie and I were busy for the next few minutes, letting them come to us and putting them down. I had an awkward moment when a crawler and walker came at the same time. I wound up hitting the walker and stomping the crawler on the head.

"Hey, a twofer," Charlie said as he slammed a zombie against the wall, crushing its skull and leaving a brain smear as it slid down.

"It's a gift," I said as I nailed a zombie with a baseball swing, picking off another that crowded close with the backswing. Black splatter covered the hallway and Charlie and I were hemmed in by a small hedge of now-motionless dead.

"Déjà vu," I said, remembering Coal City as I swung at what used to be a hospital security guard. His large gut was a gaping maw of shredded flesh and hunks had been bitten out of his arms and legs.

"It seems like all we do is hunt zombies and kill zombies," Charlie said, knocking down an elderly man. "We never do anything fun anymore."

"What are you talking about? I'm taking you on a cruise, aren't I?" I said, knocking a nearby corpse over a crawler.

"It's not the same. We're still killing zombies," Charlie said petulantly.

"What do you want, then?"

"You wouldn't care if I told you."

"Try me."

Charlie sighed. "I just want to do something that lets me know I'm special to you, that's all." He batted his eyes at me, something I never thought he could do.

I couldn't help myself and burst out laughing. Charlie joined me after a second and we both finished the last zombie.

"Don't tell me Rebecca is already giving you that nonsense." I said, wiping off my stained pick.

"Must be a female thing. The world ends and I still have to entertain her. Simply surviving is just not enough, I guess. Next thing you know, she and Sarah will start a book club or something and we'll have to go find books for the town." Charlie wiped off his 'hawk.

"God help us."

I moved forward, keeping an eye on the hallway as I climbed over the corpse pile. I didn't expect to see anything more in the immediate vicinity, since our little fight would have attracted every zombie within earshot. Coming up to a janitor's closet, I stopped and tried the door. It was locked, so I spent a minute breaking it open. Charlie looked at me, then kept his eyes on the hallway. We could hear shuffling sounds coming from the cross hall, but nothing was coming into sight yet.

Opening the door, I looked around quickly at the cleaning supplies, wrinkling my nose at the bleach and ammonia smells, as well as the anti-bacterial cleaner that made hospitals the world over smell like a jar of handy-wipes. I grabbed a small bottle of ammonia and headed out, Charlie in tow.

We reached the hallway junction and I looked around the corner, jerking back as a bloodstained hand shot forward, trying to grab my face. I took a step back as a zombie came around the corner. It was a woman in nurse's clothing, the stethoscope still dangling out of her jacket pocket. Her lips were peeled back, revealing cracked, yellowed teeth. Her slightly glowing eyes were open wide and her nostrils would have been flaring, if she still had a nose. A huge hole was in the center of her face, and it dripped black mucus down her face. I had a bad moment when she first appeared, since she was roughly the same size as Ellie, but I relaxed a bit when I saw she was too old. I avoided her grasping hands and rapped her in the forehead with my pick. She stumbled back, giving me enough room for a more forceful hit. When she bounded off the wall and came at me again, I was ready and planted her for good.

Charlie was finishing off another zombie who would have caught me from behind had I been alone. "Thanks, man," I said.

"No trouble," Charlie said. "Any idea where we are going? If you plan to check every room, three hours ain't gonna be enough."

Actually, I had thought about that. Ellie had told me the designer of the building had a wife who was a nurse. She influenced him enough to make sure there was a decent lounge for the nurses, as well as the doctors. The designer went one further, giving the nurses of the hospital not only a lounge, but a balcony as well. Most of the other staff, especially the doctors, never knew it existed, since they had their own little world. Ellie had said the balcony was her favorite place since she could sit out there and feel the world go by. The balcony faced south and she told me she liked to "pretend she could see our house and watch over her little boy" even though she was at work. If she was anywhere, she would be on that balcony. I braced myself for the possibility that if she was there, she wasn't going to look good after a summer and winter exposed to the elements.

"We need to head to the third floor, then look for the nurse's lounge." I squirted ammonia down one hallway, then the other. The scent was nearly overpowering and Charlie and I ducked into the stairs. I hoped the ammonia would mask our scent and prevent us from having to fight our way back to the boat. We only had about two hours left before we had to go swimming.

24

In the stairs, it was fairly dark, with only a little light filtering down from a skylight on the roof. I could smell death on the stairs, but it wasn't the decaying smell of the zombies. There also wasn't any blood smell lingering in the stairs, so I wondered what the story was. I pointed my flashlight down towards the basement and didn't see anything out of the ordinary. I looked at the doors and realized the zombies would never be able to breach this sanctuary given the steel doors and small windows. As long as they couldn't operate a doorknob, we were pretty safe.

We moved cautiously up the stairs and saw on the second floor landing what the cause of the smell was. A hospital worker had apparently been trapped on the stairs by the zombies, dehydrated, and then died there on the landing. Charlie quickly went through his pockets, but came up empty. "No keys, huh?" I asked.

"No, but it would have been helpful," he said, straightening.

I nodded and we reached the third floor landing. I snuck a quick peek out into the hallway through the window, but it was hard to see anything. The stairs looked out into a hallway, but the only thing I could see was a wall. I really didn't want to burst out into a floor full of zombies, but I had little choice. Charlie and I held a brief powwow and we agreed that it would be better to blast through the door and kill anything on either side.

I was going to take the left, Charlie was going to follow me for a step, then take the right as the door closed. I braced myself with my rifle, making sure magazines were within easy reach and unobstructed. I also made sure my weapon light was ready. No point wasting shots in the dark if I could help it.

Charlie pushed the door open and I slid out, moving forward enough so Charlie could let the door close behind us. Immediately to my front was a small gaggle of zombies, loitering around the nurse's station. They turned to look at me, then as it registered what I was, they let out a collective moan that sounded like a roar in the small hallway, and started shuffling forward.

"Fuck you very much, thanks for asking," I said as I fired into the group. A doctor-looking zombie took the round in his eye and fell to the ground, tripping two more behind him. Another zombie fell from another shot, and a third as it got up from falling. The immediate threat over, I waited for a better shot as Charlie opened up on his side, firing two shots close together, then two more. I would have chastised him for wasting ammo if I didn't know he had just nailed four zombies. No more firing from his side as two more advanced on me. I put their diseased carcasses down for good, then motioned Charlie to follow me.

We moved quickly down the hall, passing a bank of elevators. I roughly knew where I was going, keeping to the points of the compass. I had to hit the end of the hallway, then turn south. That back hall should have the nurse's lounge. It was the only wall that faced south and if my directions weren't totally screwy, we should be able to find it.

Coming to a main hall crossway, I looked around the corner and nearly lost my cookies. I had seen a lot of carnage since the Upheaval, but this was unbelievable. It was if someone had thought to insulate the hallway in blood and entrails. The guts didn't look like they had been merely torn out, they looked like they had been tossed aside after being torn out. Body parts lay everywhere and all of the parts had teeth marks or bites taken out of them. The slaughter was immense. I couldn't imagine what this must have been like, the screams and moans must have driven anyone witnessing this to insanity.

Charlie bumped me with his elbow. "Down the hall movement." He turned on his light and aimed down the way. "Aw, hell."

I flicked on my light and looked for myself. "Dammit," was all I had to add to the conversation.

At the end of the hall was a sign that read "Welcome Friends!" It was brightly painted to alleviate the fears of the admitted patients. As I looked at the advancing horde, nothing could have prepared parents for what had actually happened. It was a children's ward and the little victims were headed this way, looking for revenge.

"No time," I said to Charlie as he let out a breath to begin firing. He stopped himself just in time. "We'll deal with them on the way out." I squirted some ammonia to keep the scent off and we passed the hallway of horrors.

Rounding the corridor corner, I popped a zombie lurching towards the junction, his glowing eyes like beacons in the dark. My bullet entered his right eye, blowing his slightly glowing brain all over the wall behind him. A chorus of little moans answered the shot and the sound gave me the chills.

"Found it!" Charlie said, opening he door. He jumped back as a zombie fell out, it must have been leaning against the door. Charlie quickly stomped the Z in the head, killing it. He looked over at me with a slight grimace on his face, but a quick check with my flashlight showed the Z wasn't Ellie. I shook my head and Charlie's shoulders sagged a bit in relief.

As I moved towards the door, another sign got my attention. 'Medical Supply' was on the door and I opened it to find a virtual cornucopia of drugs and supplies. Charlie looked over my shoulder and said, "I'll get what I can, the doc can sort it out later." He grabbed a sheet from a nearby room and began placing boxes of supplies in the center.

I moved into the nurse's lounge and quickly scanned it for additional surprises. There weren't any and I made my way through the couches and chairs to the balcony doors. I opened the door and let in a great deal of sunlight into the lounge.

On the balcony, there were several tables and chairs, all of them empty. My heart fell as it looked like Ellie wasn't out here. I was going to have to leave without closure after all. I turned back to the door and looked over to the corner of the balcony. A chair had been overturned and it looked like something was in the corner, hidden by the chair.

I walked over, and as I got closer, I saw a body was in the corner. Hoping against hope, I approached the body, the light of the sun blocked by the floors above.

I reached out a hand to move the chair, and I was surprised at how nervous I was. I pulled the chair away and looked down at a small body. It was curled up on its side, seeming to be sleeping. One look at the skeletal arms and head and I knew this person had been dead for a long time. The elements hadn't been kind, wasting the body away to a thin, dried out skeleton. I stood up and was about to walk away when something sparkled at me. I knelt down and pulled the left hand closer. When I got a look at the ring on the finger, I dropped to my knees and took off my goggles and mask.

"Oh, Ellie." The ring on her finger was the little wedding band I had bought when I had no money and worked part time to get extra cash for her ring. It was a small diamond, but Ellie had told me at the time that it looked big to her and that was all that mattered.

I gathered her into my arms as I knelt there and just held her for a moment. It didn't matter that she was dead, that she was just skin and bones. It mattered that I had lost her, that my world had been turned upside down. But I lived and our son lived and part of her would always be alive in him. "I kept my promise, Ellie. I kept your baby safe. You probably know that, but I just wanted to tell you. He'll grow to a fine man. I promise." New tears fell on her face as I cried. "I'm so sorry I couldn't save you. I'm so, so sorry. Please forgive me." Sobs racked my body as I held her close, shaking the two of us.

25

After a long moment and a deep breath, I gently laid her down and put my mask and goggles back on. I took her wedding ring and engagement ring off and put them in my breast pocket. They were for Jake when he wanted to get married. His mother would have approved. I picked Ellie back up and brought her into the lounge where I wrapped her in a blanket and laid her down on the couch. I had no intention of bringing her out, but I did intend to bury her as I left. As I stood up, I thought I felt a gentle touch on my cheek and my heart inexplicably felt lighter. I immediately knew I had done the right thing and I also knew I was forgiven.

"Get busy living," I said to no one in particular. Patting my pocket, I headed for the door just as Charlie burst in.

"We gotta go and we gotta go now!" He panted, stealing a glance at the door. He was carrying a huge sack over his shoulder like a kick-ass, zombie-killing Santa Claus. He looked down at the couch. "Did you..."

I nodded. "I found her. I'm good."

"Are you bringing her with us.?" Charlie asked.

I shook my head. "No, but I'm going to make this place her funeral pyre. It killed her, now I'm going to kill it," I said, the rage building inside.

Charlie put a hand on my shoulder. "You'll die in that mood. Get your head on 'cause we got trouble."

"What are you talking about?" I calmed down slightly.

"Those zombie kids are on the loose and they are fast. I saw one of them move quick enough to be considered running," Charlie said.

That was bad news. Fast zombie children in the dark was a literal nightmare come to life or unlife, as the case was.

"Fuck it, let's move," I said, swinging up my carbine, with Charlie doing the same.

I moved into the hallway and headed back towards the stairway. Glancing over my shoulder, I saw several pairs of glowing eyes moving quickly behind us. They weren't running, but they were darn faster than any zombie I had seen before. I paused for a second at the corner and snapped a shot at the gang, blowing a small head apart and causing others to fall as they got tangled up in the falling body.

"Move, move, move!" I yelled to Charlie and we both sprinted down the hall towards the stairs. On the other side of the hall, other small shapes were advancing rapidly. High-pitched moans reached my ears as we made the stairs. Charlie threw the door open and dashed inside, the big bag of supplies knocking me back a step. I pulled the door shut as the first little zombie slammed into the door, managing to get an arm wedged in the opening. The grayish arm grasped wildly, trying to get purchase on something. I pulled hard on the door as half a dozen little hands grasped the edge and started to pull. I braced myself and put a leg up on the door jam, pulling desperately. I could hold it closed, but the arm prevented me from closing it completely.

Not sure what to do to resolve the situation, I was relived when a large arm holding a handgun appeared in front of me and aimed through the door opening.

"Pardon," Charlie said as he fired several rounds, the shots echoing up and down the stairwell. The owner of the arm was thrown back against others and the brief respite allowed me to close the door completely. Severed fingers dropped down on the floor. I slumped against the door and caught my breath as little clawed hands scratched against the small glass window in the stairwell door.

"Thanks, man," I said as I followed Charlie down the stairs.

"Told you they were fast," Charlie said.

"No kidding. That would explain the carnage. Wonder why they're fast, but the adults aren't."

"No idea. I'm still getting used to the glow-in-the-dark eyeballs."

We reached the ground floor and moved quickly. I stopped again at the janitor's closet and grabbed some liquid soap. Charlie and I ran down the hall and burst out into the sun at the top of the ramp leading to the landing, which led down to the dock and the missing boat.

Both Charlie and I looked at the dock, then each other, then the dock again. Tommy and Angela were nowhere to be seen.

I immediately thought the worst, that Angela had fooled us all and had killed Tommy and taken the boat. I had no proof, no signs of violence, nothing. I looked at my watch and we were a full hour early, so Tommy would not have taken off with the bad news.

Charlie must have been having the same thoughts I was, he was gripping his rifle so hard it shook

I could hear him muttering, "...hunt her down...long as it takes..."

I thought about it for a minute, then gave up. I had something else to do. I walked down the sidewalk towards the door by the dock. I figured it was a maintenance shed and after a minute jimmied the door. I pulled out an empty gas can and poured the liquid soap into it. I dug around and found an old, greasy rag and tied it around the handle. Moving back to the ramp dock, I knocked on the small fuel tank that was used to refill the ones on the ferry boat and was gratified to hear gas inside. I took out a hollow spike from my pack and a small ball peen hammer. I chose a spot near where I thought the gas level was and used the spike to punch a hole in the tank. Gas spilled out through the tube and I quickly moved the can into position to fill it up. Once it was finished, I let the gas spill out of the tank before retrieving my spike. I washed it in the canal before replacing it in my pack.

I took the can and ran it back inside, taking a moment to make sure the coast was clear. I planted the can near the stairs at the far end of the hall and pulled out a small book of matches. I pulled out a match and stuck it in between the other matches, then placed the book under one corner of the rag. I pulled another one and lit it, then lit the outside match. I sprinted down the hall, leaping the zombie pile Charlie and I had created earlier. Behind me, I could hear a small hissing sound as the matchbook caught on fire. I moved around the ramp wall and sighted the now-burning rag with my AR. I aimed slightly lower and fired. Nothing happened, so I figured I missed and tried again. This time, the can blew, and the fire lit the escaping gasoline nicely. The soap helped it to cling to everything it touched and soon the entire back hallway was on fire. Black smoke billowed out the ramp opening and escaped to the sky.

I admired my handiwork for a second and walked back to the dock to stand next to Charlie, who was watching me with interest.

"So that was what the soap was for," he said. "Nice one. I'll have to remember that."

"Learned it from an outdoor magazine," I said.

Charlie said nothing.

The fire burned well, spreading quickly in the hospital. Smoke began filling the air and on the second floor, a window had blown out, and flames were licking the sides of the building, trying to get to the third floor. I sat down on the dock and removed my squeeze bottle of kerosene and my pickaxe. Squirting a little kerosene on the blade, I lit it and watched it burn for a minute, flaming red as the virus burned. I dunked it in the canal to put out the flames. I did the same to my boots, an awkward exercise, but after practicing for a while, we had gotten pretty good at it. Charlie did the same for his weapons and boots.

"What do we do about getting back home?" Charlie asked, adjusting the sack on his shoulder.

I looked up the canal. "Take the boat, of course." Tommy was moving down the canal at a decent clip, steering the pontoons over to the landing. Charlie and I stepped over and onto the boat, with Charlie unloading his burden at the rear. I plopped down into a chair and leveled a gaze at Tommy, who seemed remarkably unfazed.

"Finish your business?" he asked innocently, steering the boat away from the landing and heading back down the canal. I looked back and saw flames shooting out of the windows of the nurse's lounge.

Rest in peace, Ellie. I thought. *Rest in peace.*

I nodded, then fixed Tommy with a stare. "Any particular reason why you decided to go for a cruise down the canal and leave Charlie and I to fend for ourselves?" I looked over at Angela. "I thought maybe you were a good liar and I was going to have to hunt you down."

Angela looked scared and Tommy looked hurt. "I know how it looks, but I think you'll forgive us in a second." Tommy nodded to Angela, who handed me a piece of paper. Curious, I opened it and stared. I looked up.

"What...where...how did you?" I was stunned into near silence. Charlie came over and I handed the note to him and he looked at Angela and Tommy as well.

"I can't take credit. Angela found it," Tommy said.

I looked over at Angela. If she had ever needed to prove her worth, she had just done so and in spades. "Tell me," I said.

Angela smiled and said, "It was by accident, really. I was standing over on the edge of the canal and a piece of paper floated by. It had writing on it, so I fished it out and saw it was a survivor note, like the ones families used to write when they were escaping sieges."

I stared hard at her and Angela shrugged. "My grandfather was a survivor of the siege of Stalingrad when he was six years old. His mother wrote a note in the hopes they would be found by his father. People wrote hundreds of these notes, hoping someone would find them and be able to reunite with them later.

"Anyway, I showed it to Tommy, who thought we should head upriver a bit to see what we might find. We figured you all wouldn't be out for a bit and if you were you would just wait a minute."

I just shook my head and then Tommy asked Charlie, "We called you on the radio, why didn't you answer?"

Charlie looked sheepish as he retrieved it from his pack. "Forgot to turn it on," he said, fiddling with it. I couldn't blame him since I forgot he even had it.

I changed the subject. "What did you find upriver?"

Tommy jumped in. "We didn't see anything going north, which made sense since anyone in their right mind wouldn't go to the city during the Upheaval." Tommy cast a sly glance at me before continuing. "But we saw on the other side of the bridges people had left notes and markings as they fled the city. Those that used the canal, anyway. The closer we got to the city, the more notes we saw. Then, when we were about to turn around and head back, we saw the note in your hand. Angela wouldn't have noticed it except it was so odd."

I looked down at the note. Just like my brother to do something to get noticed, even in the middle of a crisis. It read **Eagles at Fort St. Louis'** in large black print, then in smaller writing, it read *'Tell John Talon his brother lives and will look for him at the Leap.'* I turned the note over in my hands and then gently folded it and put it in my pocket next to Ellie's rings. At the moment it was precious to me, as it was the last thing my brother had left for me.

"Thank you," I said quietly to Tommy and Angela, meeting their eyes in turn. "Thank you."

"So what's the plan, man?" Tommy asked, his hand on the throttle of the boat.

I looked around and realized the city had nothing I wanted. It was a nightmare to try anything and whoever was still living in there could have it. We would just get killed if we went farther in. If I wanted a close look at the city, a better bet would be to approach from the water side, like the lake. Even now, drifting as we were, we could hear the moans of thousands upon thousands of zombies. In a few years it would be safer as the zombies decayed past being a danger. But it would take years to clean them out to make the city livable. Not my work. Maybe Jake's, in time. But not mine.

"We head back to the community, drop off the supplies and get Angela checked out and fed properly." Angela shot me a look of pure gratitude. "After that, we head south as fast as we can. My brother has been out there with his family for over a year and I want to go get him."

"Do you know where he is?" Charlie asked.

"Yes," was all I had to say. The note put an idea in my head and Charlie and I had a few things to discuss.

26

We made for Leport as quickly as we could, yet it was still late evening when we finally pulled up to the dock. Charlie and I delivered the bag of medicines to the doctor and her jaw nearly dropped to the floor when she saw what we had procured. Tommy took Angela to the doctor as well and was declared healthy enough, if not well-fed. I talked to Nate for a brief time and he told me that he had figured I was successful when he saw the smoke from the burning hospital.

I went back to my home and after a brief reunion with Sarah and Jake, I spoke about the trip I needed to take in the morning. Sarah listened, then nodded.

"You know where he is, then?" she asked, looking at the note.

I nodded. "When we were kids, we used to go to Starved Rock all the time. My dad was a big fan and liked to take us to the hidden places that most people didn't know about. As we grew older, we went back as adults with our families. If he's anywhere, he's there, and I have to say if I had thought of it, I would have gone there as well."

Sarah looked at me funny. "You sound like it's a place you want to go live."

I shrugged. "It has a lot to offer defensively and if you're into rustic living the river and forest would feed you forever. Indians had lived there for thousands of years."

"What about the community you worked so hard to build and protect?" Sarah asked.

I gave it some thought before answering. "Sometimes I get the feeling I'm outliving my usefulness. Did the community fall apart when I was gone? Did the people not get fed or get water? No, they have managed to get on with their lives. Not the way they were before, but they are learning. Me, I wake up with a slightly uneasy feeling that people are whispering behind my back, saying things like 'What has he done for us lately?'"

Sarah frowned. "That's not true and you know it. Everyone respects you and nearly everyone here owes you their lives and the ability to go on living."

"That's the point. They owe me. And people as a rule do not like owing. It works on them and they wait for the time when the debt is called, so they can shout in righteous anger 'Aha! I knew you'd call that debt in!'" I sat down and Jake toddled over to me, carrying a toy truck. His beautiful brown eyes lifted to mine and I picked up my baby, giving him a quick kiss on the cheek, my three days worth of beard tickling him.

"Where will you find peace, John? Where will you be happy?" Sarah asked, looking down at me.

I shook my head. "Maybe I never will. But I do know one thing for sure."

"What's that?"

"I want you with me wherever I am."

Jake squeaked as his daddy's lap suddenly became crowded.

In the morning, I headed down to the dock, Charlie following behind me. We were not going to take the pontoon boat this time, since we weren't really on a sight-seeing tour and there was only the two of us. We got into the North River Seahawk boat, a small, twenty-four foot aluminum craft with a small cabin on the front. It was a decent find in the warehouses by the canal and we used it occasionally for ferrying across the water. I had planned on taking it to Lake Michigan, but not right now. It would serve well as a means of transportation and a good overnight cabin to sleep in. I figured it would take us the better part of a day to get to Starved Rock since it was roughly seventy-five miles from Leport to the park.

We pulled out from the town and I waved goodbye to Sarah and Jake as Charlie waved to Rebecca and Julia. I was not as heavily armed as before, carrying my trusty M1 carbine and my SIG. Charlie had his usual armament and we were provisioned for three days as usual. We carried additional rations in the boat since I had hopes of bringing my brother and his family back. If he wasn't at Starved Rock, I was going to have to figure him gone.

We headed downstream, moving at a good clip. I hadn't expected any trouble, but we had to pass Joliet again and I had the feeling they were keeping a watch for us. We had been moving back and forth on the rails to Coal City and beyond and it wasn't much of a stretch to imagine someone trying to disrupt that process.

We passed by Romeoville and I remembered the fight we had there. Charlie remembered as well and we both shared a look. Farther south, we threw a wave to the people at Freeport, and I was surprised to see the number of people out and about, tending to gardens and making repairs to fences, windows, and such. It looked so normal that I had to do a double take. I shook my head to clear it and caught Charlie doing the same.

Half an hour later, we were on alert. We were passing close to Joslin and the air seemed tense. I couldn't put a finger on what it was, but my instincts were screaming at me to be careful. Something was wrong. I didn't see anything on the banks, save for the usual ghouls that patrolled the area, but I couldn't shake the feeling that something was waiting for us.

Suddenly, Charlie slowed the boat and headed for the canal bank. Several zombies were nearby at the parking lot for the county courthouse. I found it oddly amusing that there were more than a few that had on the blaze orange jumpsuits of county detainees.

"What's up?" I asked, jumping over the side and grabbing a rope. The zombies were about one hundred yards away and not an immediate danger.

"There's a chain in the canal." Charlie pointed along the bank and sure enough, a chain was looped around an abandoned car, the links disappearing under the surface of the water. On the other side of the canal, the chain emerged and was looped around another car.

"Nice," I said, running over to the car. I was just about to lift the chain when a shot rang out from the courthouse, whipping past my ear and plowing into the blacktop. I dove to the front of the car and hunkered down as Charlie threw up his rifle and fired twice at a second-story window. I poked my head around the car and cursed. Three orange-suited zombies were closing fast and I couldn't get up without running the risk of getting shot. Well, crap.

I stretched out on the ground in front of the car and took aim at the zombies. No good. From my angle, I couldn't get head shots. I used the only alternative I had, which was to bring them down to my level. I aimed at the nearest one's knee and fired, the .30 caliber bullet easily shattering the joint and bringing the zombie down. A second shot entered the top of its head and it stayed down permanently. I dropped the second one the same way, then ducked back as another round kicked up stinging stones in my face.

"Shit!" I yelled, spinning back to cover, wiping my eyes.

"You hit?" yelled Charlie, firing at the spot where he thought the shots came from.

"Not yet, but he's getting warmer!"

I couldn't stay where I was, because I could see more zombies headed my way and I couldn't get up because the sniper was still shooting at me. To top off the fun, still more zombies were coming this way, attracted by the shots and potential feeding and I still had yet to remove the damned chain!

I had to do something, so I rolled out and shot a zombie dead, then rolled back as a barrage of shots punched holes in the car I was hiding behind. The shots proved to be just what Charlie needed and he fired one telling shot.

"Got him!" he called.

"Finally!" I yelled back. I scampered around to the back and removed the chain from the back of the car. At least ten zombies were bearing down on me and I dragged the chain to the water and dropped it in. Charlie had fired up the boat and was moving alongside the canal bank. I ran for a small way, away from the congregating zombies, and jumped the four feet of water to land clumsily on the boat.

"Thanks," I said, rubbing a sore knee.

"No problem. We're going to need to do something about Joslin," Charlie said.

"Well, you know my solution to problems like that," I replied.

"You wouldn't happen to have been milking O'Leary's cow way back in 1871, were you?"

"Good idea. We'll try that in the fall when the winds kick up out of the south."

"You're nuts."

27

We pulled away from Joslin, keeping a sharp eye out for any additional traps or snipers. I used Charlie's scope and spotted what might have been two or three people on rooftops looking us over with binoculars. I sent a shot at one, causing them to duck for cover. It was over eight hundred yards and I would have been stunned by a hit, but I'll take a duck at that range.

"Did you elect him?" Charlie asked from the pilot's seat.

I laughed, understanding his reference. "No, but I nominated him real good."

We continued to head south, passing through familiar territory. We had been this way earlier this year and I had to shake my head at the memories. I was still amazed Charlie and I made it out of Coal City alive. *Too lucky*, I thought.

The sun was fast approaching its zenith when we moved around the bend where we had stopped to go to State Center Bravo. I wondered how Trevor was doing since he and his men had gone in search of answers at the other state center. Charlie swung the boat around to the dock we had spent the night at before and we quickly reconnoitered some additional gasoline for the boat. Our buddy from the machine shop was still there, although he looked to have been chewed a bit by local fauna.

After the brief stop, we moved on to unfamiliar waters. I was sure of where we were according to the map I had, but I had no clue as to what lay ahead regarding the towns that were on the river or what else we might encounter. The first town we were supposed to come in contact with was Morris, but since it had a major highway running through it, I did not think it would have escaped the infection. But I have been wrong before and this might be one of those times.

As we pulled under the bridge to Morris, it was immediately apparent the infection had indeed struck this town. I could see shadowy shapes flitting from building to building and the omnipresent white flags were everywhere. The town seemed abandoned, but I knew there were still occupants, although likely none living.

I shook my head at Charlie as he slowed down and we sped up again, leaving Morris in our wake. We moved down a long stretch of river with untended farms on both sides. We could see the silos of farms in the distance, but had no desire to investigate. I had to assume that since Morris had been hit, that the outlying farms and small towns were hit as well when the ghouls ran out of food in the main communities they headed out to the country. No single family home could withstand a siege from hundreds of hungry, determined zombies.

I had seen too many homes with the windows smashed in, the doors broken, and bloodstains marking the walls and floors.

The next town we were supposed to come close to was Seneca, which was a small, older community on the river. If I remembered correctly, there was a row of homes on an upper portion of the town, almost on cliffs. If they could have made a coordinated stand and blocked the entrance to the subdivision, there might be survivors.

We slowed to an easy drift as we approached the town, passing several barges abandoned at the side of the river. I couldn't see the town, but I could see the long dock on the south side of the river with many boats still moored. I took that as a positive sign. My confidence was further bolstered when we spotted a lone man standing on the bridge, a scoped hunting rifle balanced on his hip. He was waving to us and I shrugged my shoulders at Charlie and, standing on the roof of the cabin, I tossed a mooring line up to him.

The man caught it with his free hand and looped it around a bridge support, holding on to it tightly. Charlie cut the engine and the boat slowly swung around under the bridge, until we came out facing the other way and facing the man on the bridge. He was about fifty years old, dressed simply, with graying black hair peeking out from beneath a worn camouflage cap. I could see an additional revolver on his belt and the bridge had been blocked at one end with a chain link gate.

"Howdy!" the man called down to us. "Nice to see another live soul 'round these parts. Name's Josh Courtner. Where y'all from?"

I smiled at the man's southern accent although we were still in what many considered northern Illinois. "We're from Leport. I'm John Talon and my partner at the tiller is Charlie James. How's your town?"

The gentleman considered the question for a minute, then replied, "We're gettin' by. The kids are complainin' they're bored, but that's 'bout the worst of it. Did you pass Morris?"

"Yes," I said. "We didn't go in, but I got the impression it was empty, nothing living."

"We've thought so for months, but never got around to checking it out. We're too busy tryin' to make a livin' in a world gone dead." Josh seemed amused by his statement, but I didn't press him further. I had seen enough to know that unless he went in there with some decent firepower and cool shooters, someone was going to die.

"What brings y'all down the river?" Josh asked. "Not that I mind, it's great there's another town that's alive out there, we thought we were a little alone, here."

"I'm looking for my brother," I said. "His name is Mike Talon, he would have been traveling with his family. He's about my size, dark hair, and blue eyes. I'm not sure when he might have passed this way."

Josh thought for a minute. "Would this brother of yours been carrying a 9mm Beretta, by any chance?" he asked.

I brightened, suddenly hopeful. "Yeah, he would. Did you see him?"

Josh nodded. "I reckon so. He showed up along the river late last year, right before the snows became serious. He and his family looked like they had been traveling a while and some of our local boys thought to have a little sport. You brother asked for some supplies and our town idiot thought it would be a good idea to make your brother sing for it. Your brother sang, although from what I heard, he looked like he was gonna kill somebody. When the song was over, the idiot stiffed your brother, laughing and drinking a beer. Your brother waited until the dumbass was about fifty yards away then shot the bottle out of his hand. After that he got his supplies. No one wanted to mess with someone who could shoot like that."

I grinned. Mike was hell on wheels with a handgun.

Charlie nudged me. "You have any other family out there? Any more of you and we'll whip the whole damn zombie horde single-handed."

I shook my head. "Mike's great with a handgun, but can't shoot for shit with a long gun."

"Anyway," Josh continued, "he was welcome to stay, but he said he needed to get downriver and wait for his brother. Said something about a fort, although I don't know what the hell he was talkin' about. I lived here my whole life and there ain't never been no fort anywhere near here."

"This was before winter?" I asked.

"Yep."

"Thanks. We'll see you when we are heading back," I promised.

"We'll be here," Josh said, letting the line go and releasing our boat. We drifted for a bit, then Charlie righted us, and we headed farther down river. I looked at our map and saw we were supposed to clear Marseilles within the hour. The sun was moving into the afternoon and soon we would have to find a place to spend the night. I was hoping that we would have been able to reach Starved Rock and my brother by nightfall, but it was looking like it was going to have to be in the morning. We had a decent ways to go and I didn't see us reaching him soon.

28

We moved farther down the river and I was once again struck at how quiet it was. I could clearly hear the river moving along its banks, the sudden splash of fish and frogs and the increasing whine of insects. Part of me wondered if this might have been what this area was like back in the day before humans started to settle along it in force.

Marseilles was a lot like Seneca and we had a pleasant conversation with a couple of teenagers who were at the river when we passed. The town looked like most river towns, small homes with a few larger ones back in the hills. The thing that Seneca had separating it from others was the tall earthen mound that seemed to surround the town. When I inquired about it, I was told that since Seneca was a holding place for highway construction equipment, they had no trouble creating a defensive barrier, especially considering what had happened to Ottowa. They didn't elaborate further, telling me I would see when I got there, in typical teen fashion. They promised to tell their leaders about us and would hopefully see us when we came back since we had "kick-ass" gear.

Charlie and I were left to ponder this information as we moved farther down the river. The sun was sinking lower and if I had to guess, it was roughly three or four o'clock in the afternoon. The sun was starting to become a problem on the water, as it was making it more difficult to see where we were going. When the sun dipped lower, we would be lucky if we didn't hit something. There was plenty of debris in the river and thus far Charlie had been able to steer clear, but if we hit something and lost the boat, we had a long swim back home.

As we got closer to Ottowa, Charlie spotted a dock sticking out into the river. Not one to ask a gift horse to open wide, I suggested we moor there for the night and head out first thing in the morning. It would give us a chance to stretch our legs and walk on dry land for a bit.

As Charlie steered us close, I jumped off the boat and tied us up at the dock. The dock was a serious structure and I noticed a concrete reinforced pylon which I assumed would have been used to keep the barges from taking out the dock. Interesting, but it still didn't explain why the dock was there.

Charlie and I walked along the pier and followed a service road until we could see where we were. On our left was a farm and on the right looked like a power plant or manufacturing plant. I didn't have any desire to figure out what it was and Charlie didn't either. If no one wanted this place, it would eventually crumble into decay. Most places would be like that, I guessed. We simply did not have the people left to bring things back to exactly the way they were. A lot of places would have to be abandoned. Maybe if we survived another twenty years, humans could make a comeback and use what we left behind. All speculation at this point. We had to survive those years, first.

Charlie pointed towards the plant and I could see movement around the doors. A lone figure was walking out of the building and even at that distance, I could see the telltale shambling walk of a zombie. I shook my head sadly, realizing this area had been hit by the infection as well.

"We've come so far, I kind of hoped we would have found an area that the infection didn't touch." Charlie said, echoing my thoughts.

"No such luck," I said, turning back to the dock. "The infection touched everything, one way or the other." To emphasize my point, four more came strolling out of the building.

We moved back the way we came and rounded a grove of trees, blocking us from the sight of the zombies. With luck, they would lose interest and go wander off and chase a bug or something.

We went back to the boat and untied one of the mooring lines, letting the boat drift along until the second line went taut, keeping us tied, but safe from attack. We were about thirty yards from the pier and safe in deep water.

Charlie and I passed the time cleaning our weapons and arguing which kung-fu movie was best. As the sun dipped below the horizon, we settled in to sleep.

29

In the morning, I got a nasty surprise. I stepped out of the cabin to stretch and I found myself faced with about fifteen zombies. They were standing on the pier and when they saw me they raised a ghoulish chorus that echoed across the water. Much to my dismay, I heard an answering chorus downriver. Charlie came out of the cabin with his gun ready, but I pushed it down. The zombies were just standing on the pier, but they clearly wanted to get to us. I thought it was interesting that they retained enough intelligence to recognize water. I told Charlie to start the motor and when he was ready, I would cut the line.

Charlie started the engine and at the sound, the zombies became more agitated. One fell into the river and drifted dangerously close until he finally sank under the surface. The boat eased forward and when there was slack in the line, I quickly severed it and Charlie slewed the boat around, taking us away from the dock of the undead.

As we approached Ottowa it was easy to see that the city had been hit hard. Given its proximity to the interstate, I really wasn't that surprised. What did surprise me was the crowds of zombies standing along the edge of the river. There had to be hundreds, if not thousands, and they were standing wherever they could. The bridge spanning the water was packed with zombies as well and they were held in place by a *huge* pile of debris. If it was twenty feet high, it was an inch. As we moved underneath the bridge, I could see movement on the south side of the river. I looked closely and saw living people. I waved a hand in greeting and they tried to wave me over, but I shook my head. "We'll be back," I said, the words sounding unnaturally loud over the stillness of the morning. The zombie crowd took up a moaning that rebounded off the cliffs and hills. If there was a zombie within a mile, they heard that undead song.

We sped away and headed downriver and I was getting anxious to reach the state park. Starved Rock got its name from the legend that a group of Indians had become trapped on the top of the formation by enemy Indians and they subsequently starved to death. In later years, the rock formation was home to a French fort, named Fort St. Louis which was placed there to protect French trading interests in the region. The rock was home to a hotel and after that it became a state park. A number of trails wound their way through the hills and limestone cliffs and it was not uncommon to find a waterfall or two feeding the river from forgotten streams. A lodge had been built on the cliff overlooking the river during the CCC days of the Great Depression and a visitor center had been erected in recent years to educate the tourists about the history and wildlife of the area.

In all honesty, I wasn't sure I was going to find my brother. For all I knew, he had moved on, figuring me for dead. But I needed to at least try and that was the point of this journey. I decided to put the boat in at the far end of the park and we would work our way through the trails, making sure we didn't miss anything. Just because my brother said he was going to be at Fort St. Louis didn't mean he was going to sit on top of a rock until I showed up.

We brought the boat into a small inlet and beached it. Charlie cut the engine and we jumped ashore, bringing the remaining mooring line to tie up to a tree. I wasn't exactly sure where we were, since I didn't have a map, but the good news was maps were all over the trails, letting you know exactly how far from your car you were. The vegetation was not yet full, as summer had a month to go before being in full swing, but it was still pretty greened over. The large trees bracketed the trail and brush reached in from the sides. Large ferns were growing and would eventually cover the ground. I could hear movement from small animals as we headed west, jumping out of our way, chattering their disapproval. The morning sunlight made the tops of the trees light up like they were on fire while the ground was still dark. We had to move through this and I was hoping we had arrived unnoticed.

We moved quickly along the river, our progress fairly silent, save for the occasional water dweller that dove for safety as we passed. Charlie nudged me as we went past a trail marker and said, "Something's not right."

I stopped and looked around. "What do you mean?" I said in a low voice.

Charlie scanned the area with his rifle and scope. "Something's watching us."

"Zombie?" I asked, raising my carbine.

"Don't know. How much farther?"

I looked at the marker. "Maybe three quarters of a mile, maybe more."

"Good. This is giving me the creeps," Charlie said.

That made me nervous. Anything that could creep out a guy like Charlie who had seen and done the things he had, was something worth avoiding.

We moved forward, with our senses on higher alert. I could feel something out there as well, but I couldn't get a read on what it was. I held my carbine low, ready to snap it up and fire in an instant. We moved quickly, but carefully. And all the while we checked all around us. I thought I saw a ghost of movement in the shadows down a trail to a canyon and brought my gun up, but didn't see anything else.

Charlie saw my movement. "Anything?"

"No. But you're right, something is out there, I'm sure of it." To emphasize my point, something large moved suddenly in the brush behind us, but it was still too dark to see clearly.

"We're being hunted" Charlie said, gripping his rifle tighter.

"You're right." I stepped forward again. "We are. We'd better get moving to some open space. Keep your eyes open, check everything, especially the trees. Too many places to hide up there."

We doubled our pace, moving past a stairway to an overlook, heading west. The beauty of the forest was marred by the ominous feeling we got from the darkness. The sun was getting higher in the sky and the forest was becoming lighter, but there were still plenty of places to hide. In all honesty, I would have rather had a zombie gunning for me than whatever it was out there. At least a zombie was predictable.

The trail wound inward and if anything else that made it more tense. When the trail was by the river we didn't have to worry about an attack from water which left three sides to worry about. Now we had to worry about all sides.

After about a quarter mile, Charlie spoke suddenly. "I wish whatever the hell is out there would just get it over with. This stalking shit is getting on my nerves."

I nodded, but his sentence struck a nerve. Stalking. It raised a question I had never considered before. What happened to the animals in the zoos? Sure, most of them would die of starvation after a while or freeze to death, but what about those that had the ability to get out? If I had to guess, we were being stalked by a large animal, possibly a cougar or other exotic animal.

I related my thoughts to Charlie as we moved up towards another overlook.

Charlie shook his head. "It's fucking crazy, but it makes sense. As if we didn't have just the zombies eating us to worry about, now we have to worry about big cats eating us."

"Could be worse," I said.

"How the hell could it be worse?" Charlie said, stepping over a fallen tree branch.

"Zombie cougars." Even though I was joking, there was a serious side. If the virus jumped species and made zombies out of animals, we had a whole shit load of new problems to worry about.

We moved up a stairwell to Eagle Cliff Overlook and looked out over the expanse of water that made the Illinois River. The rising sun glanced off the water, sending small shafts of light back to the heavens. The forest spread out in front of us and we could see the roof top of the lodge from where we were.

"We're close," I said, heading back to the stairs.

"So is that," Charlie said, pointing. A treetop suddenly swayed and another moved just as suddenly, as if something heavy had jumped from one tree to another. Watching the spot, I headed back down the stairs, but when we went around an outcropping of rock, the spot I had marked was empty.

"We know you're there..." I said, moving forward again.

"Here, kitty, kitty, goddamn kitty," Charlie said through gritted teeth, tightening his grip on his rifle.

We moved away from the overlook and headed deeper into the woods. It was unnaturally quiet and my nerves were quickly becoming undone. I had faced hundreds of zombies, but I had never been this nervous. From the sweat I could see on Charlie's face, he felt the same way.

A rustle in the trees caught my attention. In a flash I brought my rifle up and fired a shot, the echo blasting through the forest. Charlie whipped his rifle up, ready to cover me. I saw a tawny shape disappear into the brush and it was then I knew what was stalking us.

"Did you get it?" Charlie asked, still trying to find something to shoot at.

"No, but I scared the crap out of it," I said, staring hard at the spot where it had disappeared.

"What was it?"

"Cougar."

"You sure?"

"Go look if you doubt it," I said.

"Screw that. Where do you think it came from?" Charlie asked.

"Probably from a zoo, followed the river and ended up here. Can't fault it for its choice of hunting ground."

We moved forward again, angling west more. I figured that shot would have alerted anyone in the vicinity that someone was here. Carbines are notoriously loud and mine was no exception. If my brother was here, he had to know someone was in his backyard by now.

The heavy brush started to thin out and I could see some clearings up ahead. If memory served correctly, we were pretty close to our objective.

A few more yards and we were in the clear. I looked around and noticed a pair of legs sticking out from under a bush. Moving closer, I saw it was a zombie or what used to be a zombie. Its grayish skin and bloodstained clothing gave it away. However, it was dead because of the massive bite in its neck and the large bites which had penetrated its skull. Chunks of meat had been ripped of it, leading me to believe this zombie had met our little kitten in the woods.

30

The Visitor Center was visible from where we were and the trail to the top of Starved Rock. I figured to check out the Visitor Center first, as it would be a place I would hole up if I had to. Starved Rock itself was a great site to visit, but was lousy for long term habitation. I moved forward with Charlie taking the rear, casting worried glances over his shoulder as he did so. When we reached the Visitor Center, I looked carefully into the dark interior. I could see the gift shop and the model table, but not much else. I tried the door and found it unlocked. I eased myself into the foyer with Charlie right behind me.

We stood stock still for a moment, getting our bearings. I knew there was a small café on the other side of the center, but I wanted to make sure we were alone. Hearing nothing, I slung my carbine over my shoulder and drew my SIG. Anything that happened here would be extreme close quarters. Charlie followed suit, but pulled his twin tomahawks rather than his Glock.

I moved over to the historical section and shined my flashlight around, giving myself a small start when the light played over the mannequins dressed as French explorers. Charlie checked out the book section, then walked back. His foot struck a walking stick on the floor and sent it clattering across the hall.

I looked at Charlie and he shrugged sheepishly. I was about to comment when I heard something. I raised a hand and pointed to my ear and Charlie nodded. He had heard something, too.

The sun was higher in the sky, allowing for more sunlight to stream in the doors and filtered skylights and I moved through the center on silent feet. Getting closer to the heavy wooden doors that separated the café from the information center, I heard more clearly what I thought I had heard before. There was muted whispering and what sounded like whimpering. I tried to look through one of the panes of glass in the door, but could only see tables and chairs. I pushed the door open slightly and the noise suddenly stopped and I heard scuffling. Somebody was alive in here.

I pushed the door wider and whispered, "Hello? Is someone in here?" I stepped back to the side in case whoever was in there wasn't friendly.

Nothing happened and I waited for a second. "Hello? Anybody there? We're here to help." Charlie cocked an eyebrow at me but I ignored him.

Suddenly the door flung open and a large bearded man burst through, pointing a handgun all around. He didn't immediately see us, which allowed me to step up to him and put my SIG against his temple. "That's enough. Put it down."

The man breathed heavily, then lowered the gun. Charlie stepped up and took it from his hand. I stayed on the side, keeping an eye on the man's hands. I took in the man's appearance and he looked like he had been through the ringer. His clothes were filthy and matted and his hair was long and unkempt. I expected the man to react, but I never expected him to drop to his knees, cover his face and start to cry.

I stepped back, fearing a trick, as the man sobbed into his hands. "Take what you want, but please don't hurt my family. Please."

The voice, while raspy, was familiar. I holstered my SIG and squatted down in front of him. I didn't worry about him trying anything since Charlie was there.

"Hey," I said, looking hard at the man.

He looked up and I found myself looking into my mother's eyes. Only they didn't belong to my mother. They belonged to my brother. I had found him. By all that's holy, I had found him.

"I found your note," I said. "You were supposed to be looking for me at Eagle Cliff." I took off my goggles and balaclava and at the moment of recognition, threw my arms around my brother. Charlie stepped back and I had a hard time keeping the tears from my eyes as I held my baby brother.

Mike drew back, wiping his eyes. "Thank God. You came. Oh, thank God," he kept saying over and over.

We stood up and Mike motioned us to follow him. We went through the doors and into the gift shop. There, hiding in the corner, was Mike's family. Nicole was there, holding a whimpering Annie, and Logan was bravely standing in front of his mother, tears down his cheeks, trying to protect her from the bad guys.

I knelt down in front of Logan and said, "Hi, little buddy. Your cousin Jake misses you." It took a minute for him to recognize me, then he threw his little arms around my neck and hugged me tight. I held on to him as I stood and gave Nicole a hug as well.

I put down Logan and introduced Charlie to everyone. Logan was as impressed as a three year old could be and asked to touch Charlie's gun.

I spoke with Mike and Nicole for a few moments and realized that they had holed up in the visitor center when the cougar first came stalking. After that, it was touch-and-go as they finished their supplies and worked their way through the stores kept in the café. Once those ran out, Mike had been making runs to the lodge, bringing back what he could from the restaurant. Those runs became more dangerous as zombies from the town across the river began to cross the bridge and realized food was nearby. They had actually run out of food three days ago and were on the brink of collapse. When they heard us, they thought we were zombies at first, but when I had opened the door, they thought we were looters. Mike was actually out of bullets, so he had been hoping to surprise whoever had come in. When that didn't work, he had just reached the end of his string.

I took off my pack and handed out the food and water I had in there and Charlie did the same. The family gratefully accepted the stores, making sure their children ate first. We had more in the boat, so I wasn't concerned. Besides, we were going back to Leport as soon as possible.

I spent the next several minutes talking about what had happened to me since the Upheaval and Charlie jumped in as necessary. When we had finished, my brother looked at me with new eyes. "When did you become such a dangerous person?" he asked.

"'Bout a year ago, give or take a month," I said. "Believe me, if I had a choice, I'd have kept things the way they were."

After the family had assuaged the worst of their hunger, I started to head for the front door, nearest the parking lot, when my brother grabbed my arm.

"What are you doing?" he hissed, looking furtively out the window. "There's at least six zombies out there!"

I shook my arm free. "I just found my brother after thinking he was dead for over a year. I'm taking you home and if you think six zombies will stop me, you have no idea what your brother has become." I signaled to Charlie and he came over, standing on a chair and looking out of a high window overlooking the parking lot.

"There's seven by the front door and five more out in the parking lot. Two just disappeared around the corner, so I'm guessing they're checking out the back." Charlie stepped down. "How do you want to play it?"

I thought for minute. "Let's wait for the two to get to the back, deal with them quietly, then we'll hit the front like we did with the trailers at Coal City."

Charlie nodded. "You want to go first again?"

I shook my head. "You can this time."

"What about the ones in the lot?"

"One on one, I'll take the left side."

"Deal."

My brother just stared at me with an open mouth as I readied my gear. I topped off my carbine and loosened my pickaxe in its holder. Charlie checked his gear, then signaled he was ready. I repositioned my balaclava and goggles.

I motioned to Mike to come over and Charlie handed him his gun back. "It's fully loaded now, so you can defend your family if it comes to it. If something happens to us, take the trail to Horseshoe Bend. The boat is beached there. Take it and get your family to Leport. Don't stop at Joslin, and don't hesitate. Clear?"

Mike just nodded and Nicole just stared at us with wide eyes.

"Ready?" I asked Charlie.

Charlie nodded.

Pushing open the door to the information center, I headed towards the back door. The two that had headed that way from the front were just ambling past the doors, not finding anything of interest to them. I stepped to the back door and nodding to Charlie, burst out onto the sidewalk. The two zombies turned as one and came at us.

I didn't waste time and planted my pick into the skull of the first one, a heavy man with grey skin and deep gashes on his shoulders. Charlie crushed the skull of the other Z with a well-placed blade to the temple. We wiped off our weapons and split up with me taking the left side and Charlie taking the right. I unslung my carbine as I moved, making sure I stayed close to the walls to avoid having my shadow reveal where I was.

About twenty feet from the corner I stopped and shouldered my weapon. I walked out away from the wall and kept my eye on the corner. I moved until I could just see part of one of the zombies and stopped. When Charlie opened up, I wanted to be out of the way, but in position to support him if needed. Out in the parking lot, the other zombies saw me and started in my direction. They were about two hundred yards out and not yet a threat.

I waited for about five seconds, then heard Charlie's rifle bark. He was very methodical and four shots rang out. I waited a second, then stepped forward and faced three zombies whose backs were to me. At the first shot, I dropped a teenage girl who had moved quickly to the corner. The other two, probably her parents, turned at the sound and headed for me. I shot the father first, then the mother, both of them falling beside their daughter.

The fusillade of shots stirred the Z's in the parking lot to move faster-and both Charlie and I took a moment to shoot the ones nearest to us. Mine seemed to be whiter than usual and as I ran to engage the remaining zombies I noticed that the reason he was white was because he was covered in maggots.

Charlie reached a zombie first and jumped high into the air to bring his tomahawk down on its head. I reached my second one and, ducking under its clawed hands, swept its feet out from under it, slamming it onto the pavement. Stepping up to it, I drove my pickaxe into the top of its head before it had a chance to recover.

The next two were going to present a little bit of a problem because they were close together. They were two women, dressed in tank tops and jeans, with lank, filthy hair hanging down their faces. Deep scratches covered their arms and one had a tear in her shoulder. The other had a hole bitten in her thigh, the opening torn and bloodied. Their hands and arms were blackened with dried blood and they moved in an almost coordinated fashion. They advanced with their arms outstretched, allowing very little room to maneuver. This was going to take some timing. I waited until they got close, then I swerved to the side, placing one behind the other. I shoved the head of the pickaxe into the face of the blonde one, knocking her into the brunette and tumbling them both to the ground. I moved around again and slammed the heavy blade end of my pick into the top of the blonde. She lay still as her companion crawled towards me, standing up on unsteady feet as she faced me. Her arms came up again and I kicked her back over her friend again. I moved and slammed the pick down more forcefully than I had intended and caved in half her skull. Her reaching hands immediately fell to the side and she looked like she and her friend were now sleeping.

Charlie came over after he finished his zombie. "All done with your threesome?" he asked, wiping off the 'hawk.

"Yeah. Wasn't as fun as I thought it would be," I said, scrubbing my pick on the grass.

I looked around and didn't see any threats. I knew the cougar was still out there, but that was a danger I could live with if I had to.

"Come on," I said. "Let's get the family moving. I want to show you something before we go."

We went back to the Visitor Center and gathered up Mike and his family. They watched with wide eyes as Charlie and I dragged the bodies to the parking lot and set them on fire. I used the opportunity to cleanse my pick and Charlie did the same with his weapon. As the fire was burning out, I took Charlie up to the lodge, where we scouted around for a bit. Not finding any enemies, living or otherwise, we stood on the expansive patio that ran the length of the building. The Illinois River Valley stretched before us and the water of the river lazily wandered by. In the middle of the river was an island, about a mile long, with trees and long grass.

"What's on the back side of this place?" Charlie asked.

"Farms and another state park," I said. "A little more rustic than this one, but very nice."

"What are you thinking?" Charlie asked.

"I'm thinking this is where I want to be. It has everything. Land for crops, land for animals, perfectly defensible positions if needed, water all year long, lookout points for the river. I would move here in a second. There's a horse farm nearby. Might have some horses left."

Charlie thought for a second. "What about your brother?"

"He's alive and will stay that way. Unless I miss my guess, he and his family will want to get to some semblance of civilization soon. They would be a welcome addition to the community."

"What about Sarah.?"

I thought about that. "She'll resist at first, but I think she'll come around."

Charlie gazed out over the water and the forest. "Want some company?" he asked.

I laughed. "You been feeling the same thing?"

Charlie looked at me. "The 'I'm not meant to run a community' feeling? Yeah, I've been feeling that. I was looking to head out earlier, but didn't know where to go. Now I do."

"Yeah, me too. This place feels right, better than any other."

"Exactly."

"Still have a lot to do back at Leport."

"Yeah, but we'll get here."

We headed down the stairs to where Mike and his family were waiting. We had a lot to do, but we had another success under our belts. I was eager to get back to Starved Rock and settle in, but we had to go to our old home first before we made the trip to our new one.

For the first time in a long while, I felt an odd sense of peace. I hoped it would last.

31

We moved my brother and his family quickly back to Leport, stopping briefly at Ottawa and Seneca to speak with the survivors there. We established communication protocols and traded information about towns we had visited to the south. I figured once we cracked the nut of the huge distribution center to the north, we would be in a great position to share what we had with towns that needed it.

Joslin proved to be no trouble on the way back, although we did hear gunfire and saw many zombies still in the area. I was again curious as to the viability of restarting the power plant, but that would only occur after the danger had been taken care of.

At Leport, there were plenty of hugs to go around and I moved my brother and his family to a house just down the road from where Sarah and I lived. Logan was delighted to see Jake again and Jake thought Annie was just the greatest thing. We spent several nights just catching up on things, sharing stories and shrugging our shoulders at the way things turned out. The one sour note was we had no idea about our parents, but even I wasn't crazy enough to try and head in that direction.

After a few weeks of readjusting and settling back in, I finally got around to talking to Trevor about his trip to State Center Alpha. Trevor had insisted that he wouldn't talk to anyone until he had talked to me first and I put it off for a while. I knew he had found several towns that were on the brink of extinction and had managed to bring back over a hundred people. For that alone, he was a hero in anyone's eyes, as well as the rest of the crew that accompanied him.

I sat down in Trevor's living room and waited for him to organize his thoughts. I was in no hurry, although I was very curious as to what he found. Outside, summer was past its high point, and every once in a while, you felt a breeze that let you know fall was on its way. Plants weren't as green as they used to be and overall there was a dustiness to the air.

Trevor leaned back in his chair and launched into his report. "We didn't run into anything we couldn't handle on our way to the center. We worked our way around some roadblocks, but didn't hit anything serious until we came to the outskirts of Alpha. We approached pretty much the same way you did, keeping an eye on the cars and building, looking for movement. The gates were closed, however, and we could see the buildings were occupied. Thanks for the map, by the way, Alpha was built just like Bravo."

I nodded.

Trevor continued. "We moved in and checked things out. The dorms were full of zombies, but they couldn't get out. The main office building had labs like you said and some offices. It was in the offices that we found the information you suspected was there."

I leaned forward. I had my suspicions about those centers, but kept them to myself, telling only Trevor about them when I sent him to the center. My biggest question was how the state had managed to build the centers without anyone knowing about it and how had they managed to build them so quickly after the outbreak of the virus? To me, that smacked of prior knowledge, which meant the virus could have been contained had we just been warned earlier.

"The center wasn't for keeping people safe from the zombies. The centers was for the study of zombies. Everyone who came through those gates was not supposed to leave alive. They were supposed to become zombies and be experimented on."

I kept my face passive, but inside I felt like I had been sucker punched. How the hell could the government do this to their own people? This knowledge created more questions than answers.

"Here's the thing," Trevor said. "The federal government never figured the virus to go as out of control as it did. The creation of the centers was to weed out a segment of the population deemed expendable, those people without any usable skills or any inclination to self-preservation. They would be the ones to run for a shelter because they lacked the wherewithal to manage on their own.

"The purpose was to understand the virus, then try to understand the zombie. What motivated it, why did it eat humans, what were its weaknesses?" Trevor sounded older, like the knowledge aged him.

"When the centers lost contact with their federal masters after the central government fell to the virus, the centers just shut down, and most of the staff left. The commander you found had a sense of guilt and shot himself for what he had participated in." Trevor finished with a sigh. "But that's not the worst of it."

I doubted anything could have made me more disgusted than what I already heard, but I had a feeling Trevor was about to prove me wrong. "What was the worst?"

Trevor held up binder that he had been holding by the side of the chair. It was plain grey with red lettering that read "Operation Zero Friday". "If the government had been able to contain the virus, the plan was to use the zombies to control the rest of the population into compliance. Remember the line the President's Chief of Staff liked to use? 'Never let a good crisis go to waste?' They wanted to use this crisis to solidify absolute control over not only the United States, but the rest of the world as well."

I shook my head. "A power play. Billions dead for a power play. Somehow, I'm not surprised."

Trevor stood up to drink some water. "The last of the reports talked about a regrouping of military forces, so it's a safe bet they're still out there. A side note talked about possibly a safe haven for those in Washington, but nothing specific."

I stood up and offered my hand to Trevor. "Good work. You're a hell of a fighter and a good friend. This community is grateful and so am I."

Trevor smiled as he shook my hand. "Thanks. Coming from you that means a lot."

"We'll let the rest of the community know as soon as possible. Some of them have family that went to those centers and they deserve to know the truth." I headed for the door. Part of me was disgusted by what our so-called elected leaders had tried to do and another part was glad they had failed.

I left Trevor's house and walked right into a zombie. We collided together and I managed to catch myself on the door of the house and draw my gun as the Z fell backwards and onto its back. It scrambled up faster than I had ever seen a zombie move, then raised its hands over its head as it yelled, "Don't shoot!"

I stared hard for a second, not believing I had just heard a zombie speak, then lowered my gun. It was Carl Witry, our acting coach and resident zombie impersonator. "Jesus, Carl! You're gonna get shot walking around dressed like that!"

Carl wiped off his rags. "Tell me about it. You're the fifth person to throw down on me since I came to get Trevor."

"What's up?" I asked, holstering my SIG.

"Nothing. Trevor is late for training and Nate sent me to come get him." Carl was upright again and none the worse for wear.

"Alright, I'll be at home if anyone needs me."

"Righty-ho," Carl said as he knocked on Trevor's door. As I walked away, I heard, "Don't shoot!" coming from Trevor's house once again. I laughed and hoped Carl would survive his errand.

Back at home, Sarah and Jake were waiting for me. I laid down on the floor and let Jake crawl on me while I played Daddy monster and made him giggle. I told Sarah what Trevor had told me and she just shook her head.

"You know, when you think about it, what we have here is pretty much the best we could hope for. If the government had won, we'd be virtual prisoners of the state, forced into slavery, threatened with the possibility of being turned into a zombie or torn apart by them if we resisted," Sarah said.

"That's what I was thinking, too. As rough as life has become, all it would have taken for it to get rougher would have been the government getting involved," I said, tickling Jake on his tummy, eliciting a squeak of protest.

"Change of subject," Sarah said.

"Go for it."

"When are we moving?" she asked.

I smiled. "Been talking to Rebecca, have you?"

"Can't help it. We're women. Besides, Charlie is much less resistant to Rebecca's charms than you are to mine." Sarah slid down on the floor.

"Guess you'll have to just work harder," I said, wiggling my nose into Jake's.

"Answer the question," Sarah said, taking a turn tickling Jake.

"Probably at the end of the week. Charlie and I have to find another boat so we don't deprive the community of one and we have to make sure we have everything packed and ready to go. I want to be firmly established before the fall comes and I want to make sure we are able to survive the winter. Plus, Charlie and I need to secure the area as much as we can."

"Anyone else coming along?"

"Not that I know of." I had spoken to very few people about our plans as I wanted to avoid any conflicts, but I was starting to feel a bit crowded in our current community. I know Charlie felt the same way, which was why he had asked to come with to our new home.

I broke the news at the next council meeting. I didn't expect a lot of resistance, but there was a lot of 'Are you sure?' 'Did someone offend you?' 'We still need you." and so on.

"I appreciate the sentiments, I really do," I said. "But in a strange way, I feel like my work here is finished and I need to move on, maybe help another community get things together. I will not fade from the scene entirely, as Nate knows, we have a final campaign scheduled for this coming winter and I will definitely be here for the fun. For right now, though, I am moving on."

We finished the meeting with a few hours worth of planning for the upcoming offensive and as I left I felt the familiar pang of regret when I made a big decision. Was it the right thing to do, was it right for Jacob, etc. In the end, though, my gut told me it was time to move on. I had done what I had set out to do here, now I needed to see if I could do for myself.

32

The week passed quickly with a lot of well wishes from most of the community. We had a lot of supplies to load and I was surprised at the amount of stuff we managed to accumulate. It was a far cry from the beginning of my journey when I had packed up my belongings and my son on a bike and headed out into the zombie world.

Charlie and I were still looking for a boat after three days and it was becoming frustrating. We had found several small boats, but we didn't want to take more than one trip. So we were looking for something a little bigger. I had suggested we try some of the boat storage facilities, but lacking a trailer, we had no way to get the boat to water. Which left us with searching many homes, usually finding bass boats and small fishing boats, but nothing useful like the boat we took to Starved Rock in the first place.

We were driving down 191st street, very close to the Condo Community we had started in Frankfort after we had left the school when I had a bit of inspiration. "Pull in here!" I shouted to Charlie.

Charlie cursed and hit the brakes, causing us to swerve slightly as the tires squealed in protest. We came to a stop and Charlie swore again.

"Dammit, are you trying to kill us?" he said, irritated.

"You're driving, you're the one who nearly caused an accident. I was just navigating." I tried to sound contrite, but I didn't think it would work.

Mollified, Charlie asked, "What are we stopping here for?"

I pointed to the small industrial park. "Sometimes the guys who own the businesses store their toys in their unused space. I remember a sealant company having a large boat in the warehouse owned by the same guys who owned the business back when I worked for a living as a kid."

Charlie shrugged. "Couldn't hurt to look, we've struck out so far." He pulled the truck into the parking lot and cruised to a stop in a parking space. I smiled when I saw he had avoided the handicapped space.

Old habits never really go away, I thought.

We got out of the truck and I looked around. The little industrial park was laid out like a couple of squares with a road passing in between the buildings. There weren't the usual signs of violence or infestation, so I took that as a positive sign. Across the road was an identical business park, but it looked like it had some problems. Several windows of the businesses had been broken into and there was an abandoned van slewed across the front of one area. I nodded to

Charlie in the direction of the van and after a moment's look he nodded. We'd keep an eye on that area. In our experience, a vehicle parked in front of a door like that meant someone was trying to keep something out.

I pulled my crowbar and went to work on the nearest door. It was a paving business and the door opened easily after some persuading. Taking a quick look around, I made my way past decorative piles of brick samples and to the back room. I knocked on the steel door and held my ear to it.

I heard nothing, opened the door and looked around. There were large pallets of bricks and other types of paving rocks, as well as barrels of tar and repair kits for driveways.

I met Charlie and shook my head. No dice on this one. We checked the next two in line and found nothing of interest. The businesses were actually interconnected, so one business could actually occupy two or three spaces. It also allowed us to access each business without having to go outside every time.

On the last business, we got hopeful. It was an insulation company and Charlie noticed a lot of stuffed fish on the walls. I looked around and saw a couple of family photos that showed several smiling people sitting on a largish boat.

"Maybe, maybe," I said, working my way to the back door. I opened the door and shined my flashlight around. At first I didn't see anything except piles of insulation, but tucked out of the way was pay dirt. It was a beautiful Bayliner Express Cruiser, thirty two feet long with twin engines. I moved over and climbed aboard. It had two cabins, one fore and one aft, a full galley, and a small dinette area. The deck had a nice U-shaped lounge area, and a low diving platform. It was, in a word, perfect. Well, almost. It had been christened "Wetter Dreams", obviously by someone who thought they were being clever.

Charlie came over and inspected the boat, giving me an approving nod and the name of the boat an eye roll. We inspected the trailer and we were pretty sure we would be able to tow the boat, but as to the route back to Leport to put it in the water, we weren't so sure.

We argued back and forth about possible routes and alternates, each one having its merits, although none easy, since there were still hundreds of cars blocking easy access.

I was about to make a remarkably poignant argument when a knock on the garage door stopped us cold.

I looked at Charlie. "Did you order take out?" Another knock.

"Not me. I hate Chinese food." More knocking.

"Hmm." I went over to the back door and put my ear against it. Sure enough, there sounded like a few people were walking around out there. The door didn't have a window, so I couldn't see what was happening. I didn't worry about anyone on the outside getting in, since these warehouses generally had doors without handles on the outside, offering only a deadbolt for entry.

I started to leave the warehouse when something caught my eye and I ducked back into the darkness. Charlie was right behind me and we collided in the gloom. Shaking his head, he assessed the situation correctly. "How many?" he asked.

"At least four by the front windows and if they see us they'll be on us in no time," I said.

"Four isn't too bad," Charlie mused.

"That's just what I could see. I'm pretty sure there's more out back." I said, trying to keep quiet.

"What's the plan, then?"

"Hold on. I'm going to see if we can get to the roof." I headed back to the storeroom and looked around. No luck. We checked the other storerooms, being very careful to avoid being seen. The last one in line had roof access, so we headed up and carefully looked around.

The roof was a simple affair, with a three foot false front around the front and sides of the buildings. There was nothing of note on the roof except for a couple of bodies in the corner. I approached them carefully and Charlie did the same, but we relaxed when we saw they were dead and staying that way. I looked closer and couldn't see a cause of death, although they were both just skin and bones. They were lying with their arms around each other and judging by their clothes, they were just teenagers.

"What do you think?" Charlie asked, tilting his head towards the couple.

"If I had to guess, they got chased up here and died of dehydration. Not a pretty way to go. Wonder why they didn't hole up in the storerooms until the zombies lost interest?" I mused.

"They were just scared kids. They weren't thinking all tactical like you do," Charlie jibed.

I ignored the barb. "Let's take a look at our friends." We walked over to the front side and carefully looked over. The four I had initially seen had been joined by four more, making the equation a little more untenable.

Moving over to the side of the building, I looked over and my shoulders slumped. There had to be twenty of the fetid things wandering around and bumping into each other, standing by the wall, and generally making a mess of things. I could smell the nasties all the way up on the roof, and ducked back before they could see me. Charlie looked over and shook his head.

"Where the hell did they come from?" Charlie asked. "They weren't here twenty minutes ago when we pulled up."

I shrugged. "My guess is they were over in the other building, saw us pull up, and located us by our conversation in the storeroom."

"Are we shooting?"

"Don't know as we have much choice, except we'll attract every Z in the neighborhood and we still have to get the boat out of here, not to mention the truck." I looked over the roof edge again. I checked my ammo supply. "I haven't got enough ammo for a long fight," I said.

Charlie felt himself and confirmed a lack of ammo. "We could get these guys, but if another swarm shows up, we're screwed."

I was beginning to understand how the dead couple wound up where they were.

Suddenly, Charlie brightened. "I'll be right back." He headed down the ladder, leaving me wondering what the heck he was up to. Two minutes later he reappeared with two large bricks from the paving business.

I immediately caught on to what he was going to do. "Oh, you magnificent genius," I said, relieving him of a brick.

Charlie grinned like a kid who found his dad's porn. "It just came to me. Let's see if it works."

We went over to the front of the building and looked over. Two of the zombies were in sight, the other two were nowhere to be seen. Charlie waited until one was within range, then hurtled the brick down at the corpse. The brick slammed into the Z's head with a sickening thud and the body dropped heavily to the ground. We waited for a few seconds to see if it would get up again, but given the serious dent the brink had put into its skull, I doubted that Z was going anywhere soon.

The small commotion caused the second zombie to come over and investigate and I launched my brick. The zombie, a grayish, older specimen that might have been a black woman once, happened to look up at the last second and took the brick right between the eyes. The impact knocked her completely off her feet and drove her head to the ground. She lay there with a brick sticking out of her head and moved no more.

"Nice one," Charlie said as we headed back down to grab some more bricks.

It took the better part of half an hour, but we managed to bring up a number of bricks and paving stones to deal with the zombies. We had a good pile by the side of the building and looking over the side, it seemed like our little swarm was starting to disperse. We needed them to get closer to the building as I had no illusions about my ability to hit a moving zombie at thirty yards with a rock.

"Any ideas?" Charlie asked as he hefted a brick.

"Just one," I said. Leaning over the side, I waved my arms and yelled, "Oh boys! Lookee what I got here!"

Charlie smiled and leaned over. "Where the white women at?"

That worked. Zombies came shuffling over, moaning and grasping at the air. Charlie and I both took aim and started throwing bricks. Meaty thuds and smacks reached our ears as assorted zombies fell to our missiles. Some took more than one hit, as our aim wasn't perfect on every shot and we learned you had to actually throw the bricks, just dropping them didn't do sufficient damage to permanently put them down. It stunned them and took them a moment to recover, but they got up again and clamored for our flesh.

After about ten minutes of playing Whack-a-Zombie, Charlie and I found ourselves without targets. We waited for another ten minutes to see if any of them moved, but they were still.

We moved quickly, pulling the truck around and moving the boat into position. I was glad to have Charlie with me, I had no idea how to hitch a boat and watched intently as he went through the process. I was paying such close attention to Charlie that I nearly got nailed by the two zombies we hadn't accounted for earlier. They came shuffling around the garage door and I only noticed them when I saw a shadow moving that shouldn't have been moving at all.

I turned around and lunged back as the first zombie reached for me. Its hands grasped empty air as I backpedaled. The second zombie turned and made for Charlie as I moved to place some insulation between the first zombie and myself. It was a gruesome sight. Fat maggots wiggled out of gaping holes in its flesh as its dead eyes fixed themselves on me. Yellowed teeth bared from blackened lips and it's groaning was hampered by a large chunk out of its neck. Bluish dead veins spider-webbed its greenish-hued flesh, and lank hair swayed as it lurched forward.

I threw a bundle of insulation at the Z, knocking it over and giving me a second to unhook my crowbar. As it unbent I took a baseball swing and smashed it in the side of its head, spinning it around and dropping it on the floor. I stepped up quickly and delivered another blow to its head, finishing it for certain. I stepped back, ready to engage the second one, but on the other side of the boat, I saw a tomahawk rise and fall, then saw a dead zombie slump to the floor with a caved-in head.

I stepped over to the truck just as Charlie popped his head over the bed.

"That it?" he asked, wiping off his blade.

"God, I hope so," I said, wiping of my crowbar and re-securing it in place. "Let's get out of here."

We started up the truck and pulled out just as another stray zombie wandered around the corner of the storeroom. Charlie didn't even bother to try to avoid it, he just drove, crushing it to the pavement. If it was still moving after the truck, it was finished when the boat trailer pulverized it.

We stopped briefly at the condo complex for a quick reunion and a chance to burn off the zombie glop from our weapons. We exchanged stories and news and found out that the group had been especially active in finding other survivors and killing zombies. The entire area south of the complex was clear and I could see for quite a ways, as many buildings had been burned down. The fence was still in place, as there was the occasional roaming Z, but the people were happy and prospering. I told them about the other towns we had encountered and shared the belief that there was no reason not to think that far more people had survived than we thought.

33

Charlie and I drove back to Leport after another argument about the best route. We ended up taking the same route we took when we first headed out nearly a year ago. We got nostalgic as we passed the little house where Dot used to live and we shook our heads when we passed the home where we first encountered Dane Blake.

We reunited with Duncan briefly and there was lots of well-wishing and wishing in particular. I told Duncan he was welcome to join us when he finished and he said he was sorely tempted. He gave us a letter to give to Tommy and we rolled on to Leport. We ignored the burned out home where we first encountered the lunatics from the home improvement store who had eventually killed Kristen.

Charlie and I brought the boat to the dock and unloaded it. We got some approving glances and a few envious stares. But no one said anything, as we were the ones who went out and got the damn thing.

By the next morning, we had packed up our belongings and were ready to head out. Jake and Julia were happy as clams to wander around the inside of the boat and Rebecca and Sarah had their hands full chasing those two little demons and keeping them out of the cabinets. Just as we were about to pull out, Tommy came strolling by, with Angela in tow. Those two had become closer as the time had gone by and Angela rarely left Tommy's side.

"Ready to go?" Tommy called as I gathered up the lines and Charlie worked the controls.

"Just about," I called back.

"Nice place you're headed to?" Tommy said.

I looked sideways at him. "Pretty nice," I said carefully.

"Safe?"

"Needs work, but I'm bringing my son if that means anything."

"Big place?" Tommy asked.

I grinned. "If you don't get aboard, we'll leave you behind."

Tommy whooped and grabbed his duffle bags, which he had stashed out of sight. Angela hugged me as she passed and climbed aboard. Charlie slapped Tommy on the back and Sarah hugged them both.

I climbed aboard and gave Charlie the thumbs up, settling back into a lounge chair.

"What made you decide to come with?" I asked Tommy.

Tommy smiled. He pulled out the letter Duncan gave him. I opened it and it just said 'Stay with John. I'll join you later after the winter.'

"Wouldn't have it any other way," I said.

My easy cruise was short lived, as we came up to the outskirts of Joslin relatively quickly. I kept my Enfield trained on the buildings on the West while Tommy kept his on the right. Sarah and Rebecca were below with the little ones and Charlie kept the big boat moving steadily. The chain had not been replaced and I did not see anyone watching us. We heard the undisputed cry of thousands of hungry ghouls and saw many of them lining the canal, watching us drift on by. I wondered if the ghouls had finally won against the holdouts in Joslin and the city was truly dead. Given the number of Z's we were looking at right in front of us, trying to find the answer would be deadly.

We moved down the canal, joining the river and moving past the towns that Charlie and I previously passed. Since that visit and the one we were making, we had established communication via ham radio and had actually sent some trade envoys down. Apparently the town of Seneca had a surplus of bread products and we traded regularly for flour and wheat.

Sarah, Rebecca and Angela took advantage of the lazy trip and the sunlight to get a little tanning in. They surprised us by disappearing into the cabin and reappearing in very slight bathing suits. Charlie nearly ran us aground as he had a hard time keeping his eyes on the river. I didn't blame him a bit.

Jake loved the river ride and laughed as the water slapped the side of the boat. Julia was enthralled as well and gave Tommy the fits as she repeatedly tried to jump into the river.

We rode for a while and the sun was reflecting off the water as it started to work its way into the evening hours. The warm day had begun to cool off and a breeze from the south promised a comfortable night. By my watch, it was about three in the afternoon when we finally made it to Starved Rock. Charlie steered us closer to the monument itself, bringing the boat into a small inlet in the shadow of the Rock. Tommy volunteered to jump into the water to secure the boat, and we maneuvered the big craft up as close as we could without grounding it.

Securing the boat and hauling off our supplies, after a brief wait for the women to gear up, we headed into the woods towards the lodge. I didn't get the same creepy feeling I got the last time we were here, although I still walked with my rifle at the ready. Sarah let Jake walk beside her and he and Julia shared happy baby sounds as they toddled through the woods.

We reached the first clearing and I glanced up at Starved Rock. I thought I saw a flash of tan fur in the sunlight, but I couldn't be sure. As long as he left me and mine alone, I had no problem with a cougar in the backyard. We did see another zombie that had been chewed up by the cougar, so as long as he earned his keep, I was fine with him.

We settled into the main lodge itself after taking a while to secure the rooms. By the time we had finished, the sun was nearly down, and the evening light cast long shadows over the countryside. I figured we would take rooms on the second floor, just in case, and use the restaurant's kitchen for food storage and preparation. The huge common area, with its enormous wooden beams and massive central fireplace was reminiscent of a medieval hall. Just outside the main hall was the paved porch area, which overlooked the entire preserve and gave us unfettered views of Starved Rock, the Visitor Center, and Plum Island. The land dropped away just beyond the patio, falling straight down by more than fifty feet. On the east side of the lodge was a small canyon which had a waterfall not twenty yards from the lodge itself, solving our water problem and providing additional security.

The front of the lodge was surrounded by forest, with an open parking lot area immediately outside, providing an unobstructed firing zone if needed. There was ample room for growing food and the island across the way would be perfect for livestock if we decided to keep any. In a word, the lodge and surrounding area was perfect. Standing on the patio, as the sun cast pink and red hues across the clouds in the sky, I watched as Jake walked with stumbling feet around a wrought iron gazebo likely used in the past for weddings. Sarah was with me and I wrapped an arm around her shoulders as we took in the view.

"Well, what do you think?" I asked, nodding to Charlie and Rebecca who were sitting on the lounge chairs watching Julia roam around. Tommy and Angela were exploring the park with an express caution about the cougar.

"I feel like we're in a fairy tale," Sarah said. "We live in a manor and are surrounded by our fief. Across the river there are monsters."

I hadn't considered it that way, but I thought it sounded pretty good. "You know, in the old days of this country, whoever could back up and hold a claim to land eventually was titled to it. These days, I would think the same rule applies. If you can hold it, it's yours. I'd say unless things change dramatically, this lodge and land is ours as long as we can defend and keep it."

"No trouble there," Charlie growled.

I hoped so. My gut told me this was the place to stay, that this was the place I had been looking for. My family was safe, my friends were close, and we had what we needed to get on with our lives.

The wind picked up suddenly, swaying the treetops and causing a rustle to pick up from the leaves. If I had been poetic, I might have thought the land was saying "Welcome home."

34

We settled in relatively quickly and made several forays into Utica. The town had largely been abandoned when the Upheaval hit, so we were able to secure a decent amount of supplies. There were, of course, the usual skirmishes with zombies, but I have to say, we were getting fairly good at dealing with them. They weren't the horrible boogeymen they were in the beginning and we treated them more like vermin to be exterminated. Large, smelly, kill-you-if-it-bites-you vermin, but vermin nonetheless.

Tommy managed to find an old style water pump which allowed us to pull up water from the waterfall basin near the lodge. Charlie got it in his head to try and rig up a waterwheel to a generator to try and provide some low wattage power, but by fall he was still working that one out, getting mostly soaked for his trouble.

When fall finally came, the forest was ablaze in colors, as far as we could see. Charlie and I took Sarah and Rebecca on a surprise trip to Seneca, where Josh steered us in the direction of the local minister. Charlie and I had picked up rings during one of our trips to Utica and eschewing tradition, simply told the women we were getting married. They made a half-hearted attempt to object, but once they realized we were serious, they lined up pretty quickly. After the vows were exchanged, we headed back to the lodge to break the news to the children, who really didn't seem to care. Jake put a stuffed animal on his head and walked around the main room in celebration, at least we think that's why he did it.

Christmas was actually a pretty happy affair. We selected a small pine tree from our abundant supply, and decorated it with trimmings gleaned from a few of the abandoned houses. It took a few tries, because some of those people had really bad taste. Jake got some new cars and Julia got some new stuffed animals. I raided a bookstore for Sarah's gifts, and Charlie did the same for Rebecca, except he went to a craft store. Tommy had made a run to another town, and came back with several dresses for Angela. It was almost normal, except for the cougar growls that drifted upwards from the river valley floor.

We celebrated Jake's second birthday around this time and since we had no idea about Julia's birthday, we celebrated hers as well.

Three weeks later, Charlie, Tommy and I were back in the boat, heading north. The ground was covered in snow, and ice chunks bumped into the hull every now and then. We were headed back to Leport to take part in a massive push to clear the area of zombies. Nate and I had planned this push for months, realizing that if we moved when the zombies were frozen, we would stand that much better of a chance when the weather turned warmer. Plus, with all the towns that had survived and the communication network we had set up, we were able to coordinate a massive assault on the undead.

As we ventured farther out, we were meeting with more people and towns that had survived the initial Upheaval. What we needed to do was to make it safe to travel and to let people get on with living, not just surviving. That was why the towns on the railroad were clearing up their counties, marking them safe as they pushed out farther. With luck, we hoped to have an area of over twelve hundred square miles cleared of the Z's by spring. Next winter, we would do the same. A big hope was that a majority of the zombies would eventually decay to the point of uselessness within a few years.

The three of us were standing with Trevor and his band of merry men on the outskirts of Bolingbrook, a heavily populated suburb of the city. It had been bitterly cold the last two weeks which was perfect for zombie hunting. The ones we encountered were pretty much frozen, moving slowly if at all. There wasn't the heavy snowfall yet, so we didn't have to worry about zombies under the snow.

I stood with my long crowbar in my hands, my faithful M1 Carbine slung over my shoulder. There were two pickup trucks waiting behind us and more waiting beyond them. My orders were simple. Eliminate the zombies, drag them outside, and mark the doors according to what was found inside the homes. F if there was salvageable food, W if there were weapons or ammo. Other items would be recovered later to be distributed as needed or sent to the towns on the river or railway.

In a way, it was funny. There was so much stuff that we couldn't possibly use it all. Much was going to go to waste, but I guess that was the price to be paid for a society that was consumed by consumerism. More of everything, whether we needed it or not.

The cars were being moved to the edges of the roads and placed on their sides to form a wall. Gas was removed from the cars and added to a tanker truck that followed along. Any leftover zombies in the cars were summarily executed.

I looked at the rows of homes with their torn and frayed white flags fluttering from mailboxes and sighed. *Gonna be a long day.* I thought, hefting my crowbar. I looked at Tommy and Charlie and gave the order.

"Move out."

We separated into pairs and I went with Trevor. All around me was the sound of men breaking into homes and dispatching zombies. Doors were spray painted, and then the trucks fired up. In the first three homes I didn't find any zombies, but Trevor found a decent horde of canned goods. That was the way we ran it. One would go in, check only for Z's, while the other looked for usable goods. It was cold enough that the zombies were pretty much popsicles; some could move, albeit very slowly.

Some homes had that broken-into look, with interesting blood sprays on the walls and ceilings. Body parts were here and there and in some homes you could almost read what happened in the way things were left. One house had a father lying in his bed with a neat hole in his forehead, the bodies of his wife and children in their beds, tied with rope and each sporting a ventilated skull as well. My guess was the family had turned and the father committed suicide after finishing them off.

We found little in the way of arms and ammo, but we had plenty of canned and dry goods. The majority of the trucks taking supplies were laden with food items. We had no use for the vehicles we found, but we rolled them out to the end of the driveways in case we needed them.

The day went fairly smoothly and the sun was beginning its evening decent when Trevor and I approached our last building. It was an older two story home that looked like it had been renovated before the Upheaval. I popped the door open and Trevor stepped inside. He immediately dropped from view, landing with a crash in the basement. I stepped up and saw that the floor had been removed from the front hallway, leaving only studs. Trevor had managed to fall neatly through the studs to the cellar below.

"You okay?" I called down, trying to keep myself from laughing.

"Yeah, I'm fine." Trevor grumbled from below. "Just my pride...Oh, Jesus!" Trevor screamed.

I dropped through the boards and landed heavily next to Trevor, my crowbar clanging loudly on the cement floor. I sprang up, holding the bar in front of me. The basement was dark and cluttered with only the thin light from the upstairs door and window wells providing any illumination. I could hear them shuffling in the dark and I could see what startled Trevor . I saw several pairs of glowing eyes in the darkness and as I looked further, more eyes slowly opened up. A quick count revealed at least fifteen ghouls in this basement. They were coming around corners and crawling out from under workbenches. One was even slowly rising from a large wooden box, unfolding itself. It was all in slow motion, like the worst nightmare someone could have come up with. As I looked, several more pairs of glowing eyes opened up and started to move forward in the darkness. These were just the ones I could see. Chances were, more without glowing eyes were down there as well, shuffling slowly forward, hunger driving them on and on. The noise in the basement suddenly intensified as the dead struggled forward. I had no time to wonder why so many Z's were in this particular basement.

I swung the crowbar viciously at the nearest one, cracking its skull and killing it.

"You bit?" I hissed at Trevor as the eyes moved slowly forward. This basement had been relatively protected from the cold, so these zombies would be moving a little faster.

"I don't know!" Trevor cried. "Something got me on my ankle when I fell!"

Inwardly, I cringed. If Trevor had been bit, he was as good as dead. I quickly looked around and didn't see any Z's near us. I did see a board with nails sticking out of it, so it was possible Trevor had fallen on that. I didn't care at that point. We needed to get out of this hole. There was so much clutter and too many zombies to make a stand. They might have been slowed by the cold, but not enough.

I hauled Trevor to his feet and yelled in his face. "You gotta get up out of here now!" I swung the crowbar at another zombie that poked its head around a box of National Geographic magazines. The crowbar impacted with the sound of an axe hitting a log and the zombie fell to the floor.

Trevor jumped for the support beam and I swung his legs up, allowing him to hook his leg over and pull himself out of the cellar. That left me. I hooked the rounded end of the crowbar over the top of a stud and jumped up, catching two of the beams. As I swung my legs back, another zombie lurched slowly into view. I used my momentum and slammed my feet into the zombie's chest, hurling it back over the box of magazines and crashing it to the floor at the feet of the rest of the Z's. I swung my legs up and through the studs, hooking them over the top and pulling myself through the boards.

I took a moment to catch my breath. I carefully balanced myself and stepped over to the threshold and open door. Trevor was outside, inspecting his leg. I knelt down and reached to retrieve my crowbar.

The bar jerked in my hand and I fell forward, catching myself on the stud. One of the zombies had grasped the crowbar and jerked it down as I pulled it up.

"Not bloody likely." I growled, lifting the bar up and shoving it forward, catching the zombie in the eye and impaling it neatly. The zombie fell back, the bar making a nasty squelching sound as it exited the Z's skull. I stood up and looked down at the group of faces staring up at me, putrid faces and decaying limbs reaching up. I reached into my pack and retrieved my kerosene bottle. Squeezing a line of fluid down over their faces and into the box of magazines, I sprayed over the studs and on the walls I could reach. I also squeezed a little on the ends of my crowbar.

I pulled out a Strike-Anywhere match and used the grasping grooves of my SIG to light it. Tossing the match inside, I stepped back as the flames erupted and started their work. I lit both ends of my crowbar, and holding it by the middle, I wandered over to Trevor while the house behind me started to smolder and smoke.

Trevor watched me approach with my flaming bar and smiled wryly. "You planning on joining a luau soon?"

I grinned. "I look lousy in a grass skirt and a coconut bra. You okay?"

Trevor nodded. "Landed on a nail. I'll probably die of infection."

I turned serious. "All the same, you're quarantined for three days. With that many zombies in that basement, one of them might have stepped on it, too."

Trevor turned ashen. "Didn't think of that. Oh God..."

"Just a precaution. Try not to think about it."

Trevor looked down. "John, if the worst happens, could you...?"

Knowing what he meant, I placed a hand on his shoulder. "Yeah."

We finished up and headed back to the regroup point. I filled in the rest of the team and there was a lot of concern expressed for Trevor, but a lot of hope as well. He should be okay, but if he turned, it was my job to put him down.

We moved through subdivision after subdivision, through office building and school. We killed the zombies where we found them, fought them if needed. We cleared more area than would have been possible a year ago and managed to safeguard more of the surrounding area. We had supplies to spare and were well-situated to not only survive the storm, but to actually start living as well.

35

Six weeks after the start of the offensive, the weather began to get warmer. I called a halt to offensive operations and we went back to our homes. I spent a week with my brother and made sure he and his were taken care of. He hadn't taken to the training as well as I had hoped, but he was a natural at organization, so he was invaluable with all of the supplies and materials our push was bringing in. I invited him and his family back out to Starved Rock, but they wanted nothing to do with that place.

Mike had nothing but praise for me and what I had done. He said he had never been more proud to be related to me than he was now. I didn't know what to say. I just always did what needed to be done.

Reports came in from the other towns and they all had success stories. We did lose several to the zombies, but I would have been stunned if it had been otherwise. Trevor got a nasty infection from the nail, but recovered in time to take part in the last three weeks of the operation.

Charlie, Tommy and I were on the boat, rolling back to Starved Rock. I hadn't seen my son and new wife in two months and that was two months too long. We had laden the boat with supplies and were looking forward to planting some crops and making a serious go of our land. Sarah and Rebecca and Angela had gone to one of the other towns and learned how to can food for storage.

As we pulled into our little cove at Starved Rock, I felt a sense of home I hadn't felt in a long time. We didn't bother unloading supplies right away, we just headed to the lodge, each of us looking forward to our reunions.

Three weeks later, I stood on the patio, holding Jake and looking over the trees of the park, noting the emergence of a green haze which marked the beginning of spring and new growth. Jake was walking all over the place and babbling constantly. He loved his new home and loved the toys I had brought back.

Several days later, I was clearing out the Visitor's Center when a heavily laden truck pulled into the parking lot. I stepped out onto the sidewalk, keeping a hand near my ever-present SIG. The truck door opened and the driver got out. I dropped my hand as Duncan walked over to me.

"Your orders have been carried out, sir. Request permission to rest," Duncan said as he saluted me.

I wrapped Duncan up in a bear hug and lifted him off his feet. As I put him down, I shook his hand and reminded him of what I told him a while ago. "You're always welcome where I live. C'mon up to the lodge. Charlie and Tommy will be glad to see you, old son." We walked up to the lodge, where Duncan was greeted like the long lost prodigal.

The summer breezes ran lazily over the treetops as the sun dipped into the horizon. Scarlet rays turned the green leaves crimson and the purple clouds raced each other to the far side of the world. Sarah moved up close to give me a hug and kiss.

"Thank you," she said.

"For what?" I asked.

"Saving us all."

I shook my head. "I didn't do anything special."

Sarah took my face in her hands and looked deeply into my eyes. "You reminded us that we were alive once and gave us the will to live again. Don't ever deny that because that is what you did. Everyone knows it and you should too."

I looked down. "I lost a lot of people too."

Sarah hugged me. "You never worried about ghosts before, why bother now? It was never your fault. You did what you could."

She was right. We were alive and we were living. It was the best revenge we could have against a world gone dead.

As I closed my eyes and breathed Sarah in, I heard a far-off moan carried on the evening breeze. I had managed to get a lot done, but there was more work to do. I still had a promise to keep and we had more to take back.

I made another promise that day. The white flags of the dead might be still out there, but they were no longer a symbol of surrender. They were a rallying cry, to take back what we had lost and reclaim our lives and land. They had tried their best and failed.

We were taking it back. One ragged step at a time, but we were taking it all back.

I looked in and watched Jake play on the floor of the lodge. I thought about his mother, and how far we had come in such a short time. Across the river, next to the abandoned school, I saw a ragged flag flutter in the wind. I knew what I had to do for my son, what I needed to do for everyone still alive, still struggling to keep the monsters away.

I had to step up, rip the country away from the rotted fingers of the virus, and spit in the eye of the infected who haunted the darkness.

I had to take it back.

AMERICA THE DEAD

BOOK 3. WHITE FLAG OF THE DEAD SERIES

Coming soon from severed press

Sixteen hundred miles of infected territory. Sixteen hundred miles over terrain which may not have seen a living human in nearly three years. Millions of infected souls, waiting with the hungry patience of the dead.

John Talon and his crew of survivors, torn away from their loved ones by a mission of urgency, must make a journey across the country to save their one small chance at rebuilding a nation. At stake is the soul of a nation, the binding ideals which could remake the country in the hands of whoever possesses them.

Racing against time and a madman who will not allow anyone, living or dead to get in his way, John and his friends will discover whether or not America the Brave has become America the Dead.

THE LIVING END
James Robert Smith

One Hundred and Fifty Million Zombies.

Sixty Million Dogs.

All of them hungry for warm human flesh.

The dead have risen, killing anyone they find. The living know what's caused it-a vicious contagion. But too late to stop it. For now, what remains of society are busy shutting down nuclear reactors and securing chemical plants to prevent runaway reactions in both. There's little time for anything else.

Failed comic book artist Rick Nuttman and his family have joined thousands of other desperate people in trying to find a haven from the madness.

Perhaps refuge can be found in the village of Sparta or maybe there is salvation in The City of Ruth, a community raised from the ashes of Carolina.

In the low country below the hills, a monster named Danger Man changes everything.

While watching over it all, the mysterious figure of BC, moving his gigantic canine pack westward, into lands where survivors think they are safe

And always, the mindless hordes neither living nor dead, waiting only to destroy.

There will be a reckoning.

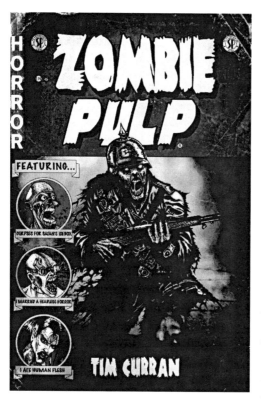

WHITE FLAG OF THE DEAD
Joseph Talluto

**Book 1
Surrender of the Living.**

Millions died when the Enillo Virus swept the earth. Millions more were lost when the victims of the plague refused to stay dead, instead rising to slay and feed on those left alive. For survivors like John Talon and his son Jake, they are faced with a choice: Do they submit to the dead, raising the white flag of surrender? Or do they find the will to fight, to try and hang on to the last shreds or humanity?

Surrender of the Living is the first high octane instalment in the White Flag of the Dead series.

DEMONMACHY
Brant Danay

As the universe slowly dies, all demonkind is at war in a tournament of genocide. The prize? Nirvana. The Necrodelic, a death addict who smokes the flesh of his victims as a drug, is determined to win this afterlife for himself. His quest has taken him to the planet Grystiawa, and into a duel with a dream-devouring snake demon who is more than he seems. Grystiawa has also been chosen as the final battleground in the ancient spider-serpent wars. As armies of arachnid monstrosities and ophidian gladiators converge upon the planet, the Necrodelic is forced to choose sides in a cataclysmic combat that could well prove his demise. Beyond Grystiawa, a Siamese twin incubus and succubus, a brain-raping nightmare fetishist, a gargantuan insect queen, and an entire universe of genocidal demons are forming battle plans of their own. Observing the apocalyptic carnage all the while is Satan himself, watching voyeuristically from the very Hell in which all those who fail will be damned to eternal torment. Who will emerge victorious from this cosmic armageddon? And what awaits the victor beyond the blood-drenched end of time? The battle begins in Demonmachy. Twisting Satanic mythologies and Eastern religions into an ultraviolent grotesque nightmare, the Messiah of Death Saga will rip your eyeballs right out of your skull. Addicted to its psychedelic darkness, you'll immediately sew and screw and staple and weld them back into their sockets so you can read more. It's an intergalactic, interdimensional harrowing that you'll never forget...and may never recover from.

Available at www.severedpress.com, Amazon and most online bookstores

The Official Zombie Handbook: Sean T Page

Since pre-history, the living dead have been among us, with documented outbreaks from ancient Babylon and Rome right up to the present day. But what if we were to suffer a zombie apocalypse in the UK today? Through meticulous research and field work, The Official Zombie Handbook (UK) is the only guide you need to make it through a major zombie outbreak in the UK, including: -Full analysis of the latest scientific information available on the zombie virus, the living dead creatures it creates and most importantly, how to take them down - UK style. Everything you need to implement a complete 90 Day Zombie Survival Plan for you and your family including home fortification, foraging for supplies and even surviving a ghoul siege. Detailed case studies and guidelines on how to battle the living dead, which weapons to use, where to hide out and how to survive in a country dominated by millions of bloodthirsty zombies. Packed with invaluable information, the genesis of this handbook was the realisation that our country is sleep walking towards a catastrophe - that is the day when an outbreak of zombies will reach critical mass and turn our green and pleasant land into a grey and shambling wasteland. Remember, don't become a cheap meat snack for the zombies!

BIOHAZARD
Tim Curran

The day after tomorrow: Nuclear fallout. Mutations. Deadly pandemics. Corpse wagons. Body pits. Empty cities. The human race trembling on the edge of extinction. Only the desperate survive. One of them is Rick Nash. But there is a price for survival: communion with a ravenous evil born from the furnace of radioactive waste. It demands sacrifice. Only it can keep Nash one step ahead of the nightmare that stalks him-a sentient, seething plague-entity that stalks its chosen prey: the last of the human race. To accept it is a living death. To defy it, a hell beyond imagining

"kick back and enjoy some the most violent and genuinely scary apocalyptic horror written by one of the finest dark fiction authors plying his trade today" HORRORWORLD

Lightning Source UK Ltd.
Milton Keynes UK
UKOW05f1806181113

221352UK00001B/75/P